MOONGLOW ROAD

A CITY OF FOUNTAINS NOVEL

C.J. JOHNSON

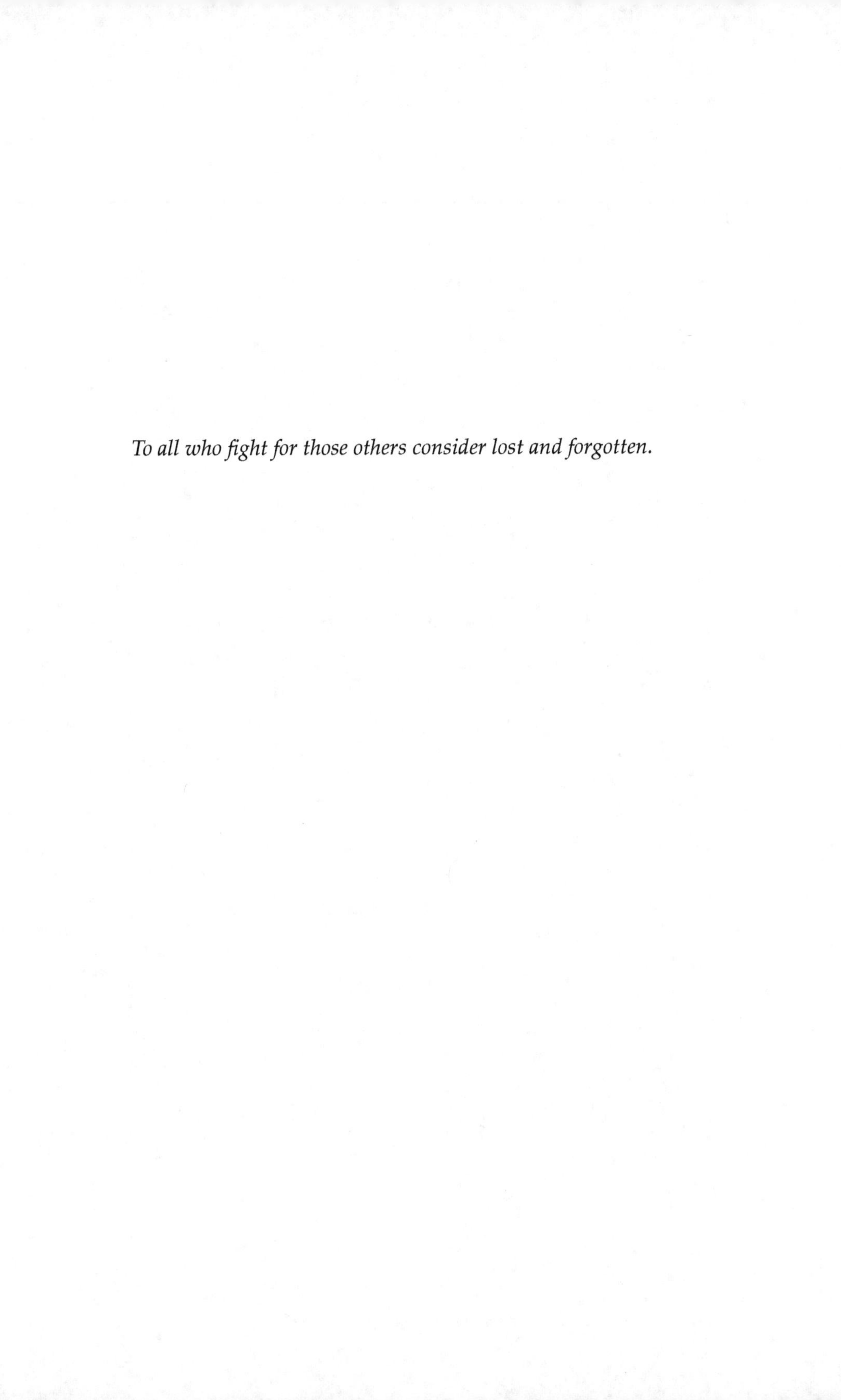

To all who fight for those others consider lost and forgotten.

CHAPTER
ONE

FINLEY THREW her backpack over her shoulder as she walked out the front door. Rubbing her cheek, she vowed this was the last time she would be hit. Finley's foster mom looked the other way when her boyfriend got mad and knocked the kids around. With only one year of school left, Finley thought she could put up with the punches, but the night before her foster mom's boyfriend had come into her room after everyone was asleep. Finley, asleep on her side, heard him step into the room and felt him sit on the bed. She did not move when he ran his hand along her hip and up her body, grazing her breast. She gripped the knife she kept under her pillow, prepared to plunge it into his body if he tried anything. Just when he lifted the blanket, the baby began to cry, and he was gone. That was the moment she knew she had to leave.

Her foster mom thought she was walking to school, but Finley had other plans. Instead of textbooks, her backpack held her journal, a couple changes of clothes, and money she had saved from babysitting the neighbor kids. She told her foster mom she had a field trip with her summer school class and would be late getting home. If everything went well, she would be on a bus far away before anyone even knew she was gone. Her boyfriend said a ticket would be waiting for her at the bus depot. Twenty minutes after walking out the door, Finley was on the Greyhound bus heading north to Kansas City.

At the first stop a woman sat down next to Finley and said, "I'm going to see my daughter in Omaha."

As the woman spent the next ten minutes talking about her daughter, her daughter's "lowlife" husband, and her grandchild, Finley let her mind wander. She could hardly believe she was on a bus, and she was finally going to meet Wes face to face. After months of talking and exchanging photographs, they would be in the same room. It seemed surreal to her.

"It's been almost a year since I've seen them. I really hope my grand-baby remembers me." The woman stopped to take a breath and then asked, "Where are you heading to?

"Kansas City," Finley pause and then added, "To meet my boyfriend."

"How sweet. How did you meet?"

Finley thought about her answer, wondering what the woman would think. Finally, she said, "He started messaging me on Instagram."

CHAPTER
TWO

WHEN SHE GOT off the bus, Finley looked around the busy station. She did not see the boy she had been talking to online but about the time she began to panic, a man approached.

"Are you Finley?" the stranger asked.

"Who are you?"

"I'm Hudson. My boy, Wes asked me to pick you up. He had to work today and asked me to take you to see him. He wasn't kidding, you really are pretty."

The hair on the back of Finley's neck prickled, but she looked at the old man, shook off her concerns and said, "Okay."

Finley followed Hudson to his truck and climbed in with her backpack securely on her lap. She looked out the window and watched the people walking on the broken sidewalks. After a short drive, Hudson pulled into the driveway of a house that looked to be abandoned.

"Where are we?"

Hudson evaded the question and said, "Wes works here part-time taking care of an old man. Come on inside with me."

Finley hesitated. Wes hadn't told her he took care of an old man, but Hudson said it was part-time, so maybe Wes had forgotten to mention it. Hudson was on the porch by the time Finley got out of the truck. He looked back and motioned for her to come inside.

"Here, let me get the door," Hudson said.

Finley walked in and heard the distinct sound of a lock click behind her. She turned back towards the door, but Hudson grabbed her and pushed her into a dark room. A hand covered her mouth when Finley started to scream.

"No one will hear," Hudson said. "And even if they did, they wouldn't help you."

Hudson began to grab at Finley's clothes, but he wasn't prepared as she struggled under his hands. Her backpack had fallen to the ground, and Finley knew if she could get to it, she could get away. She kicked and pushed Hudson's hands away, doing everything she could to keep him from getting under her clothing. Tiring of the fight, Hudson put his hands around her neck and squeezed.

"I didn't want it to be like this."

Finley barely heard the words as she faded into the darkness. She did not know how long she had been in the house when she regained consciousness. Finley grabbed at her body, noticing the rips in her shirt and bare skin below her waist. Finley's body ached from the struggle and the violation. She moved quickly and quietly, feeling around in the dark for her bag and jeans, careful not to wake the sleeping man beside her. With her bag and jeans in her hands, she tiptoed from the room, unlocked the front door, and began to run.

CHAPTER
THREE

FRANCESCA "FRANKIE" Thomas sat on a bench, looking around the town square she called home as a child. The shell of the square was the same, but a few things had transformed in the 27 years since she had moved away. The First National Bank building on the corner had changed names more than once and was no longer a bank. The once-coveted storefronts from her childhood were different, and a couple of the buildings had been razed, but her memory filled in the gaps. The thing most notable to Frankie, was the once bustling small town was showing signs of age and loss of patronage. Signage had faded and sidewalks were cracked, however, two things remained the same: the courthouse, and the town theater. Frankie had spent thousands of hours in the theater as a teenager watching movies with her friends, rehearsing for school musicals and plays, and even performing with the opry a few times.

The theater had been a place of fun and creativity, but it was a tour to the courthouse with her first criminal justice class that sparked an interest in Frankie that would grow and eventually develop into a career. Light from the setting sun bounced off the historic buildings and created a golden hue around the courthouse sitting center stage in the square. Frankie could still smell the furniture oil liberally applied to the wooden railing which separated the gallery from the attorney's tables and the bench where the judge sat. Walls were adorned with framed portraits of judges who had sat on the bench over the years. The leather seats were a dark brown and soft to the touch. Frankie and her classmates took turns sitting in the various places throughout the courtroom but when Frankie sat in the judge's seat, she immediately knew whatever path her life took would lead her back into a courtroom.

A warm breeze brushed Frankie's forehead, and a faint odor of honeysuckle floated through the air. She was about to leave when a bright red convertible caught her eye. The top was down, revealing two young girls in the front seat laughing and singing along to a song on the radio. To the outside world looking in, the two girls did not have a care in the world. Frankie followed the car with her eyes, stopping as they drove past the old bank building. She thought she saw a familiar figure in the lot and started to walk that way but when she got closer, he was gone.

CHAPTER
FOUR

Twenty-eight years earlier

FRANKIE SAT behind the wheel of her little red convertible. The top was down, and her best friend Beth sat in the seat beside her. The hot July breeze wreaked havoc on their hair, but neither seemed to mind. The grass around the courthouse was a lush green, and the dust in the air looked like flecks of gold glitter. The storefronts surrounding the square were closed and the parking spaces surrounding the town square were empty as they drove around the block looking for their friends. After coming full circle, they headed back through town and saw an old pick-up with KC off-road lights on the roll bar pull into the First National Bank parking lot on the corner. The driver stuck his hand out the window and waved at the girls.

"Hey, there's Brent and Patrick," Beth said. "Let's see if they want to ride around with us!"

Frankie pulled up next to the driver's side and after a short back and forth between the foursome, Beth jumped in the backseat of the convertible with Brent, allowing Patrick to sit shotgun next to Frankie. They cruised through town and the car was filled with chatter about end of summer plans and the upcoming school year. Brent and Patrick were planning to play football, and camp was only a few weeks away. Frankie and Beth had cheerleading camp the same week at a nearby university.

"Where's the camp this year?" Patrick asked.

"Warrensburg. What about you guys?"

"Same. Maybe we can hang out some while we're there," Patrick said.

"That would be fun," Frankie said softly.

Sensing a need to change the subject, Patrick asked, "Did you all hear about Julia?"

"What have you heard?" Beth asked.

"I heard Craig knocked her up, and she left town," Brent said.

Beth thought for a second and then said, "That doesn't sound right. Why would she leave town? I mean, it sucks, but she wouldn't just take off."

Frankie kept quiet. She had known Julia since they were in preschool. Julia's house was by Frankie's family's farm and growing up they had been inseparable during the summers...until they could drive. Julia started dating Craig, and then it seemed like they saw each other more often cruising town than at the farm. Frankie did not mind; both were busy with jobs and after school activities, and cars made staying home less of a necessity.

Frankie had been friends with Craig since he moved to town in 3rd grade. He and Julia started dating at the beginning of their freshman year and showed no signs of slowing down. Julia had not said anything to Frankie about being pregnant. The last time they talked about their relationship, she said she and Craig had not had sex. But Frankie kept quiet. It was possible things had changed, and she didn't want to betray Julia's confidence.

Patrick said, "I heard her dad got pissed off, so her mom was taking her to stay with family in Arkansas or Tennessee. Lance said they left this week."

Frankie asked, "This week?"

To herself Frankie thought, *Surely, she would have said good-bye. I can't believe she would have left without telling me. We've known each other too long for her to just disappear without saying anything.*

"I saw Craig yesterday, and he was freaking out because Julia wasn't returning his calls," said Brent. "He said her dad finally answered the phone and told him to quit calling,"

"Frankie? Frankie!"

Beth's voice brought Frankie out of her thoughts. Blinking she said, "What?"

"You drove right past the Sonic. I thought we were going to stop for a drink and some onion rings."

"Yeah, sorry. I guess I got distracted."

CHAPTER
FIVE

THE SUN SETTLED into the earth and other than streetlights and headlights, the town was dark. The hours passed quickly and, one by one, the cars began to disappear. Couples found their way to empty cornfields and deserted country roads, some headed to the levy to drink beer, and some congregated in various lots throughout town, listening to music and dancing until the law came and ran them off.

Frankie had just parked in one of the lots when someone mentioned a levy party. Frankie had a hard and fast rule to stay away from those because they always got busted, and she didn't need her mom breathing down her neck for having a run-in with the cops. She declined Patrick's invite and took him and Brent back to their truck so the boys could go. Beth and Frankie were having a sleepover, so they did a couple more laps through town then went back to the old farmhouse and sat outside to watch for shooting stars.

Bored and hot, the pair decided to take a walk to the creek and dip their toes in the cool water.

"I see where the name came from," Beth said.

Lost in her own thoughts, Frankie said, "Huh?"

"Moonglow Road. It's like God hung the moon in just the right place so that it would light this road."

"Mmhmm, that's exactly what my dad says. Sometimes, when I'm here, I forget the rest of the world exists."

Beth thought about what Frankie said and whispered, "Magic."

The girls walked silently for a few more minutes, then Frankie asked, "Do you think Julia really is pregnant?"

"You know her better than I do. What do you think?"

Frankie debated on what to say, but Beth was her best friend, and she knew she would keep her confidence. Eventually she said, "I don't buy it. Julia told me she and Craig hadn't had sex, which makes it kind of hard to get pregnant."

"How long ago was that? I mean, it only takes once, right?"

"We just talked a couple of weeks ago. I think something else is going on. I'll give her a call tomorrow. Or maybe I'll just stop by her house. I noticed it was dark when we drove by."

"Yeah. I looked as we drove by, too, but it's late, so I figured everyone was just asleep," Beth said.

"She would have been out tonight..." Frankie couldn't shake the feeling something was amiss.

CHAPTER
SIX

FRANKIE LOOKED in the direction of the dark barn overlooking the creek, thinking of the sleepover she and Julia had planned a few weeks earlier. When they were in fifth grade, Frankie asked her father to build a playhouse on the tree line that separated their property from Julia's. Frank knew Frankie, and later her siblings, would outgrow a simple playhouse, thus he wanted to build something that could be used long-term even after the kids were adults. Shack creek cut through the property at the bottom of the hill and during the warmer months, they all enjoyed an occasional swim to cool off. Frank decided whatever he built needed to compliment the creek. Hidden in the trees along the edge of the property line, just above the flood line, was an old barn with a view of both properties.

Frank spent several weekends working towards his plan. He painstakingly removed trees that threatened to fall into the building, but kept the ones that would provide shade, and natural air conditioning in the hot summers and keep the space somewhat hidden. While he was clearing, he created a path from Moonglow Road to the barn, just wide enough a full-size truck could get through without scratching the paint. Once the ground was clear, he and his brother, Michael surveyed the exterior of the barn, then made their way inside. The old wooden posts that held the roof were joined together with thick wooden dowels and the building was sound. The floor was a fine, black dirt that had not seen sunlight for decades and seemed impervious to movement. The building was built to withstand time and, Frank's best guess was it had lasted over 100 years.

Frank and Michael added a couple of trusses for more security, created a space for extra storage, and room in the back to pull in their trucks and other farm equipment as needed. They built a ladder for the loft which covered the open space and added a rail in case one of the kids decided to climb up. In the front of the barn was a small room with an old wood floor that had been a living quarters or office at one time. Frank decided that was where they would make the playhouse.

Cabinets and a non-functioning sink lined one wall, but the rest of the room was a blank slate. Frank and Michael talked about tearing the cabinets out but, in the end, they cleaned them up and put a solid wood countertop over where the sink had been. Frank put out some rodent deterrent and added a small table with a few chairs. Windows on each side, caked with years of dirt, gave way to views of both farms. Frank bought a chalkboard from an old, abandoned school and hung it on the wall opposite the cabinets.

Outside the door they built a small wooden deck facing Shack Creek. It was just big enough for a couple of chairs and a cooler and after they finished with their work, Frank and Michael, sat on the porch, raised a cold Budweiser, and watched the sun set into the creek below. Over the next few years, it was common to find Frank and Michael on the porch while the kids played inside the playhouse or in the fields and creek around the barn. It would become a place each family member used to escape their daily life and enjoy the slow steady rhythms of the creek.

When Frankie and Julia were young, they would spend hours playing school and other games, letting their imaginations run free in the barn and the area surrounding it. By junior high, they were spending nights camped out on the floor, talking about boys and dreaming about their futures.

"Frankie?"

Looking over at Beth, she said, "Huh?"

"Did you hear anything I just said?"

Frankie had not, but took a guess and said, "You were talking about cheerleading camp and hanging out with Brent."

"Nice save."

Frankie and Beth continued to dangle their feet in the icy water of Shack Creek. When they were done laughing, and sufficiently cooled off, they returned to the house for sleep.

CHAPTER
SEVEN

THE WEEKEND PASSED and Frankie didn't see Julia. She tried to call the house several times, but no one picked up the phone. Monday afternoon Frankie finally knocked on the door. She heard someone scrambling inside, but no one answered.

The rumors continued to spread among Frankie's friend group and eventually through the school and town through the remaining weeks of the summer. Julia was pregnant, and she had gone to stay with family in Arkansas. Julia had run away because her dad was mean. After a couple weeks, the stories became more ominous. When Julia's mother did not return, people began to say she and Julia had both ran away because Julia's dad was physically abusive towards her mother. Then it was because he had been beating them both. Her mother was having an affair and ran off to live with the man she was sleeping with and took Julia with her. As time wore on, people said they were both dead. Julia's older sister, Lauren did not live in the area, but no one seemed to think of reaching out to her to try and learn the truth. Frankie thought of calling Lauren, but they had not been close, and somehow it seemed wrong to call her out of the blue because of rumors.

As the stories grew, Frankie began to notice changes at Julia's house. She didn't want to fuel the rumors that had already taken over the town, so she kept her observations to herself. A few days after Frankie knocked on the door, Julia's father, Warren, ripped out carpets and threw them into the burn pit adjacent to the farm. The smell of the fibers burning filled Wolf Hollow for a full day when Frankie decided to get a closer look to investigate the smell.

Frankie had not been to the barn in a few weeks but knew she could see the fire pit clearly without being easily seen. She expected cobwebs to be covering the doors but when she got to the entrance of the little playhouse-apartment it looked like she and Julia had just left minutes before. Frankie opened the door slowly. The countertop looked as if it had just been cleaned. Books she and Julia exchanged were neatly stacked in the corner and the camping lamp was sitting in the center of the table. Reflexively Frankie looked to the chalkboard where she and Julia had often left notes for one another. A familiar Phil Collins song lyric was written in Julia's neat cursive.

I was there and I saw what you did. I saw it with my own two eyes. You can wipe off that grin. I know where you've been. It's all been a pack of lies.

Frankie didn't recall the lyric being on the board the last time she was there. For a moment she wondered if it was intended to be a message, but if it was, what? Looking around the familiar room, Frankie noticed a leather book laid on top of the books and made a mental note to look at it later.

Frankie stepped over to the window and looked in the direction of the fire pit. She was surprised to see a piece of a mattress sticking up among rolls of carpet. Burning trash and household goods was not an uncommon occurrence among the houses on Moonglow Road, but something felt weird about this. Frankie wondered if she should tell her dad.

Frankie's imagination ran wild with possibilities as she watched the fire burn. When the sun hit the windowpane, she knew it was time to go. The walk to the house wasn't long, but when the sun set, it quickly got dark in the woods, and in the twilight hours the animals started moving. She had listened to the wails of bobcats and coyotes on many occasions, but always from the safety of the porch with her dad by her side. She didn't want to meet one in the dark on her way home.

EIGHT

WHEN FRANKIE GOT to the house, she noticed a light on in her dad's workshop. The familiar and comforting smell of stale oil and dust floated through the doorway as she pushed it open. Frank looked up from the engine of the car, grabbed an old rag and said, "Well, if it isn't Francesca Elizabeth. It's been a while since I've seen you in this shop."

Frankie smiled at her father's use of her full name. She would never tell him, but she loved the way it sounded when he said it. "Hey dad. What's wrong with Jody's car now?"

"Oh nothin'. I was changing the oil then decided to do a little tinkering." Frankie's dad looked up from the engine, grabbed a dusty red rag and asked, "Is dinner ready?"

"I don't know. I just got back from a little walk." Frankie paused, then asked, "When was the last time you were up at the barn?"

Frank wiped his hands and said, "Shoot, it's probably been a few months. Why?"

"It looked like someone had been there recently, that's all."

Before Frank could say anything more, the youngest Moretti child bounded through the door and said, "Daddy, it's time for dinner." Surprise filled her face when Sophie saw Frankie standing by the car. Sophie squealed and grabbed her sister around the waist, "Frankie! I thought you had work."

Frankie returned Sophie's hug and said, "Not tonight kiddo."

"Does that mean we can read Narnia tonight?"

"Of course," Frankie said.

By the time Frankie and the family finished dinner, she had convinced herself she was imagining things and there was no need to tell her dad what she had seen. She had forgotten to look at the journal, but figured she would go back the next day and get it.

Present day

"LAST ONE TO the parking lot buys breakfast."

Frankie looked back over her shoulder and giggled. She enjoyed her daily runs often with her friend, Jim Craven. Frankie was a detective assigned to Sex Crimes and she had met Jim, a special agent with the FBI, while working a rape involving an organized crime syndicate. They had become close friends, often spending time together off duty.

"Better have your wallet ready," Jim responded, picking up the pace.

Frankie and Jim made it to the parking lot at the same time. Both laughed as they collapsed against the side of Frankie's Jeep and grabbed their water bottles, gulping the cold drink as they caught their breath.

"Pancakes at the City Café?" Jim asked.

Frankie looked at her watch and said, "I can do a quick breakfast, but I have to get to the office early today."

Ten minutes later the pair were sitting in their favorite booth overlooking the area of town known as the City Market in the City of Fountains. Cup of coffee for Jim, Diet Coke for Frankie, and water for both as they waited for their breakfast to be delivered.

"You realize neither of us ordered pancakes?" Frankie asked.

"You know this southern boy prefers grits over pancakes any day," Jim laughed.

Jim was from a small fishing village on the coast of North Carolina and had moved to Kansas City with the FBI. He had not lived in North Carolina in 25 years, but Frankie could still hear the hint of a southern accent, especially when he got excited or angry.

Frankie and Jim ate in companionable silence, watching the patrons come and go from the small diner, not feeling a need to fill the silence with chatter. Although there were closer places for breakfast, Frankie enjoyed the quaintness and location of the tiny diner, and Jim swore by their grits, often commenting on the similarity to those his grandmother would make.

Hesitating slightly, Jim asked, "How is Danielle doing?"

Frankie did not immediately offer an answer. Her daughter, Dani had gone to spend the summer with her father and recently she said wanted to go to school in the small town where he lived. Frankie suspected there were outside forces influencing her decision, but she couldn't prove it and was unsure what, if anything, she could do about it.

"She told me she wants to stay there for the school year."

Jim considered what Frankie said then asked, "How do you feel about it? What about Tyler?"

"I'm trying to see it from her perspective, but it's hard. I mean, she does have a more normal life there. Her dad is home every night, and her stepsister is putting a lot of pressure on her and constantly telling her what she will miss out on if she moves back to the city with us. Tyler is angry and somehow thinks it's his fault no matter how often I tell him it's not. It doesn't help she has missed the last couple of scheduled weekend visits."

"What happened?"

Frankie moved the food around on her plate as she weighed her words carefully, then said, "They offered her something better, so she stayed."

Jim reached his hand across the table and touched Frankie's. When she looked up from the plate, Jim could see the sadness in her eyes. He knew how much Frankie loved her children and how difficult it was for her to let Danielle leave for the summer. He did not have children of his own but could imagine the pain Frankie felt at the permanence of Danielle staying with her dad for the school year.

Changing the subject, Jim asked, "What do you have going on today?"

"Mia and I have an interview on a case I caught this weekend." Frankie did not technically have a partner in the Sex Crimes Unit, but she and Mia Boden were as close to partners as one could get. Frankie had trained Mia when she transferred from patrol, and since then they had been through a lot together. Frankie considered Mia more than a partner or friend; she was family.

"What about you?"

"A lot of paperwork, unfortunately. I have a case I need to get ready for submission to the US Attorney this week, and I am behind on some of the recordings we snagged. Y'all want to come and help me listen to the wires?" Jim laughed out loud knowing Frankie hated sitting behind a desk more than he did.

Before Frankie could answer, the waitress dropped the check on the table. Neither needed to look at the total, as their order and the total had not changed since they started meeting there for breakfast years earlier. Instead, they each pulled a ten-dollar bill from their pockets and laid it on the table, allowing for a generous tip for the waitress who made sure they were well-cared for but knew when to stay back and give them space.

"Where's Tyler tonight?" Jim asked as they walked to their cars, silently hoping he could entice Frankie to meet him for a beer after shift.

"He's down at the farm with my brother Jake. Tyler asked him to go four-wheeling, so I dropped him off last night. Jake's going to bring him home on his way to work tomorrow."

"Let me know if you and Mia want to meet up at Kelly's after shift."

Frankie climbed into her Jeep and replied, "Will do. Hopefully tonight will be…"

Jim interrupted, "Don't finish that sentence kid, or you know it will be an all-nighter."

CHAPTER
TEN

FRANKIE PULLED into the lot moments before Mia parked. She grabbed her bag and waited.

"Have you talked to the day shift yet," Mia asked.

"No. You?"

"No, but Erik got called in on a warrant. All they told him was it was for Special Victims. I don't know if it's us, Domestic Violence or Crimes Against Children. If it's us…"

"Don't even say it. I know –"

"Guess we'll know soon enough," Mia said as they started the climb to the fourth floor.

Frankie and Mia entered the door together, dropped their bags on their respective desks, and watched the flurry of activity in the squad room. Their supervisor, Sergeant Myles Baker, was in a closed office with Sergeant Jeff Kramer from their sister squad. The office had a large picture window, and based off Baker's uncharacteristic animation, it was not hard to see he was unhappy.

"What's going on?" Frankie asked.

"Baker is pissed off because there's a scene, and you all are going to have to deal with it. The call just came in about an hour ago. Patrol is with the victim at County. Based on what they told us we secured a warrant. Hell, Baker should be thanking us from keeping you all from having to run down a judge after hours for something that is probably a bunch of bullshit," said Larry Wilhelm.

Frankie could almost taste the blood from biting her tongue so hard. This was not the first time Wilhelm, or any of his squad for that matter, left a mess for her and Mia to clean up. Or the first time she heard them refer to a case as "bullshit" before investigating. Just as Frankie was about to respond, Kramer opened the door and nodded at Wilhelm, signaling it was time for them to leave.

When he was sure they were clear from the squad room, Baker walked out and said, "Thomas. Boden. Good thing you came in early."

"What do we have Sarge?" Mia asked.

"Best I can tell it is an 18-year-old girl who was abducted and raped. She ran from an abandoned house off of 9th Street and flagged down patrol. They got a warrant and should have gone out there, but..." Baker sighed. "You know how they are."

"What's her name?"

"Finley Garrett."

"Wilhelm said he thought it was bullshit. What's up with that?"

"Not surprising. Vic has a record as a runaway and for petty theft. Honestly, if the call would have come in earlier, he probably would have closed it out."

"Tell TAC to stand by until Mia and I talk to this girl." Frankie knew the Tactical Response Team would gladly execute the warrant, but it didn't sound like there was an active threat inside. Just a crime scene.

"Already done. Couple of the guys from TAC are watching it to see if anyone comes or goes. They know not to make a move until we get up there."

"Thanks, Sarge. We'll call you when we have an update."

CHAPTER
ELEVEN

MIA NAVIGATED the city streets deftly, pulling into a parking spot at County Hospital just as her cellphone began to ring. Putting the car in park, she reached for her ringing phone and answered on the second ring.

"Sex Crimes, Boden."

"Got any sex?" The deep voice on the other end of the phone made Mia laugh.

"Hey, Killer," Mia said, referring to the reporter that called the unit at least once a day. "We don't have anything right now."

"I heard there may have been some badness off of 9th street today. Any truth to the rumor?"

"Like I said, we don't have anything."

"Got it. I'll check in with you later."

"That didn't take long," Frankie said. "I wonder who tipped them off."

"Probably heard it on the scanners…or Wilhelm tipped him off."

"You don't really think he'd do that, do you?" Frankie asked.

"Not really, but if he thought it would make our lives more difficult, he might."

The two women walked through the Emergency Department, saying hello to the nurses and doctors they routinely worked with on their way to the examination room designated for sexual assault forensic exams.

The door opened as they approached the room, and a petite young woman peeked around the corner.

"Oh, hey Frankie. Hey Mia."

"Hi, Grace," Frankie said, greeting the young woman who had recently started a job with the local rape crisis center as a victim advocate. Suddenly noticing a tremble in Grace's hand, she asked, "Are you okay?"

"Yes. I came out to get Finley some water." Grace's voice quivered and tears filled her eyes as she said, "This was a hard one. The victim is pretty young."

Mia and Frankie shared a look then Mia asked, "Do you need a minute?"

"No. I think they're almost done. Will you be taking her to your office?"

Frankie thought about the question briefly and then said, "I think I want to ask her a few questions and see if we have to do a full interview now or if we can give her a day or two to rest. She's been through a lot. I don't want to push her unless it's necessary."

Before they could knock on the door, the nurse stuck her head out. Frankie was happy to see the face of the matronly nurse, Jennifer Jacobsen. Over the years she had taught Frankie about forensic examinations, bedside manner, and humility. Frankie had watched Jennifer take a drunk to task in one breath and comfort a terrified rape victim in the next. She did not suffer fools and made sure every patient understood every step of the invasive process involved in a forensic exam and what their options were. She never forced a patient to do anything he or she did not want to do.

Jennifer nodded and said, "Detectives. Finley is about to get a shower and get dressed. She'll be ready to leave in a few minutes."

"Can we talk to her real quick before she showers?" Mia asked. "We may be able to let her go home after and then come to our office later this week."

Jennifer said, "It's up to her," and stepped back into the examination room. After just a few seconds, she cracked the door and motioned the women inside.

A halo of curls outlined the face of the child lying on the bed. Her thick, red hair fell across the pillow and cascaded past shoulders. The nurse said she was just under 18, but in the hospital gown, she looked much younger. Her cobalt eyes were rimmed in red, and her freckled skin was splotchy in the harsh fluorescent light.

Once the introductions had been made, Mia asked, "Do you mind if we sit down and ask you a few quick questions?"

Quietly, Finley said, "Sure."

Frankie and Mia sat in a chair on either side of the bed.

Frankie said, "We want to talk to you about what happened today. We know you've been through a lot and probably want to get home..."

"I don't have a home..." Finley stopped herself, unsure how much more she should say.

Frankie and Mia looked at one another. What they said next could make the difference

between Finley cooperating or shutting down.

Frankie said, "Hey, we don't care if you were squatting. Or even if you were trying to make a date. We are here to talk about what happened to *you*."

"I wasn't trying to make a date. I ran away. He was supposed to be taking me to meet my boyfriend."

FRANKIE LISTENED INTENTLY as Finley described leaving her foster home, getting on a bus and ultimately being taken to the house off of 9ᵗʰ Street. Frankie and Mia made sure their expressions did not reveal any shock or judgment as Finley talked. Knowing they would do a more thorough interview at a later time, Frankie did not push for details, but instead listened for information that would guide evidence collection.

Just as she was finishing, Finley said, "I think he took pictures or videos. I saw flashes."

Frankie looked up from her notebook just in time for Jennifer to bring in discharge papers.

"Do you have any reason to think the man may still be there?" Frankie asked.

"He was lying on the floor when I left, but I don't know," Finley said.

"You said he had a truck?" Mia asked.

Finley nodded and provided a brief description of the truck before Jennifer asked the detectives to leave so she could give Finley her meds and discharge instructions.

While they were waiting, Frankie and Mia discussed where they should take the runaway. Jennifer called child protective services, but Frankie was afraid if Finley was placed with a foster family she would run again. There was a local shelter for displaced youth, and after a few phone calls, Frankie had a bed secured.

Frankie dialed the number for the social worker Jennifer had called. The man answered on the second ring, "This is John."

"Hi John, I'm Detective Thomas with the Kansas City Missouri Police Department. I'm assigned to the Sex Crimes Unit and am at County with Finley."

"I'm still about thirty minutes out Detective."

Frankie explained her concerns and plan to the overworked social worker and after just a few minutes she had convinced him to allow her to take Finley to the shelter. John could meet with her the following day after she had gotten some food and rest.

Once Finley was discharged, Frankie and Mia explained their plan to Finley.

"Will they make me go back to my foster family?"

The fear in Finley's voice was evident but Frankie knew better than to make promises she had no control over. Instead, she said, "I want you to be honest about your experience. This shelter is a safe place, and they have programs for kids your age. Programs to help you transition out of foster care and onto your own. Talk to one of the social workers at the shelter and see if they can help you."

Finley nodded.

CHAPTER
THIRTEEN

"HEY, SARGE," Frankie said into her cell. "It sounds like the house is vacant. The vic didn't get much of a look at the house but said it didn't look like anyone lived there."

"We'll have TAC make entry first just in case. Any weapons?"

"She didn't see one. She said he was supposed to be taking her to meet some guy she met online. She's a runaway," Frankie said.

"Rape?" Baker asked.

"Likely. He strangled her unconscious, and when she came to, her jeans were off, and her body was sore."

"How did she get away?"

"He was asleep, so she snuck out."

"You said she's a runaway?" Baker asked.

"Yes. I talked to the social worker, and he agreed to let us take her to Synergy. She was adamant about not returning to her foster family in Springfield. Synergy said they would see what they could do to help her. We'll get a formal from her tomorrow, but I think she needs food and sleep tonight."

"Agreed. Come on back here to brief TAC, and then we'll head over."

In the car, Frankie said, "I hope the jerk is there, and we can get the cellphone off him."

The pair drove in silence for a few minutes before Mia asked, "Do you really think he's still there?"

"I don't know."

Frankie circled headquarters looking for a place to park, finally locating one near the courthouse. She parked and looked up at the dark building with only a few lights illuminated on each floor.

CHAPTER
FOURTEEN

FRANKIE AND MIA watched as Bobby LeGrande and his partner Mark Andrews made entrance into the house with their team following. Frankie said a silent prayer for their safety and then waited for LeGrande to radio all clear. Less than five minutes passed and LeGrande was waving them to the porch.

"The house was vacant," LeGrande said. "Just like we expected."

"Looks like people have been squatting inside. We saw a bunch of garbage, and there was a mattress in one of the rooms on the main floor. Did she say anything about going out back?" Mark asked.

Frankie looked at her notes, then said, "No. She said as soon as they were inside, he locked her in and pushed her into a room on the main floor. Why?"

"It may be nothing," Mark began. "But there was a 55-gallon drum just outside the back door. At first, I thought it was an old burn barrel, but there was a lid and barrel clamps."

"Interesting," Mia said. "We'll have Crime Scene look at it."

As if on cue, Joel Pallerhinoshki and his partner pulled up in their white van. Frankie had worked with Joel, or Rhino as everyone called him, since she had been with the department. At almost 7' tall, he had played football for the University of Missouri. A knee injury sidelined him from going professional, so he pursued a master's degree in forensics from George Washington University instead.

Rhino filled the doorway when he entered the room, and his personality and heart matched his physical size. He was good at what he did, so Frankie and Mia were always glad when he showed up on a scene.

"Well, if it isn't the dynamic duo," Rhino said, his voice booming. Rhino reached out and gave each woman a side hug, then asked, "What do we have today?"

Frankie briefed Rhino and his partner with the information she received from Finley at the hospital. Rhino took notes, then grabbed his camera and began to shoot photographs of the exterior.

They were beginning to walk to the back of the house when Mia said, "Don't forget the barrel."

"Barrel?" Rhino asked.

"Yeah, Mark noticed it. It's probably unrelated, but it's odd."

"Okay. We'll take a look before we leave."

Once inside the residence, Frankie and Mia made notes of the evidence and its location while making small talk with the crime scene techs. They fell into an easy rhythm, finishing just before their shift ended.

"Ready to pack it up?" Mia asked.

"We're about done," Rhino said. "My partner took some photos of the barrel. It was empty, but I had him take a few swabs around the rim for DNA and dust for fingerprints. It didn't look like there were many of value. It looked pretty clean."

"Thanks, Rhino," Frankie said as the group walked to their respective vehicles. When they were inside their car, she looked at Mia and asked, "Want to grab a drink at Kelly's after we drop the car?"

"Mind if Erik joins us?"

"You know I don't," Frankie said. "Wonder if Sam will be there?"

Samantha Ryan was one of the prosecutors assigned to the Sex Crimes Unit in the prosecutor's office. She was a petite woman, with long black hair, classic Italian beauty, and moxie. Sam had been in Kansas City for less than a year, but in that time she, Frankie, and Mia had become an unstoppable team.

"Are she and Jim dating?" Mia asked.

"I don't think so. They went out a time or two but neither mentioned it being serious." Frankie said.

"Of course, *he* didn't..." sarcasm dripped from Mia's words.

Frankie asked, "What do you mean by that?"

"You seriously don't see it, do you?" Mia asked.

Frankie gave Mia a look full of question.

"He's waiting for *you*."

Frankie laughed out loud, then said, "You're crazy. He and I are just friends. I think you're seeing things. He's never so much as hinted about being attracted to me."

"Maybe because you are a busy single mom and, given your history, he wanted to respect your boundaries. I've seen the way he looks at you when you're not paying attention. And the way he drops everything anytime you call."

"I think you need your eyes checked sis."

Before Mia could respond, Frankie's phone rang. She didn't need to look to know who it was. Mia listened to the chatter and smiled to herself. Even if Frankie couldn't see it, Jim Craven did not want to be in the friend zone.

"Hey, Jim. Yeah, we just finished the scene and are on the road to HQ. Mmhmm, I think Erik is going to join us, too. Is Sam there? What, Sophie's out? Tell her she owes me a beer! Okay, see you in thirty."

"What time is Jake bringing Tyler home tomorrow?"

Frankie smiled at the mention of her younger brother and son. "Way too early. By the way, Jim said Sophie is at the bar."

"What's your little sister doing at a cop bar?" Mia asked. Laughing she added, "Has she lost her mind?"

"I guess I shouldn't have introduced her to our world. I think she's gone out with Craig Jenner a few times. So far, he seems to be treating her okay. If I hear otherwise, I may have to enlist your help in kicking his ass."

"You won't even have to ask."

FRANKIE WALKED into the bar and scanned the room for familiar faces. It didn't take her long to see Sophie, Jim, and Sam sitting at a high-top table by the dartboard with bottles of Bud Light on the table in front of them. Frankie stopped at the bar, grabbed her own and sauntered over to the trio.

"Where are Mia and Erik?" Jim asked.

"They weren't far behind me."

"Maybe if you didn't drive like your hair was on fire…" Sophie teased as she threw her arm around Frankie's shoulder, smiling as she looked down at her older sister.

"Are you driving topless tonight?" Jim asked with a wink.

Smiling, Frankie answered coyly, "Is there any other way?"

"Jim said you caught a new case today." Sam said, not amused at the subtle flirtation.

"Yeah. Teenage runaway came to the city to meet a boy she had been talking to online. When she got to the bus depot an old man was there instead of the boy. He took her to an abandoned house in Northeast."

Sam asked, "Anyone in custody?"

"No."

"Any leads?"

"Not really. We'll do a canvas tomorrow but I'm not going to hold my breath. The people in the neighborhood around the house aren't big fans of ours."

Sophie piped up and said, "Okay, enough shop talk. Let's put some tunes on the jukebox and maybe get my sis out on the dance floor. Liven the place up a bit."

Craig Jenner walked up behind Sophie, put his arms around her waist, and said, "Girl, you liven up a room just being in it."

Sophie smiled, collected change and requests from everyone at the table, and headed for the classic jukebox a few feet away.

Frankie smiled, looked around the table, and thought about how things had changed over the past few years. It hadn't been that long when she and Tyler's father, Brad…

"Frankie… Frankie?" Sophie nudged her shoulder.

"Huh? What?"

"Where'd you go? I was asking if you wanted another beer?"

"Sorry, just lost in thought. Thanks. Need some cash?"

"I got you," Sophie said.

The time crept closer to closing, and one by one people took their leave. Mia and Erik were the first to go, having stayed for only one beer. Sophie and Craig left separately, acting coy, as though everyone had not figured out that they were going together. Left behind were Frankie, Sam, and Jim.

"I should probably head out, too," Frankie said, suddenly feeling awkward and like a third wheel. "Jake is dropping Tyler off early in the morning."

Sam smiled and said, "Let's grab lunch this week Frankie. It would be great to hang out."

"I'd like that, Sam," Frankie answered. "I'll give you a call."

Jim, always the gentleman, stood up and asked, "Want me to walk you to your car?"

"No, it's okay. I parked close. I'll be fine." With a laugh Frankie said, "Besides, I think I can handle myself."

Giving her a hug, he said, "Girl, I know you can. Drive safe. Text me when you get home."

Returning the hug she had once thought brotherly, she said, "Okay dad," exaggerating the word dad.

Sam took note of their interaction. It looked to her as though Jim wished he were leaving with Frankie as he watched her walk away.

CHAPTER
SIXTEEN

THE ALARM SOUNDED JUST as Frankie heard the passenger door of Jake's truck slam shut. She hopped to the floor and unlocked the door at the same time Tyler began ringing the doorbell.

"Hey, mom. You look like you just got out of bed. Me and Uncle Jake have been up for *hours*," Tyler said, stretching out the word hours for effect. "I need to go get my stuff for camp. Thanks, Uncle Jake. I had fun."

"Anytime, bud. I had fun, too." Jake said.

Tyler could be heard as he darted down the hall, "Love you!"

"Love you, too," Jake said loudly. Turning to Frankie with a hint of laughter in his voice, he asked, "Hey, sis, rough night?"

"No, just late. Had a scene, then went and grabbed a beer after work. Guess who came out on a school night. One hint, she looks just like you."

"Sophie? I'm not surprised she was out, but I am surprised she was hanging somewhere your friends would hang. That's a pretty rough crowd."

Jake, who was built like a linebacker and stood almost a foot and a half taller than Frankie, moved to avoid the punch he knew would come from his older sister. Frankie was several years older than Jake and Sophie and was very protective of her siblings.

"She was with a cop, Jake. I knew I shouldn't have introduced her around."

"He a good guy?"

"Yeah, I guess. He's green, but from what I hear he is pretty good."

"I didn't ask what kind of cop he is; I want to know if he's a nice guy."

"He seems to be, but I haven't spent much time with him."

"Good. Keep me in the loop because you know she won't," Jake said. "Before I go, I had a visitor down at the farm last night. He asked me to get a message to you."

"Really? Who?"

"Your buddy from high school, Patrick. Didn't you two date for a while?"

"Not really. We just hung out a lot as friends."

"Seemed like more than friends to me, but what do I know? I was just a kid. Did you know he was back in town?"

"Someone may have mentioned it, but I haven't talked to him in a while." Frankie said.

"Rumor around town is he just got out of the military and was thinking about putting in a bid for sheriff," said Patrick.

"No kidding?"

"Have you ever thought of running for sheriff? Or is that too small-town for you?" Jake asked.

"Too political," said Frankie. "I wouldn't have thought Patrick would have any interest either."

"Who knows. Because of the rumors, I figured he just wanted a donation to his campaign, but he said he needs your help with something. He gave me his number and asked me to have you call him."

"Probably just wants me to help plan a school reunion or something," Frankie said.

"I don't think so, Frankie. He said it was about Julia."

A cloud crossed Frankie's face. She took the card Jake held and said, "It's been a long time since anyone has asked about her. I wonder what it's about. I'll give him a call after I drop Tyler off and let you know what he says."

"Okay. Let's plan another weekend for Tyler to come down before school starts. He's a pretty fun kid."

"Thanks, Jake, I know he loves hanging out with you. Almost as much as I do," Frankie said, slugging him on the arm. "Love you."

Jake walked away uttering a muffled, "Love you, too."

CHAPTER
SEVENTEEN

FRANKIE CLOSED the door and leaned against it, holding Patrick's number in her clenched fist and wondered if it *was* him she saw in the old bank parking lot. It had been years since she had seen Patrick and thought her eyes were playing tricks on her.

Patrick was a year older than Frankie, and she and Beth spent a lot of time with him and his best friend Brent his final year of high school. People assumed they were dating, but they were just friends. It started as group outings. They would cruise through town and got to bonfires with their group of friends but eventually it developed into something special. Frankie sat down on the couch remembering.

Twenty-eight years earlier

With August came lots of sunshine, heat, and cheerleading camp. Frankie couldn't believe the school – and their parents – allowed her and Beth to drive her car to camp instead of taking the bus. Driving to camp alone gave them a glimpse of the adult world and freedoms that were to come. Frankie smiled, put the top down, and played the music loud as they drove out of town. Beth sat next to her and their bedding, bags, pom-poms, and a cooler of snacks filling the backseat of the tiny convertible.

The hour-long drive to the university where the camp was being held went by quickly. The fields of wheat and corn waved in the wind when they passed. Frankie and Beth sang along to every song on the radio, and when the station became static, they popped in a cassette tape of one of their favorite bands.

"It's more than a feeling when I hear that old song play…" Frankie and Beth sang loudly.

Pulling onto campus, Frankie imagined what it would be like to go to college. She, like many teenagers, was in a hurry to grow up and travel far to attend college. San Diego was her first choice, but her dad wanted her to consider local options. Frankie could not wait to live in a dorm and experience college life.

"Do you know which building we're staying in?" Frankie asked.

Beth fumbled with the papers in her bag then said, "Hey, there's Brent and Patrick." She stood up in the car and waved at the two boys from their hometown.

Frankie reluctantly navigated the car towards the boys. She liked both of them but wanted to get things unloaded so they could explore campus before it got dark.

Beth barely waited for the car to stop before she was out and flirting with Brent. Frankie casually made her way to Patrick, looked up, and smiled.

"Nice to see a familiar face," Patrick said.

"Same. Have you found your way around campus yet?"

"We found our dorm and the football field but not much else. We were about to grab some food and then walk around. What about you?"

"We just got here. Beth was looking for the name of the dorm when she saw you two and got distracted."

Patrick laughed, apologized, then said, "If you can find the name, I'll help you unload and then maybe we can all grab a bite and explore together?"

Frankie nodded and pulled the papers from Beth's bag. After orienting her location to the images on the map, she realized they were one building away from their dorm and directly next door to the football players.

"Beth, are you going to come and help us?" Frankie asked, but Beth and Brent were lost in conversation.

"What, huh? Oh, yeah, how far's the building?"

Frankie pointed to the building where they needed to check in. Unloading the car was quick work with four people. Thirty minutes later, the foursome was jumping in the convertible and off to find food.

The week passed quickly and, when they were not training, Frankie and Patrick were together. Different girls from camp thought Patrick was Frankie's boyfriend, but she couldn't figure out if he liked her or if he just wanted to spend time with Brent, who wanted to spend every waking moment with Beth.

When Brent and Beth separated from the group, Frankie and Patrick would continue to talk late into the night. By the time the camp ended, they knew as much about the other as two people could know, but neither shared their future plans. Frankie did not share her dreams of moving to southern California and, similarly, Patrick did not share his plans for after high school. Neither seemed to want to break the spell of summer by talking about what lay ahead.

The second night of camp, they sat on a blanket in the quad and Frankie told Patrick what she saw on the Hudson farm. For reasons she could never fully explain, he was the only one she told. The topic consumed many of the private conversations that followed, and they made plans to investigate further when they returned home from camp. Based on instinct and their limited knowledge of investigations (from television and mystery novels) they jotted down notes, thought of people to interview, and hypothesized on what type of evidence they might be able to find. They were driven by more than morbid curiosity. Both had a strong desire to figure out where their friend had gone, and why people had stopped talking.

Throughout the school year, Patrick and Frankie continued to spend time together and, although their friendship grew deeper, neither made any move to take things to the next level. Patrick went to the farm with Frankie, and she went to his house on the edge of town. Rumors circulated, but both denied them, saying they were just friends.

CHAPTER
EIGHTEEN

IN A BLINK OF AN EYE, the year ended, and Patrick and Brent walked across the stage to receive their diploma. They planned a blowout party to celebrate, and Frankie and Beth were two of the limited underclassmen invited.

The girls could hear the music before they saw the first car. The notes of a Top 40 song filled the air and guided Frankie to the menagerie of cars and people. Based on the size of the crowd, she thought the entire senior class must be there. Frankie recognized many of the cars parked haphazardly in the field. A stack of wood in the shape of a teepee served as a centerpiece to the graduates milling around. Summer was on the horizon, but there was still a slight chill in the late May air, making the bonfire a perfect accent to the evening.

Frankie parked the car but did not make a move to get out, instead she sat and watched the people she had known most of her life. Julia should have been there, she thought. It had been almost a year since her friend went missing and, even though the occasional rumor was spread, there had been no real leads and very few pieces of valid information. It seemed as though law enforcement had given up. Patrick and Frankie had done some rudimentary investigation of their own but had not learned much. They knew Julia and her mom had not picked up their final paychecks and didn't take any of their belongings with them. Craig told Frankie in confidence that he and Julia had not had sex, so the rumor she was pregnant was false. Julia's father continued to do "renovations" at their house, but Frankie noticed Lauren did not come home for the holidays or for the summer.

"Are you coming, Frankie?" Beth stood by the car door holding her sweater.

"Hmm? Oh yeah, let me grab my sweatshirt."

The pair mingled with the upperclassmen, hearing for the umpteenth time who was going to what college or which branch of the military, who was staying behind to work the family farm, and who had secured a job at one of the nearby automotive plants. Frankie smiled and laughed, but inside she knew things were changing, and in 12 months, she would be in their shoes. Suddenly the life she couldn't wait to start was almost there and, for a moment, it scared her.

"Hey, Frankie," a deep voice said from behind.

Turning she answered, "Hey Patrick. Great party!"

"Thanks. Brent planned it, I just got permission from mom to use the field."

The two made small talk, reminiscing about the last year of school and the hours they had spent in various places together. Before either realized it, the fire had gone out and partygoers had started to scatter. Beth had already left with Brent, leaving Frankie to drive home alone.

Looking at her watch, Frankie said, "I'm going to have to leave now if I want to make curfew. I just realized, after all the months of hanging out, you haven't said what you're doing this summer. Or this fall, for that matter."

Patrick smiled and said, "I leave for bootcamp in two days. I enlisted in the Army."

FRANKIE FELT her heart drop into her stomach. It never crossed her mind Patrick may be leaving town. In all the time they had spent together, he had never mentioned it. Aloud she said, "Following in your father's footsteps, huh?"

"Father, grandfather, uncles – they were all Army. I'm just carrying on their legacy."

"How does your mom feel about that?" Frankie knew this must be bittersweet for Patrick's mom. His father was killed in action in Vietnam, and she had never seemed to get over it.

"She was mad as hell when I first told her, but secretly, I think she's very proud. She made me promise I would call her every Sunday."

"Sounds like a mom," Frankie laughed. "What does your granddad think?"

Patrick paused then said, "He didn't say much at first. He seemed… almost disappointed. I don't know for sure if it's because of dad or because he needs my help on the farm. He finally came around though."

"What's your granddad going to do on the farm?" Frankie asked. She knew Patrick's mother and grandfather depended on him during planting and harvest.

"We've got all the crops out, but he will have to hire someone to help during harvest."

By this time the pair reached Frankie's little red convertible. She turned towards Patrick, embraced him in a hug, and gently kissed his cheek, "Be safe, Patrick. And stay in touch."

Without another word, Frankie got into her car and left. That was the last time she saw or spoke to Patrick. They exchanged letters throughout Frankie's senior year, but eventually they wrote less and less frequently until they finally lost contact.

CHAPTER
TWENTY

Present Day

FRANKIE SAT on the porch and watched the neighbor's kids play, turning the card over in her hand. She hadn't seen or heard from Patrick since the note he sent for her graduation. Beth told her he served in Desert Storm and made a career in the Army, but their paths hadn't crossed. Frankie had no idea why Patrick would need her help, but they had been close in high school, and it felt wrong not to see what he wanted. Carefully, she dialed the unfamiliar number.

"Hello?"

"Patrick? This is Frankie. Frankie Thomas… uhm I mean Moretti. Jake gave me your number. Said you needed me to call."

"Hey, girl! It sure has been a long time," Patrick said.

The two exchanged a few pleasantries before Frankie asked, "After all these years with no contact, I know you didn't call to make small talk. What's going on, Patrick?"

"Never one to suffer fools. I always liked that about you, Moretti. Truth is, I heard you were a detective and I need your help. Can you meet?"

"What do you need *my* help with?"

Patrick paused for a moment and then said, "I wanted to talk about this in person, but if my hunch is right, I've uncovered some corruption in town, and I think it may be connected to Julia's disappearance."

Frankie was stunned and unable to find the right words to respond.

"Are you still there?"

"Yeah. You just took me by surprise. I'm booked pretty solid today, but I'm off tomorrow. I drop my son at camp at 8, but I'm free after," Frankie said. After making plans to meet, she said, "I look forward to catching up."

"Me, too."

Frankie watched the kids playing in the sprinkler and thought about the hours she and Julia had spent running through Shack Creek, splashing in the pools that formed after a rain. She could hear the laughter as they ran through the hayfield, catching fireflies and putting them in jars. In her memories, their skin was sun-kissed and their eyes bright and innocent. They had shared the wishes and dreams of childhood, their hope not yet dulled by age and experience.

The alarm sounded on her phone and jolted Frankie out of her thoughts, letting her know it was time to get ready for work.

"Talk about reality. Guess I better get ready to face mine."

CHAPTER
TWENTY-ONE

CLARA STEPPED off the Metro bus into the waning sunlight. She slung her purse over her shoulder and thought to herself she should walk straight home. Clara looked at her watch, turned and walked in the opposite direction from her house and headed to The Corner Bar.

"I'll just have one quick drink, then I'll go home."

Clara had just finished a double shift at the nursing home and was keyed up and exhausted all at the same time. One of her favorite patients had taken a turn for the worst at the beginning of her first shift and by the end of her second, he had passed. Clara had broken one of her own cardinal rules working with the elderly and infirm; she had become friends with a patient.

Haywood McDowell moved into the home a year prior. He was 95 years old, and his parents, siblings, wife, and children were long gone. He talked about the children he and his wife LaTonya raised and, although he rarely mentioned it, Clara knew both children had died. His son, William died in Vietnam and his daughter, Grace from cancer. Grace's death prompted Haywood's move into the home. Despite his many losses, Haywood was a positive, inspiring man and had lived a life full of experiences. He told stories of the civil rights movement and his involvement with the marches in Selma, Montgomery, and Washington,

D.C. He talked about the changes he had seen throughout the years and often marveled at how different, yet the same, things were.

Clara had sworn off alcohol about the time Haywood moved into the home. When she told her drunk of a boyfriend she was getting sober he left. Clara was lonely and found herself checking on Haywood at the end of her shift, eventually staying through dinner, especially when the cravings were at their worst. As a result, Haywood had become her friend.

In the weeks leading up to his death, Haywood was diagnosed with pancreatic cancer. It came as a surprise, and his decline was fast. Clara tried to talk him into treatment, but in the end, she helped him have a dignified death, holding his hand until his last breath.

Clara had not had a drink in more than 300 days, but the craving was strong tonight. She didn't want to walk into her empty house with a bottle knowing she would find herself at the bottom of it. She didn't trust herself to be alone, at least not for a little while.

Clara pulled the heavy door open, sidled up to the bar and said, "Can I get a Patron with lime?" After a beat she added, "Make that a double."

The bartender barely glanced at her face, just nodded, and made the drink. Clara was thankful he did not feel the need to make conversation. He didn't look like the kind of person who wanted to hear other people's problems and she didn't want to share hers.

"Do you want to start a tab?"

Clara hesitated before saying, "No, I'll just be having one," and laid money on the bar top.

The bartender took her cash and walked away. Clara sat and stared at the drink, using her fingers to squeeze the lime and move it around the short glass with the thin straw. She knew what the drink would taste like; how it would feel on her lips and as it went down her throat. She knew the burn that would be followed by a warm sensation and soon a sense of ease in her shoulders. Clara knew in a few minutes the pain she felt at losing her friend would be duller but not really gone. She had lost herself in that feeling when her father died and almost did not find her way out of it.

CHAPTER
TWENTY-TWO

CLARA WAS LOST in thought as she stared at the lime and didn't immediately notice the man who sidled up to the bar and sat down next to her. She was unsure how long he had been there but felt him staring at her intently. When she looked over, the first thing she noticed was the design shaved into his fade and then his size. He sat ramrod straight on the stool and her head was only as high as his chest. He looked down at her with a glint in his light, greenish-colored eyes. Her momma called eyes like his bedroom eyes. Because of the contrast and color, they were mesmerizing.

"Are you going to drink that or just stare at it," the man asked with a hint of laughter in his deep voice.

"Honestly, I haven't decided yet."

"I don't think I've seen you in here before. What's your name?"

Clara considered giving this stranger a fake name, but then said, "Clara. You?"

"Deacon, but my friends call me Blade."

"Why, because you carry a blade?" Clara asked in bemusement.

Laughing, Deacon answered, "Maybe...but more likely it's because they think I look like Sling Blade," touching the shaved section of hair.

Clara didn't see the resemblance but thought it impolite to say anything.

Clara and Deacon sat and talked, but Clara never picked up the glass. She continued to move the lime around the glass as Deacon, or Blade as he preferred to be called, talked about his job as a security officer and bouncer at The Corner Bar and the neighborhood grocery store.

"Yeah, they really rely on me over there. I mean I probably prevent at least one robbery every day. The cops are always stopping by telling me how much they appreciate me and what I do. Hell, I wouldn't be surprised if they wrote me up for some kind of award."

Clara knew Blade was blowing smoke and trying to impress her, but listening to him kept her from thinking too long about Haywood and how much she already missed him. She looked at her watch and back at the glass sitting in front of her and then slid off the stool where she had been for the past hour.

"I think it's time for me to go home. It's starting to get dark, and I have to work tomorrow. Thanks for the conversation, Blade. Maybe I'll see you around."

"I'll walk you home," Blade said. "It's a service I offer all the nice young women who come in here alone." Looking at the bartender, he said, "I'll be back in ten minutes."

Clara noticed he did not give her a chance to refuse his offer. She considered saying something but decided the company would be nice. She also wondered how he knew he would be back in ten minutes. She hadn't told him where she lived, but then she figured it was a good assumption that she lived close if she didn't have a car. Clara grabbed her bag and walked out into the twilight with Blade close behind.

CHAPTER
TWENTY-THREE

CLARA BEGAN WALKING in the direction of her house and Blade followed. At the first crossroad, he said, "I need to run by and get some weed for after work. Want a little? I can get you some from my guy. It's primo."

Clara did not immediately answer. She smoked occasionally but only when she did not have to work the next day. She started to explain but then said, "I don't have any extra cash on me right now."

"It'll be my treat. I really want you to try my guy's stuff." Blade pointed down the street away from Clara's house and said, "He lives this way."

Clara hesitated, but then followed Blade. When they got to the house, she noticed the front door had a piece of plywood over it, and there were no cars in the driveway. She stopped at the end of the driveway and did not move; a feeling of dread ran down her spine.

Blade walked ahead of her, turned around and gestured towards the front door, "Don't worry about that. Someone broke in the other day, and he hasn't had the time to get a new door. This was a short-term solution until he can get to the hardware store. He knows I'm coming and left the backdoor unlocked. Come on."

"I can just wait out here for you."

"You don't want to do that. Henry will think you're a cop. He's watching us right now, and if you don't come in, he won't give me any. Besides, you'll like him."

Clara felt the hair on the back of her neck stand up, but Blade had been nice and said he was a security guard. She should be able to trust him. She tentatively walked behind Blade, following him into the back door of the dark house. Once inside, Blade gestured for Clara to step out of the doorway and before she realized what was happening, he had grabbed her by the arm and hit her on the back of her head. Everything went black as she fell to the floor.

When Clara woke up, she couldn't move. She was lying on a mattress that reeked of urine and God knew what else. Her hands were bound behind her and there was something in her mouth so a scream would be muffled. Her purse was gone, but even if it wasn't, she didn't know how she would get her cellphone out.

Clara was unsure how long she laid there before she heard the back-door of the house creak open. Her shoulders and head hurt and as he approached, his entire body filled the doorway, and hers filled with terror.

CHAPTER
TWENTY-FOUR

BLADE PRODUCED a large switchblade and cut the ties from Clara's arms and legs.

"One word and it will be your last," Blade said and then removed the gag from her mouth.

Clara didn't know what time it was, but she assumed it was after midnight since he told her he worked at the bar, and she thought that was when it closed. The man who cut the ties was not the same man she had talked to at the bar. The mesmerizing bedroom eyes from earlier now reflected pure evil and elicited fear.

For the next several hours, Blade raped Clara repeatedly, in every way imaginable and always with the switchblade in reach. When he finally tired of degrading and hurting her, he laid back on the mattress and picked up a glass pipe.

"Want a hit?" Blade casually asked, as though the coitus had been pleasurable and wanted by both parties.

Clara did not answer but held her breath as her pulse raced.

"Suit yourself," said Blade.

"I'm cold," Clara said softly.

Blade picked up Clara's pants and shirt and threw them at her.

"Thank you."

Blade hit the pipe until the substance was gone. Eventually he closed his eyes, and his breathing, which had been labored, slowed to a steady rhythm. Clara waited, thinking he must be asleep. Very slowly and carefully she began to move off the nasty mattress onto the equally dirty floor. She had planned to run to the back door and try to find help, but when she reached the doorway to the room, she heard his low, deep voice.

"Where the hell do you think you're going?"

Without answering, Clara ran. The layout of the house was unfamiliar and instead of running into the kitchen, she ended up in what must have once been a living room. Blade was close behind and almost within arm's reach. He grabbed her, but Clara kicked and screamed, fighting as though her life depended on it. When she was able to wrench free, she ran straight to the plate glass window, bursting through it into the early dawn of morning.

Clara was almost sure Blade wouldn't follow, but she didn't stop running until she was standing on a neighboring house's porch. She alternated banging on the door and pulling glass from her pants and arms. Clara repeated this at several houses until she saw a police car driving down the street towards her. She stood in the middle of the road in her blood-stained clothes, waved her arms, and screamed with everything she had until the car stopped.

CHAPTER
TWENTY-FIVE

FRANKIE DID NOT MAKE it to the office before her cellphone began ringing. She glanced at the caller ID and then answered, "Sex Crimes, Thomas."

"Did you say Thomas?"

"Yes. This is the Sex Crimes Unit."

"This is Officer Gordon from Metro. I am out on a scene."

"What do you have?"

Frankie listened as the officer briefed her on the scene, then asked, "Is she still there?"

"Yes. The paramedics are looking at her now. She has a lot of blood on her, but it seems like...what? Detective, my FTO wants to talk to you."

"Okay."

"Hey, Frankie!"

Frankie would have known that voice anywhere. "Hey, Bobby, what's up? You couldn't give me five minutes to drop my stuff before calling?"

Anthony "Bobby" McClendon had been Frankie's partner when she was on patrol. Frankie graduated from the Police Academy a class before Bobby and, after he finished the required time with his Field Training Officer, or FTO as they were called, he and Frankie were moved to the same sector and thrown together as partners.

Frankie always felt very fortunate to have Bobby as a partner. They complimented one another well. Neither was afraid to fight if needed, but both found value, and took pride in talking their way out of situations. Their shifts were long and, when they were not answering calls for service, they were usually laughing about something.

After Frankie left the field, Bobby became a FTO and routinely cycled through recruits. Bobby was tough, but fair. He wanted to make sure every recruit went home at the end of their shift, so he challenged them as much as he could. Bobby answered up for the harder calls, but he would not let his recruits show up just to write reports. His philosophy was, if they couldn't handle it from beginning to end, then they should wait for the next one.

"This scene is pretty messy, Frankie. Do you remember Blade?"

"That guy off 36th and Walrond that had the lightning bolt shaved into his fade?"

"Yeah."

"I thought he was in prison."

"He was," Bobby answered. "But it sounds like he's out and hasn't changed much."

CHAPTER
TWENTY-SIX

THIS WAS NOT Frankie's first encounter with Deacon Jackson, or Blade as he was known on the streets. It was not even her second encounter. This was someone she had dealt with on patrol and two more times in her current role as a detective. Blade took great pleasure in threatening, beating, and cutting women and once he got them completely under his control, he would rape them.

Frankie and Bobby had not been partners long when they were dispatched to County to meet one of Blade's first rape victims. Frankie did not think she would ever forget the woman she met that night. Olivia Joy Westin was her name. She was covered in blood and had the beginning of bruises and slash marks on her arms, legs, abdomen, and face. Frankie didn't think she looked like she would make it through the night, but Olivia survived and said she would testify in court. Months later, the case got tossed on a technicality, and Olivia never got over it. Frankie encountered her periodically on patrol and was saddened when, two years after the attack, Olivia died by suicide.

There were other victims of Blade, however the cases didn't seem to stick. The victims were either too scared, or prosecutors were worried about how they would present before a jury. Finally, Frankie encountered Blade when she was a detective. She put together a solid case, and after a brief trial he went to prison. Frankie was shocked to hear he was out.

"Ugh. Is the vic going to the hospital?" Frankie asked.

"She hasn't told us much yet. She's pretty shaken up but doesn't have any life-threatening injuries that we can see. I think she's in shock," Bobby explained. "And got lucky."

"Do you recognize her?"

"No, I think she might have been trying to score but she and my boot didn't exactly connect. If she was, she isn't going to tell *him*."

Frankie smiled at the term Bobby used to refer to his recruit, boot. They both hated it when their FTO referred to them by that name.

"Is he in custody?"

"No, she said he took off when she ran through the plate glass window."

"Window? What? Never mind, text me the address. Is it her house or his?" Frankie asked.

"Abandoned. We found the owner though, and they gave us consent to search, so you shouldn't need a warrant," said Bobby.

"You are a lifesaver. I just pulled up to HQ and need to see who's working. I'll let you know who's coming and how long it'll be. Keep her there if you can."

Frankie thought about the interview she had scheduled with Finley and growled. She wanted this scene. Frankie tossed her bag onto her desk and briefed Sergeant Baker on the scene waiting. Baker was familiar with Blade and his history, and they had a full squad, so they could divide the work. Before he started barking orders, he said, "Frankie, your vic from last night called and asked to reschedule. She said she needs another day."

Frankie nodded, secretly relieved.

"Wheeler, you and Coleman will ride out to the scene in one car. Frankie and Mia, you'll take the other. I want the two of you to get a good statement from the vic and get her to the hospital for a full forensic exam, even if he didn't rape her. Wheeler, you and Coleman will meet crime scene techs to process the scene. Don't shut it down or let crime scene go until you've talked to Frankie and Mia to make sure you haven't missed something."

"Copy," the detectives said in unison, each checking their duty bags to make sure they had the supplies they needed.

"I'll be here trying to figure out how the hell this guy got out of prison and what we need to do to put him back inside before he kills someone," Baker said. As an afterthought, he said, "Don't forward the phones. I can handle them."

TWENTY-SEVEN

MIA PULLED up to the small white ranch-style house twenty minutes after Frankie took the initial call. The ambulance was gone, and a single patrol car was left behind. Crime scene tape was up around the front of the house, and a woman they assumed was the owner stood at the edge of the drive talking to Bobby.

"Look at the window," Frankie said, nodding at the shattered plate glass window on the front of the house.

"You think she really went through that window?"

Before Frankie could answer, they saw Clara pacing at the back of the patrol car, rubbing her arms and biting her lower lip. Her ebony hair stood out from her scalp in disarray. The skin that was exposed was the color of caramel and was streaked with tears and blood. Both of her arms were wrapped in white gauze from the elbows to her wrists. Her pale blue shirt and pants were torn and had dried blood on the fringes.

"I think that answers your question," Frankie said nodding at Clara.

On the way to the scene, the pair had discussed taking the victim to headquarters to get a preliminary statement and then transport her to the hospital. After seeing her, those plans quickly changed.

"Let's take her to the hospital and do a prelim there," Mia said.

"You read my mind," Frankie replied.

Frankie got out of the car, donned a pair of latex gloves, grabbed a lint roller from the glovebox, and rolled it across the seat to eliminate potential trace evidence she left while sitting there. After transporting Clara to the hospital, they would use trace lifters to capture any physical evidence that may have dropped from her clothing.

"Hey, Frankie. Mia," Bobby said. "This is Laura Jacobs. She owns this house and has given us permission to process the scene."

"Nice to meet you, ma'am," Frankie and Mia said in unison.

"Likewise," Laura said. "I need to get a handyman out to board up the window. Do you know how long this is going to take?"

"Detectives Coleman and Wheeler are right behind us. They called Crime Scene and are going to work with them to process the scene." Looking at her watch, she added, "I can't imagine them not being done by dark, but I don't want to make any promises since I haven't been inside and don't know how long it'll take for techs to get out here. Can you leave your number – or your handyman's – and we'll call when they're wrapping up?"

Laura handed Frankie a business card and said, "Please call this number when you are finished, and I'll call John."

Mia walked over to the woman pacing by the patrol car and introduced herself. Clara stared back at her with vacant eyes. The recruit motioned for Mia to step over to where he was standing.

"She's been like this since the ambulance left. I finally stopped trying to get her to talk, thinking maybe she was afraid of me or that maybe I made her uncomfortable."

"It's not you. I think she's in shock. Why don't you go check and see if Bobby needs you to do anything, and I'll see if I can get her to come to my car."

MIA APPROACHED the woman with a slow gait. She scanned the area and noticed neighbors were standing in their yards or sitting on their porches, not even hiding the fact they were watching the scene play out. They would canvas the area for witnesses, but Mia was not hopeful they would find anyone to cooperate. More likely they would hear lots of complaints about Ms. Jacobs and her lack of attention to the property.

Mia got within a few feet and stopped, careful to give the woman space so she didn't feel trapped. She stood at the edge of the car for the count of five and then asked her name.

"Clara," was the soft response.

"Clara, I'm Detective Boden but you can call me Mia. My partner, Frankie Thomas, is over there talking to one of the officers you met earlier." Mia knew the neighbors were likely trying to overhear their conversation and added, "There are a lot of people standing around, and it's pretty warm today. Do you want to go sit in my car?"

Clara gave the question some thought before asking, "Will I be locked in? Are you arresting me for breaking that lady's window?"

Mia had not considered that as contributing to Clara's fear but quickly said, "No, you can get out of the car any time you want to and no, you are not under arrest. I'm here to talk about what happened to you today."

Clara's shoulders lowered slightly, "I guess it would be alright then."

Mia opened the door and invited Clara to sit in the front seat, then walked around to the driver's side and sat down. She turned the car radio off and turned the patrol radio down so it could barely be heard and would not interfere or distract from the interview.

Mia asked a few demographic questions, identifying where Clara lived and the best ways to contact her. She kept the conversation light and superficial, hoping they would build rapport and she would earn Clara's trust or at the very least make her feel comfortable so she would share the details of her experience.

"Do you mind if I record our conversation today?" Mia asked.

"No, I don't care," Clara mumbled.

Mia turned the recorder on, provided the date, time, location, and names of the persons present, then said, "Clara, can you please tell me happened today?"

"It kind of started yesterday. Well, last night really. I...I ... uh I don't know where to begin."

"That's okay. Start wherever you feel comfortable starting and just tell me what you remember, how you remember it. Oh, and Clara, I am here to find out what happened to you. So, I don't care if you were using, trying to score, or even if you were trying to make a date. I'm not going to arrest you. I just want to hear what happened to you."

Clara leaned back in the seat, took a deep breath, and said, "He said his name was Deacon."

TWENTY-NINE

"I WAS at The Corner Bar after work and started talking to the bouncer. This guy came up and started talking to me. He never said his last name but said everyone calls him Blade because of the designs in his fade. I was having a bad day. He was nice looking and seemed okay.

"Before I knew it, it was dark outside. I told him I was going to leave because I hadn't had dinner and had to work the next morning." Clara began to panic and reached for the car door. "Oh, no, what time is it? I don't have my phone. I'm going to be late. I can't lose this job!"

Mia paused the recording and asked, "Do you want to use my phone to call your boss? I'm sure they'll understand."

It took a few minutes for Mia's words to register with Clara. It wasn't until Mia extended the phone that Clara took her hand off the door.

"Thank you." She dialed the number from memory and said, "Hi Tony, put Laquisha on the phone." Clara was quiet for a few seconds. "I need to take a personal day…I know I'm off the next couple of days, but I'm on my way to the hospital. I was attacked last night. I'm with the detective now."

Clara shoved the phone towards Mia and began to sob.

"Laquisha, this is Detective Norris. Mmmhmm, yes ma'am, I'm going to take her to the hospital. I'm not sure, but I'll tell her you want a call when she's discharged. Mmmhmm. I'll tell her." Mia ended the call, looked at Clara and said, "Miss Laquisha said to call her when you get released, and she'll come pick you up. She also said to let her know if you need anything."

Clara wiped the tears from her face, smearing blood from her cheek, and said, "Laquisha is a good boss. She's tough, but she cares about her staff."

"Do you feel up to continuing?"

"Yes. So, I went to leave and noticed he followed me to the door. I didn't think a lot about it because he was the bouncer. I figured he was just going to sit by the door, but I was wrong. He yelled to the bartender he'd be back and told me he wanted to make sure I got home okay. He said it was a service he offered. I thought it was probably a line but didn't mind having the distraction for a few more minutes. Once I was outside, I told him I had walked there but only live a couple blocks from the bar. We got a block or so away and he said he needed to make a stop on the way. That should have been a red flag, but I figured there was no harm and kept walking. Man, I wish I had told him no...."

Clara stopped talking, leaned back against the seat, and closed her eyes. Her lips quivered as she took a deep breath and said, "He didn't take me home. He walked to a different house. When we got to the corner, he told me his weed guy was close by and he wanted to get me some as a gift. I do like to smoke a little weed, but not usually when I work the next day. I told him that. He told me he had to go out of town for a couple days, and he really wanted me to have this for my days off. When we got to the house, I told him I would wait by the road, but he said the guy wouldn't give him any because he would think I was a cop. Then he said his guy would give him a little extra for free if I went in and said hello. I was so stupid...I followed him around back and went inside. The front door was boarded up, and once we got inside, he hit me on the back of the head. Next thing I remember I was laying on a nasty mattress with something stuffed in my mouth. I had a headache, my hands were tied behind my back, and he was nowhere to be seen."

"I DON'T KNOW how long he was gone. It was dark, and there were no clocks or televisions. He finally came back, and he was acting…different. He definitely was not the same guy I had talked to at the bar. His eyes were wild, and he was acting…crazy.

"He had a switchblade and cut the ties off my hands and legs. He told me, 'One word and it'll be your last.' I wanted the gag out, so I nodded. I was already thinking ahead and trying to figure out how I could get away. That was when he started doing stuff to me."

Clara provided Mia with a thorough description of the multiple rapes she had experienced throughout the night, requiring few follow-up questions. Mia would share the details with Coleman, Wheeler, and crime scene to make sure they didn't miss anything during their processing.

"He finally finished, and I thought he was just going to leave, but he laid back and pulled out a pipe. I may smoke a little weed here and there, but I don't smoke crack. My momma died from that shit, so I steer clear. I sat there and watched him get high, figuring that was my best chance to escape. I still didn't know what time it was. It was so dark inside, but it felt like it was getting lighter, so I figured it had to be daytime. He hadn't let me out of the back room, so I didn't realize most of the windows was boarded up. I can't believe I didn't notice the windows last night. Anyway, he was laying there, and I thought he was riding the high or asleep and decided to try and get away.

"I moved slowly, but he must have felt me because as soon as I got to the living room, he was behind me. His voice was so calm when he asked me what I thought I was doing. He started approaching me and I just, I just freaked out. I didn't even think. I started running to the living room and that big window without a board. He grabbed me and I thought he was going to kill me. I fought like my life depended on it. I had every reason to believe he was going to murder me and leave me in this house.

"We fought. I kicked him and screamed as loud as I could. As soon as I got loose from him, I ran straight to the window and went through it. I fell over the bushes onto the sidewalk and ran like the devil was after me. And he was. Detective, I believe the devil was in that house last night. I started screaming and banging on the neighbors' doors, and I guess one of the neighbors called the police. I saw them driving down the street and stood in the middle of the road and screamed until they stopped the car."

Mia processed what Clara had said and, when she was certain there was not more, she asked, "Did you happen to see where Blade went? Did he come out the window after you?"

Clara shrugged her shoulders and then said, "I didn't look back. I thought if I did, he would catch me."

Even though Mia was familiar with Deacon, or Blade as he was known on the street, she asked, "Can you describe him for me?"

"Like I said, he was really tall. I mean, like, taller than that cop who was trying to talk to me."

Mia made a note to ask Gordon how tall he was, "Tell me more about what he looked like."

"He was light skinned and built like a Mack truck. He had eyes almost the color of a cat. Not brown, but not quite green either. They had green and flecks of gold in them. My momma would call them 'bedroom eyes' – real sexy, you know? I don't think he had facial hair but…" Clara started to cry, "He seemed so…normal and nice. I don't understand what happened. What I did to make him change."

Mia hated this part of the job. She could (and would) tell Clara it was not her fault, and she did nothing to make *him* change, but she doubted Clara would believe her. She had yet to meet a victim of sexual assault who didn't blame themselves.

"You didn't do anything wrong. This is not your fault, Clara; this is 100% on him. Is there anything else you can tell me about him? Like, did he have any tattoos or scars?"

"He had a scar."

CHAPTER
THIRTY-ONE

"TELL ME ABOUT THE SCAR," Mia said.

"I'm not sure how to describe it," Clara said. "But I can draw it."

Mia opened her notebook to a blank piece of paper and handed it to Clara who stared at the open space. After a moment she drew an arm with a large hand. She lifted the pen to her lips and drew two lines on the forearm about an inch from the elbow.

"It almost looked like a…a plug-in. I noticed it when he was holding me down."

Mia took her cellphone and texted Frankie, *"Do you know if Blade has a scar?"*

"Probably. He got bit by one of our K-9 during his last arrest."

Mia stifled a chuckle and asked, "Is there anything else you can remember?"

Clara looked out the windshield towards the end of the block. She rubbed her eyes and looked again. Clara's breathing became labored, and her hands began to tremble. Mia noticed and asked, "Are you okay?"

"He's down there. At the corner. I just saw him. He is trying to stay out of view, but I swear that's him."

Mia picked up the mic and said, "1064 to 242."

"Go ahead for 242."

"I believe our suspect is on the southeast corner of 36th and Walrond. He seems to be pacing and trying to stay out of view."

"Copy. Gordon, stand by until I get to the car," Bobby ordered.

Mia looked at Clara and said, "I need to go talk to these officers. Do you know if he took anything of yours?"

"My cellphone and purse are missing." Clara instinctively felt for the cross necklace she never took off. Fresh tears fell down her cheeks, "The necklace my daddy gave me is gone."

"Okay. I want to go talk to them before they try to stop that guy. I'll let them know what's missing."

Mia briefed Gordon and Bobby on the missing items, then said, "He's known to carry a knife, Gordon. And he's not afraid to use it – on you or Bobby."

"This is how we're going to play it. You and I are going to get in the car and go the opposite direction. We'll circle the block and come up behind him. If he takes off running, you throw the car in park and jump out after him. If he doesn't, we'll just say we got a call on a suspicious person standing at the corner. Hopefully he'll be cooperative, and we can get him in custody without any incident."

"Yes, sir," Gordon said before climbing in the driver's seat of the patrol car.

CHAPTER
THIRTY-TWO

FRANKIE AND MIA stood next to their car. Frankie asked, "Did I just hear right? You think he's at the corner?"

"Yes. Clara thinks she saw him standing behind a tree. As if he could hide in broad daylight."

Before Frankie could respond, they heard a tone go out on the radio. Mia opened the car door and turned up the patrol radio. Through the speaker they heard heavy breathing and the sound of bodies hitting the ground.

"242," came a breathless voice. Nothing followed.

"Get out and wait here," Mia ordered. Clara's face turned ashen. "We'll be right back."

Clara was barely out of the car before Mia pulled away from the curb, tires squealing as they headed in the direction Clara had pointed. Rounding the corner, they saw Bobby and Gordon on top of Blade, trying to get his hands out from under him.

"1061, hold me and 1064 out with 242. Get a wagon headed this way. Code," Frankie said. She dropped the mic and jumped out of the car before it was in park. Mia was hot on her heels.

"319 is en route," the patrol wagon driver said before dispatch could acknowledge.

"Copy 1061, 1064, and 319 out with 242. Continuing to hold the air."

Holding the air was customary when there was a fight, car or foot chase, and other situations where radio transmissions could be urgent.

Frankie approached from the front and announced herself so Bobby and Gordon could see it was her. Their adrenaline was heightened, and she didn't want them to mistake her for someone there to do harm.

"I'm on his feet," Mia said assertively as she began maneuvering to get Blade in a leg lock.

Frankie grabbed at Blade's arm, trying to pull it out from under his body. Gordon was yelling, then out of the corner of his eye, Bobby saw Gordon pull out his taser, preparing to deploy without warning his fellow officers. Bobby yelled at Mia who began pushing Gordon away while trying not to lose her hold on Blade's legs. Frankie saw what was happening and took her body weight and helped Mia and Bobby remove Gordon from the pile. With Gordon out of the way Frankie put her knee into Blade's armpit, hoping to get a little leverage while Bobby worked the opposite arm. Gordon began to utter obscenities at Frankie, but she and Bobby continued communicating with one another, trying to get Blade in handcuffs. Within seconds of the handcuffs being secured, the patrol wagon arrived.

"Let's roll him to his side," Bobby directed.

"Just like old times, huh, partner?" Frankie asked with a wry smile.

"I'm getting too old for this shit," they said in unison.

"1061. Clear the air."

"Copy 1061. Air is clear."

"We've got him if you want to go talk to your boot," Frankie said.

"Thanks, you two," Bobby said, adding, "I need to tune this kid up."

Frankie smiled, remembering how hot-headed Bobby was when they were first on patrol. Bobby walked away to Frankie saying, "Go easy on the kid. Or at least give him hell in private."

Frankie watched and listened from where the patrol wagon was parked. She knew Bobby had Gordon's best interest in mind and someday Gordon would too.

"Don't you ever freaking pull your taser in a dog pile! And you sure as hell don't get ready to deploy it without warning, especially when other officers are going to ride the lightning with the suspect!" Bobby shouted. "That *detective* you were cursing at freaking saved your ass from riding pine. Or worse, getting written up by me and being one step closer to the unemployment line. You and me, we have some training to do. Get your ass in that car and follow the wagon to Headquarters to book that guy in, then get ready to be drilled on the taser and use of force policies. Do you copy?"

Frankie could not hear Gordon, but could read his lips as he mouthed, "Yes sir."

When the patrol wagon arrived, Frankie and Mia helped Blade to his feet. As the officer completed a secondary search, Blade glared at Frankie.

"You're the bitch that locked me up."

Frankie didn't reply.

"I didn't do nothin' then, and I didn't do nothin' now. This ain't over bitch!"

Frankie and Mia stood in silence as Blade was helped into the wagon, his seatbelt fastened, and the door slammed shut.

CHAPTER
THIRTY-THREE

FRANKIE AND MIA returned to the house to find Clara sitting on the step holding her face in her hands. Frankie looked at Mia and said, "Oh shit."

"I had almost forgotten about her. Do you think she'll agree to go to the hospital after I was so rude?" Mia asked.

"You were just doing your job. She didn't leave, so I'm going to take that as a good sign. We'll make nice with her, and it'll be okay."

"I hope you're right," Mia said.

Frankie watched Mia walk over and sit down next to Clara, speaking softly. After a few moments, Clara was nodding her head in understanding and eventually in agreement. Coleman and Wheeler pulled up at the same time as the Crime Scene van, which made Frankie's brief on what to expect and what to look for in the house much quicker.

"Clara said her phone and purse are gone. The rapes took place in the bedroom on the southeast side. Blade was smoking crack, so if you see any paraphernalia or anything, go ahead and grab it."

"Got it," Coleman said.

Almost as an afterthought, Frankie said, "Oh yeah, she was wearing a necklace with a cross. It is really important to her. If you find it, will you let me know? I'm going to see if the prosecutor will let us release it back to her."

"Will do."

"Thanks, guys. I'll text you if we get any other information on the way to County."

The drive to County Hospital was not long, but very quiet. Clara stared out the window at the boarded houses and businesses and watched as the residents of the neighborhood stood on corners talking, waited for the bus, or carried their bags to wherever they were going. When the hospital was in sight, she turned towards Mia.

"What happens now?"

"We take you inside and, if you give permission, they do a forensic examination. The nurse will go through every step with you, but the important thing for you to remember is they won't do anything without you giving your consent. Every step of the way, they'll ask for your permission and won't do anything you tell them not to do. The evidence is important to the criminal case, but in the end, the choice to participate in the exam is yours," Mia said.

"I don't know if my insurance will cover that."

"You don't have to worry about that. The exam will be covered, and you can apply for victim's compensation for any treatment separate from the forensic exam."

Clara looked at Frankie and asked, "What happens to that guy?"

"He's getting booked on a 24-hour hold right now. When we get downtown, we'll go talk to him and see what he has to say. There are two detectives processing the crime scene and interviewing the owner of the property. We'll write our reports and present it to the prosecutor in the morning. If a judge will sign off, he'll be held in jail or on bond until a trial. We'll keep you updated as we have information," Frankie said.

"We may need a follow-up interview, Clara. That's normal, so don't freak out if I call you, okay?" Mia said.

Clara nodded, then turned back to look out the window.

CHAPTER
THIRTY-FOUR

MIA PARKED the car in the garage attached to the Emergency Department, looked at Clara and asked, "Are you ready?"

Clara took a deep breath and nodded.

"I need to call home really quick. I'll meet you inside," Frankie said.

"Sounds good," Mia said.

"Hey, buddy," Frankie said. "How was camp?"

Frankie listened as her son Tyler recounted his activities at soccer camp. Tyler was attending the camp as part of the summer school program. He had resisted going at first, but Frankie insisted he do some type of activity, beyond video games, during the summer. As they got closer to school starting, Tyler was rushing Frankie out the door.

"I need new soccer shoes, mom."

"Didn't we just get shoes?" Frankie asked.

"Before summer," Tyler said. "These are getting too small, and coach wants me to play for his team this fall. He says I'm really good."

"I've been telling you that for years," Frankie said, drawing out the word years for effect.

"No offense, but you don't count. You're my mom. You have to say that."

Frankie laughed then said, "Okay. We can go this weekend if you want."

"Can't you just pick them up? I was hoping I could go hang out with Uncle Jake down at the farm this weekend," Tyler said.

"I think Danielle is coming for a visit." At least Frankie hoped so. She had been cancelling pretty frequently, and it had been hard on both her and Tyler. Frankie had hesitated to tell him because she hated seeing his disappointment.

"Yeah, right."

Frankie heard the sarcasm in Tyler's voice. She said, "I'll check with her and if she's not coming, I'll call Uncle Jake."

"Thanks, mom. Aunt Sophie wants to talk to you."

Frankie smiled and said, "Okay. I love you."

"Stay safe. Love you, too," Tyler said.

Frankie thought about what Tyler said while she waited for Sophie to get to the phone. Her little sister lived in an apartment over the garage attached to her house. Frankie knew it would have been harder, much more expensive, and a lot more stressful if she had to hire a babysitter when she was on nights. But even more important, Tyler enjoyed being with his Aunt Sophie and seemed to mind her working late just a little less when Sophie was there.

"Hey, Frankie. Sounds like you're out of the office. You think you'll be late tonight?" Sophie asked, drawing Frankie from her thoughts.

"Maybe, but I'm not sure. We have one in custody. Why, what's up?"

"No, it's okay. I have a big meeting in the morning."

"Oh man, is that tomorrow?" Frankie asked.

"Yeah, it's okay. If you don't mind, I'll just take Tyler up to the apartment with me. I want to make a good first impression." Sophie chuckled. "Showing up with bloodshot eyes from poor sleep is probably not the best way."

"Of course. I can get Tyler in the morning. Or you can send him down on the way to your meeting."

"Okay. Should be about 7:30."

"Sounds good," Frankie said. "And Soph – they would be crazy not to hire you to do the work."

"Thanks, sis. Stay safe."

CHAPTER
THIRTY-FIVE

SINCE MIA HAD INTERVIEWED CLARA, and Blade and Frankie had a history, it made sense for Mia to take lead in the interview. A couple of hours in and Blade had admitted to knowing Clara but said *she* had been coming on to *him* all night. To hear him tell it, Clara was a regular at the bar, was a drunk, and repeatedly asked him for crack cocaine. He finally agreed to take her to meet up with an unnamed man, and then she offered to have sex with him as a "thank you." Blade had no idea why Clara jumped out a window but surmised she was either crazy or the drugs made her do it. He had no explanation for why he fought officers but said he had every right to be in the house. He insisted Clara told him it was her house and had invited him in.

"What do you think?" Mia asked when they took a break.

"I think he's coming off a high and is lying his butt off."

"I agree. Do you want to take a crack at him?" Mia asked.

"Sure. Give me two minutes."

Frankie called the Corner Bar and talked to the bartender, who confirmed what she believed. Clara was not a regular and, in fact, he had never seen her in the bar before.

Frankie was about to hang up when the bartender said, "Something else was weird. She bought a double shot of Patron on the rocks with lime, but I don't think she even took a drink of it. She just kept playing with the swizzle stick, stirring the lime and ice around the cup. When she left, the glass was still full."

"That *is* interesting," Frankie said. "Did she seem high or intoxicated? Or interested in Blade?"

"No. If anything she seemed sad. Blade was coming on strong, like he always does, but she didn't seem interested at all."

"Did he come back after he said he was walking her home?"

"Yep. He apologized for taking so long. He said the woman asked him to come in and it took him a few minutes to turn her down."

"Okay, thanks."

Frankie took her notebook and a folder of photographs back into the interview room. She put both down and waited for Blade to speak. She was comfortable in the silence but knew he would not be. Frankie did not have to wait long.

"What's in that folder?"

Frankie tapped the manilla folder lying on the table and said, "This? Just a few photographs I want to show you."

Frankie removed the first photograph and asked, "Do you know how Clara got these marks on her wrists and feet?"

Seemingly needing to think, Blade rubbed his chin and then said, "I'm not sure. What, uhm, caused that?"

"I thought maybe you could tell me."

Blade began to stutter slightly, then said, "Yeah, I don't know."

"Do you have a knife, *Blade*?" Frankie asked, emphasizing his nickname.

"No. Uh, I mean yeah, I keep one for self-protection," Blade said, fumbling his words. Almost as an afterthought, Blade said, "But I think I left my blade at my house. I forgot to bring it to the bar."

Frankie pulled out a second photograph. The photo depicted a mattress lying on the floor with a knife and cut zip ties lying next to it.

"What do you make of this?"

The tendons in his neck began to stand out on his neck but Blade didn't answer.

"Is there any reason your fingerprints might be on this knife?" Frankie asked.

Blade rubbed his hands up and down his pants.

"Is there any reason your DNA might be on the knife or the zip ties?"

Blade hung his head and shook it from side to side.

Frankie continued the interview for another two hours, confronting Blade with the evidence collected from the scene. He continued to deny being in the house unlawfully and was insistent Clara had taken him to the house. At one point he accused her of framing him for the burglary, rape, and kidnapping.

"I'm telling you it's a frame job. She made it all up. This is a setup. That dumb whore was mad because I wouldn't pay her for sex and is trying to make me pay another way. This is insane," Blade yelled, slamming his fists onto the table.

CHAPTER
THIRTY-SIX

A KNOCK INTERRUPTED Blade's rant. Frankie closed the folder and picked up her notebook to open the door.

"I'll be right back, Blade." Frankie said. "We're just about finished here." Once the door was closed and locked, she asked, "What's up, Mia?"

"Crime Scene just called. A crew just finished a robbery up north and wanted to know if they needed to stop here en route to the shop. Apparently, Rhino told them about the scene and Blade being in custody. Is he going to give consent to have his body processed, or are we going to need a warrant?"

"He's pretty cocky and arrogant, so I think he'll consent. I don't think he realizes the gravity of what the crime scene will prove."

Frankie and Mia returned to the interview room with a Consent to Search form. Both sat with Blade, who looked like he could fall asleep if left alone long enough.

"What's that?" Blade asked.

"We'd like to get your consent to process your body. We'll collect a few swabs to include a buccal swab from your mouth. You can decline but if you do, I'll get a search warrant."

Blade didn't hesitate but instead said, "I don't have anything to hide. I told you what happened. Where do I sign?"

Frankie went over the document, and Blade scratched an unreadable signature.

"I'm going to go give them a call. It won't take long, and when they are done, I'll bring you some water."

Less than an hour passed before Frankie escorted Blade to the jail on the 8th floor where he had been booked in on a 24-hour investigative hold. When she got back to the office, Mia was working on the probable cause statement and a summary of Clara's interview to deliver to the prosecutor's office the following morning. Frankie started on the summary of the interviews with the bartender and Blade. The prosecutor's office would get the recordings, but these summaries would give them what they would need to determine whether to charge or release. Wheeler and Coleman had already finished the crime scene reports and the phones were forwarded to the on-call detective. The only noise in the office was the sound of typing on the keyboards.

Frankie looked at her watch. 1:00 AM. She realized she hadn't eaten since lunch. She scrounged in her desk for a granola bar to eat as she finished her report. After making copies of the photographs and videos for the prosecutors, she packaged them as evidence. Frankie hoped Mia was about ready to wrap things up so they could head home. She had not seen Patrick in years and didn't want to look haggard in the morning.

"What else do we need to do?" Frankie asked.

Mia stood up from her desk, stretched, and said, "I think that's it. Thanks for sticking around to help. No telling how long I'd be here if you hadn't."

"No problem. That's what friends and partners do."

FRANKIE WOKE up to the sound of her dog, Isabelle, barking, not in warning, but in delight. She looked at her cellphone and saw Sophie had sent a text message saying Tyler was on his way. She hopped out of bed, unlocked the door, grabbed her son when he walked inside, and embraced him in a huge bear hug.

"Good mornin', bud!"

"Ugh, mom, you're squeezing me too tight. I can't breathe," Tyler said dramatically.

Frankie squeezed Tyler a little tighter and then let him go, ruffling his hair as he walked to his bedroom with a huff. Frankie laughed, knowing that, like her, Tyler was not much of a morning person.

His voice trailing down the hall, Tyler said, "Mom, I can't be late to camp. Coach wants me to lead the team in warmups."

"You won't be late. I just need to change really quick." Frankie said. As an afterthought she said, "Unless you want me to go in my pajamas. I can walk you out to the field, too."

Frankie laughed out loud at Tyler's loud opposition to her suggestion. She looked down at her t-shirt and shorts, shaking her head at Tyler's protests. She didn't look *that* bad.

"Is Isabelle going to ride with us?" Tyler asked.

"Sure, bud. She and I can't go for a run this morning, so I should get her out for a little air while I can."

"You got to go to work this morning?" Tyler asked. Frankie heard the disappointment in his voice as he said, "I thought you had a day off."

"I am off today. We'll have the evening to hang out, okay?"

"Yeah, that'll be great. Why aren't you running today?"

"I may go this afternoon, but this morning I'm meeting up with an old friend from high school," Frankie explained.

"Is it that guy Uncle Jake was talking to the other day?"

"Yep. I didn't know you were there when they were talking." Frankie wondered how much Tyler heard.

"Only for a minute. Uncle Jake said he remembered the guy coming down to the farm to ride the four-wheelers a *long* time ago," Tyler drew out the word long for emphasis. "You know, when you were a kid."

Frankie smiled at the memory.

Twenty-eight years earlier

"Catch me if you can," Frankie yelled over her shoulder and the sound of the four-wheeler. She laughed as she accelerated and pulled away from the group.

Craig, Patrick, Julia, and Frankie raced through the woods, under tree limbs and through the creek trading places for first place, filling the air with laughter. Frankie and Julia had the advantage of knowing the woods, to include all the hidden turnouts. They had played in those woods since they were little, but Craig and Patrick were new to the terrain and were taking it slower.

They rode for hours, stopping only for a drink of water and the occasional teasing. The sun was high above the trees when they decided to break for lunch. Frankie had packed a cooler and left it in the barn in the woods. She grabbed a large quilt from the cabinet and spread it out on the banks of Shack Creek. Patrick met her at the door of the barn to help carry the food.

"Your dad fixed this up for you?" Patrick asked.

"Yeah. I think he was trying to find a way to keep me and Julia from running in and out of the house so much."

Julia bumped her shoulder into Frankie's and laughed before saying, "It didn't quite work as well as he'd hoped."

"When did you stop playing in it?" Patrick asked as they walked back to the blanket.

"Who said we did?" Julia said with a hint of amusement in her voice. "Frankie and I still meet out here every once in a while."

"What do you all do when you come out here?" Craig asked mischievously.

"Have pillow fights in our underwear," Julia said.

Craig raised his eyebrows curiously.

"Seriously though, it's a great place to get away from things. I come out here all the time. Especially when my parents are fighting."

"I didn't know that Julia," Frankie said. "I thought things were getting better."

"I thought so, too, but lately dad has been extra terrible. Mom says he's just going through a season. That's the word she used. A season. I think he's just being an ass."

"If things get too bad, you can always come to my house, Julia," Frankie said, putting her arm around the shoulders of her friend.

Julia laid her head against Frankie's shoulder and said, "I know, thanks. Enough of this depressing talk. Are you boys done eating? I think it might be time for Frankie and me to school you…again!"

The four exchanged a few friendly jabs as they picked up their trash and put things back in the barn. Once everything was safely secured, they got back on the four-wheelers and raced through the woods on the trails. Occasional laughter and screams of triumph pierced the air throughout the afternoon. The boys adapted to the terrain, and the competition got stiffer, and in the end, they had all led the charge at some point.

"Will you guys help me get these rinsed off before you head out?" Frankie asked.

"Why don't you guys go on, I can help Frankie," Patrick said.

"You sure you don't mind?" Craig asked.

"Not at all. Weren't you going to the movies or something?"

"Yeah. We're going to see *Die Hard with a Vengeance*. You two want to come with us?"

"I can't," Frankie said. "I told Jake and Sophie I'd stay home tonight."

"Maybe another time," Patrick said.

Frankie grabbed the hose and sprayed the mud off the four-wheeler she had been riding, "Have fun! Tell me how it is. It looks awesome."

"Got another one of those?" Patrick asked.

"No, but can you fill the tanks up for me?"

Frankie and Patrick fell into an easy rhythm, and within a half hour all of the four-wheelers were clean, full of gas, and in the barn.

"What are you going to do tonight?" Patrick asked.

"I'll probably play some board games with the family, then watch Saturday Night Live or an old western with my dad. I haven't stayed home lately and thought it would be fun to hang out," Frankie said. "What about you?"

"I don't have any plans."

"Want to come play games with us? I think Jody is planning to make pizza and maybe we can talk her into some caramel popcorn. It's so good," Frankie said.

Patrick went home to shower and, when he returned, they played games and ate pizza and popcorn just as Frankie had said. When the last game was played and her dad was getting ready to watch Saturday Night Live, Patrick stood up to leave.

"I think I'm going to head home."

"Drive safe, Patrick," Frank said. "Watch for deer on Moonglow Road."

"Yes, sir. Thank you for having me."

"Come back any time," Frank said.

"I'll be right back, dad."

"Don't be long."

Frankie nodded and walked Patrick out to his truck. Out of habit, Frankie looked up and noticed the moon. It was almost full, the light illuminating the road that led down to Shack Creek. Stars twinkled, lending a magic to the moment.

"Guess I'll see you around," Frankie said.

Patrick embraced Frankie in a hug. When he pulled away, he gently kissed her cheek and said, "How about tomorrow? Maybe we can go see that movie."

CHAPTER
THIRTY-EIGHT

FRANKIE HADN'T THOUGHT about that day in years. She and Patrick never did go see *Die Hard with a Vengeance* and he never kissed her again. They spent a lot of time together after, but their relationship never became romantic.

Frankie looked at her watch and said, "Tyler, hurry up or we're going to be late!"

Tyler ran down the hall with his backpack and was out the door before Frankie could remind him to grab his water bottle. She grabbed it and said, "C'mon, Isabelle."

An hour later, Frankie had showered and was in her Jeep headed to the City Market to meet Patrick. She pulled into her normal parking spot and felt butterflies in her stomach.

"He's just an old friend. Get over yourself," Frankie said as she ran her fingers through her short black hair.

Frankie saw him before he saw her. Patrick stood next to the entrance looking intently at his phone. To Frankie, it didn't seem Patrick had aged a day. He was dressed casually in khaki shorts, a polo, and flip flop shoes. His dark hair had a smattering of gray, but it lent a distinguished look that, to Frankie's dismay, was extremely sexy. As she got closer, she noticed he had applied a little cologne. The scent was light and fresh and co-mingled with the clean smell of a fresh shower.

"Hey, stranger."

Patrick looked up from his phone and a smile raised the corners of his mouth and brought a sparkle to his eyes. He immediately grabbed Frankie in an embrace and said, "Hey kid. You haven't changed a bit since high school."

"Flattery will get you everywhere," Frankie said, returning the hug. "Thank you. I was just thinking the same about you."

"We both must be living right. Let's go inside and catch up on the last 28 years!"

Frankie waved to the waitress she saw regularly and led Patrick to her favorite table. Within minutes, they fell into an easy banter, each sharing highlights of their lives.

"Two kids, huh? I haven't been as lucky. I was married for a short time, but she was more interested in dating than marriage. I guess that's why she never stopped," Patrick tried to laugh but Frankie could hear the pain in his voice. "As much as I would like to have had kids, I'm glad I never had them with her. I married the Army instead. I'm on leave now right now but will be back at Ft. Bragg for my last six months before I retire."

"What are you going to do after?" Frankie asked. She knew the rumors but wanted to hear it from him.

"You probably heard that I'm thinking about running for sheriff, but I have a couple places trying to recruit me. So, I guess the answer is I'm not sure. Right now, I'm working with a human trafficking task force in North Carolina – that's part of the reason I reached out. I wanted to see if I could get your help with a case."

CHAPTER
THIRTY-NINE

FRANKIE LEANED FORWARD, curious what Patrick thought she could do to help.

"We had a problem with some soldiers and a couple young girls a few months back. The girls said they had met online and went to party with the men. They admitted to drinking but were adamant they never planned to have sex. The soldiers, however, had other plans, and forced various sex acts on them. There were a few problems with the case, and the rapes were going to be hard to prove beyond a reasonable doubt, but then one of the girls slipped up. Two of them were talking in the interview room while I was talking to one of the other investigators. We had the cameras on and something she said caught my attention.

"I went back in and asked the one who had been talking how old she was, and it turns out she was only 16. The other girl was 17 but only by a few days. Long story short, both girls were from the Midwest and had disappeared from their homes six months earlier. It took a while, but they finally told us who brought them to North Carolina and said they were not the only ones.

"The feds came in and brought us onto their task force. The ring we've been working has been recruiting girls, mostly from the Midwest, and sending them to towns with large military bases like Fort Bragg and

Camp Lejeune. Several girls were from the Kansas City area, and two were from around our hometown," Patrick said.

Frankie sat back and considered what she was hearing but was unsure what this had to do with her, or Julia's disappearance.

"We picked up one of the lieutenants in the trafficking ring a couple weeks ago, and he said they have a contact near Kansas City. He said the guy is old and lives in the country. He befriends young girls online and then grabs the ones who talked about having a bad homelife."

"Grabbed them as in kidnapped them?"

"Yep."

"Does this guy have a name?" Frankie asked.

"Hudson. The lieutenant didn't know if that was his first or last name, and had only met him once, but based on some other evidence we found, I think it might be Warren Hudson."

FRANKIE WAS at a loss for words. Warren Hudson. Mr. Hudson? As in Julia's father? She had long thought he was a creep, but him being part of a human trafficking ring seemed far-fetched to Frankie. He was old and she didn't grow up in a made-for-tv movie kind of town… but now that she thought about it, maybe it explained Julia and her mom disappearing. As she thought of stories she heard, Frankie remembered over the years the occasional runaway or two from their county that had never been found. There had always excuses, but what if they hadn't run away? What if they had been kidnapped?

"How can I help?" Frankie finally asked.

"I want to interview the families of the missing girls from around the area. I know local agencies did interviews, but they didn't know what I know. They thought the girls were simply your run-of-the-mill runaways. Maybe with my lens we'll get some different information. I don't have any cred here; I'm just a soldier and not your typical investigator so I am going to need a local detective to accompany me. Someone they'll take seriously."

"Did you reach out to the local FBI office? They might be willing to help."

"Our taskforce sent out a lead, but all they got back were excuses.

They have their own cases and don't have time to deal with anything new."

"I know a guy; actually, he's a good friend. I think he'll help us."

"Great. Can you call him?" Frankie started to respond, but before she could answer, Patrick pleaded, "Now?"

The hair on the back of Frankie's neck stood on end. This was more than a taskforce request. This was personal.

"What are you not telling me, Patrick?"

Patrick was not quick to answer. He stirred the eggs around his plate and then stared out the window. When he looked back at Frankie, his eyes were wet.

"Patrick?"

"I have a… partner. We met the first time I was stationed at Fort Bragg and then didn't see each other for several years. A couple of years ago when I returned, we reconnected. We had both lived full lives and, in fact, he had married and divorced and was raising a teenage daughter, Sasha."

Frankie's brain filled with fog. Did Patrick say *he*? As in a man? Patrick is gay? She had no idea…although somehow it suddenly made sense.

"…and we haven't seen her since. I looked on her laptop and saw the chat log and noticed she had been talking to someone. I used some of my tools from work and eventually linked them back to Hudson."

"Wait, go back please. Sasha is your partner's daughter. She was living with her father?"

"Yeah. Well, with us. Not long after we reconnected her mother got really sick and ended up dying. Sasha moved in with us about a year ago. When she disappeared, we called local police, and they said she was grieving and probably just ran away, but I *know* Sasha. She wouldn't have left. She wasn't a troubled teen or trying to escape a bad homelife. We all got along well. She *was* still grieving the loss of her mother, but she wouldn't have run off."

"How long has it been since you've seen or heard from her?"

"Sasha came back here and stayed with my mom after school let out in May. She's really interested in animals and agriculture so we thought it would be fun for her to spend time on the farm before her senior year.

When she came back home, things had changed. She started spending more time on her computer and less time with us. She seemed… preoccupied. About a week after she got back, Sasha went to Raleigh, presumably to meet a friend at NC State for a college tour and never came home. It was June 27th to be exact, and we haven't seen or heard from her since."

Frankie did the math. It had been almost six weeks. She saw the pain in Patrick's eyes and felt it in her heart. Frankie reached across the table and placed her hand on top Patrick's. They sat for a few moments, then she squeezed gently, and let go.

Placing cash on the table Frankie said, "I'll make the call. Outside."

Patrick blinked his eyes, nodded, and followed Frankie out.

CHAPTER
FORTY-ONE

FRANKIE SAT on her back deck waiting for Tyler to come home. She had spent the entire day coordinating with Jim, Patrick, and Sergeant Baker paving the way for conducting interviews with the families of the missing girls. She was initially expecting two or three, but Patrick produced a list of more than a hundred girls who were from their hometown and neighboring communties within a 60-mile radius. The girls on the list had been missing between four weeks and 28 years. Recognizing the heavy lift of that many families, and the impact reaching out could cause, they decided to start small and narrowed down the interview list to 20 who had been missing for less than two years.

Frankie was in shock at the number of adolescents on the list. She looked it over, first with judgment then compassion. She had a teenage daughter and if she went missing, she didn't think she would be able to breathe.

Frankie looked at her watch. She still had about 30 minutes before Tyler would be home from camp, but she thought Danielle should be home. Picking up her cellphone, she hesitated, then dialed the phone number to the house. Danielle's stepsister answered on the second ring.

"Hold on," was the hateful response when Frankie asked to speak with her daughter. She heard the girl say, "It's *her.*"

Frankie did not rise to the bait, but instead said, "Hey angel-girl, how are things going?"

Danielle appeared less than thrilled to be on the phone with Frankie and said, "Fine," offering nothing more.

"I was thinking I would come and pick you up around lunchtime on Friday so we could have some extra time together."

"I have Bible quiz practice on Friday and then church on Sunday. Can't you just come take me to dinner on Saturday and bring me back home after?"

Frankie took a deep breath and said to herself, *"Don't take the bait. She's trying to pick a fight."* Aloud she said, "Your brother and I would like to spend more than an hour or two with you. You're supposed to be with us for the entire weekend."

"Mom, I can't miss practice. I've told you that before."

"What time is practice over?" Frankie asked. To herself she said, *"Compromise."*

"It's not over until nine or ten, and we may go eat after. Then, I have to come home and shower. It'll be too late."

"You know the deal, Danielle, when I'm off for the weekend, you spend the entire weekend with your brother and me."

Danielle did not immediately answer, but Frankie could hear mumbling in the background. Probably her stepmother or her stepsister. Frankie sat and waited.

"Church comes first. You would understand that if you went. I'm not going to miss practice and church to sit around your house all weekend. If you really wanted to spend time with me, you would come down Saturday and we could have dinner."

Frankie tried to hide the pain of those statements and fought the urge to say something back that would be hurtful. Instead, she took a deep breath and said, "Please call and talk to your brother. He misses you. And so do I, but I need to go. I love you."

"Okay. Love you, too." Danielle hung up the phone without saying good-bye.

Frankie felt the tears well in her eyes, but they didn't fall. Isabelle got up from her perch on the stair and laid her head on Frankie's lap.

Stroking her fur, Frankie said, "You get it, don't you girl? How am I supposed to explain this to Tyler?"

Isabelle nudged Frankie's hand and moved a little closer. Frankie wiped the tears from her eyes then continued to pet the golden, silk-like fur. With each stroke she felt her heart rate reduce. By the time she saw Tyler walking down the hill, she felt ready to put a smile on her face and enjoy the stories he would have from a day at soccer camp. He was four houses away when he realized Frankie was sitting on the deck waiting for him like she said she would be. What had been a stroll turned into a run down the street, into the yard, and up on the deck where he started regaling her with tales from his day. Tyler's laughter and quirky stories worked to dull the pain of the phone call she had with Danielle.

CHAPTER
FORTY-TWO

"ARE YOU SURE ABOUT THIS, FRANKIE?" Jim asked. "You haven't been in contact with this guy in 20 years. We don't know anything about him. What if he's some kind of vigilante?"

They had been running along the Missouri River, one of Frankie's favorite paths, and she was explaining Patrick's situation in more detail. Frankie and Jim had talked on the phone after she met with Patrick, but he didn't have time to get all the information. Jim was not one to back down from a little adventure, but he seemed hesitant to commit to helping Patrick or Frankie.

"He's one of us, Jim. He's a good guy and wants us to help him find his partner's daughter." Frankie couldn't understand why Jim was pushing back. If she didn't know better, she would think he was jealous. "I'm going to help him, Jim – with or without you." Frankie paused. "But I would prefer it to be *with* you."

Jim looked past Frankie towards the water. He knew if he looked her in the eyes, he would say yes without giving it any rational thought. A few seconds passed before he looked down and met her gaze, "Okay. When do we start?"

Without thinking, Frankie wrapped her arms around Jim and said, "Thank you!"

Jim returned the hug, feeling his face warm. He squeezed Frankie gently, released her, and ruffled her hair. "Let's grab some water and make a plan."

Frankie and Jim sat at a picnic table near the parking lot in silence while they hydrated after their run and subsequent conversation.

"How are you planning to attack this, Frankie?"

"Patrick and I are going to interview a couple of the families tomorrow before my shift. I think he wanted to go out tonight, but Mia and I have a couple of interviews scheduled that can't wait."

"Maybe I can connect with him, and we can get started tonight." To himself he thought, *"And I can see if this guy is for real."*

"That would be great! I'm off this weekend, but Tyler wants to go down to the farm. I'm thinking about doing a little recon if you're interested. Maybe take the four-wheelers out? Do a bonfire after?"

"Let me see if I can. I like the idea of going out into the woods for the day, even if it's on a case. Does Jake have enough for all three of us to go out?"

"Yeah. Mine, Jake's and Sophie's are all in the barn and I'm pretty sure my dad's is there too, but we shouldn't need it. Jake and Tyler are probably going fishing, but they'll take the side by side, instead of the four wheelers."

Jim remembered Danielle was supposed to visit that weekend and realized Frankie hadn't mentioned her. He knew it was a touchy subject and considered not saying anything but then asked, "What about Danielle? Isn't she going to be there?"

Frankie didn't immediately answer, not certain she trusted her voice not to crack. Taking a deep breath, she finally said, "She actually told me Bible Quiz practice and church was more important than spending time with me and her brother. Then she said if I wanted, I could come and take her to dinner. I told her I would see her the next visit."

"How did Tyler take the news that she was skipping another visit?" Jim knew Tyler had struggled with Danielle going to her father's house for the summer and had been angry with his sister.

"He tried to act like he didn't care, but it was pretty obvious to me his feelings were hurt. He has taken this change personally. Unfortunately, he still doesn't fully understand this isn't about him. The reality is she is being brainwashed – by her dad's wife, his stepdaughter, and God help me, the church they attend." Frankie sighed and looked up to hide the tears that filled her eyes. "Even worse, I have no idea what to do about it."

Jim didn't try to act like he knew what Frankie was going through but understood how important her children were to her. Instead of trying to fill the silence he placed his hand over hers and gently squeezed.

The sound of Jim's phone ringing broke the silence. Frankie could only hear one side of the conversation before Jim let go of her hand, got up, and walked away. He returned a few moments later and said, "We're all set for Saturday."

"FRANKIE, PHONE CALL," Coleman said as Frankie walked into the squad room.

Frankie mumbled curse words under her breath. She had to go meet Finley to do a formal statement and didn't want to have to reschedule because of a new scene.

"Sex Crimes, Thomas."

"Hey, Frankie, you have someone here to see you."

"Thanks, Dan," Frankie said to the civilian employee who sat in the lobby checking people in. "Do you have a name?"

"One of the girls from MOCSA. Alex, I think she said. I didn't get the other girl's name. She said something about saving you a trip to pick her up."

"Oh, okay. Can you please tell them I'll be down in five? I just walked in and need to get logged into the system and make sure Coleman can take the phones."

"Sure thing."

Ten minutes later Frankie was sitting across from Finley and Alex, the advocate from the local rape crisis center. Frankie took her time explaining the process and making sure Finley was comfortable before they got into the details of what was likely a very traumatic experience. Frankie listened as Finley described what happened in pieces. The things she remembered did not come in chronological order, and there were things she was unable to remember, but Frankie understood that was normal for someone who experienced trauma. Finley remembered best the things she focused on during the assault. Those were the things encoded in her memory. Anything that was a peripheral detail was not encoded and therefore was unable to be retrieved, because it simply was not there. Frankie used the techniques she had been taught, took things slow, and did not push.

An hour into the interview, Frankie asked, "Do you want to take a break?"

Softly, Finley asked, "Can I use the bathroom?"

"Of course. Alex, do you want to show her where it is?"

Alex nodded and, when the two were gone, Frankie took her notepad and went to the squad room.

"Great interview, Frankie," Sergeant Baker said.

"Thanks, Sarge. It's definitely not an easy one… but then none of them are," Frankie said.

"Has she given you any new information?"

"A few things. I don't think this kid has had the easiest of lives. How much do you want me to push about her running away?"

Baker gave the question some thought then said, "As much as is necessary to explain her being here, but not so much she shuts down and bolts."

Frankie nodded and returned to the interview room.

CHAPTER
FORTY-FOUR

FRANKIE LOOKED CLOSELY at the young woman sitting across from her. She knew, based on her date of birth that she was almost 18, but she looked the same age as Danielle. Finley told her she had met "Wes" online and left her foster home to meet him in person. She also stressed that she would run again if she was forced to return to foster care.

"Finley, I need to ask," Frankie started. "Why are you in foster care?"

Finley took a drink from the bottle of water Frankie had given her before saying, "My mom is in the ground and my dad is in prison for putting her there."

There was a flatness to Finley's statement, but Frankie heard the break in her voice. She asked, "Do you have any other family?"

"Not really. I've bounced through a few foster homes. Some bad and some awful. I'm close enough to 18 I won't go back. The social worker at Synergy said they will help me get into a program, so I don't have to."

Frankie nodded, then said, "Good. Did anything happen that prompted you to run?"

Finley fidgeted in her seat, rubbed her cheek, and then said, "I don't want to talk about it."

Frankie noticed Finley was nearing fatigue, and it was time to stop. She closed her notebook and said, "I think we have enough for now. As the investigation moves forward, I may have follow-up questions for you and will need to give you a call. Please don't be alarmed if I do."

"Okay."

"If you leave Synergy or change your number, call me, okay?"

"Okay."

"How about I take you back to Synergy?"

Finley nodded.

FORTY-FIVE

THE NEXT MORNING, after dropping Tyler at camp, Frankie sat at her kitchen table with her cellphone, a notebook, and a pen. Patrick and Jim were in the field doing interviews and trying to get information on the recent missing girls.

Frankie picked up her phone and typed, *Hey Aunt Gina. Can you please give me George's phone number?*

George was a deputy when Julia and her mother disappeared and was a friend of her aunt. Frankie hoped she could convince George to exercise some personal, if not professional, courtesy and help her get the old case files.

She had about given up hope her aunt would respond, when the message came through with the phone number and one word, *Why?*

I need to see if he has any info related to a case I'm working on. Thanks. Love you.

Frankie dialed the number to the man who had been her neighbor when she was growing up, but whom she had not spoken to in years.

"Hello."

"George, it's Frankie. Frankie Thom… uhm Moretti, your old neighbor."

A cough was followed by, "Hey, kid. Everything okay? Your mom and dad good?"

"Yes, sir, everyone's fine but I need your help. Remember the girl up the road who disappeared? Julia Hudson?"

"Of course, I do."

"I've got a case I'm working that might be related. I was wondering if you'd help me and get me copies of the case files on her disappearance."

Frankie's request was met with silence.

"George? Are you…"

"You'd be best to let sleeping dogs lie, Moretti," George said and then disconnected the call.

CHAPTER
FORTY-SIX

ZOE WAS NOT sure where she was or what time of day it was. She wished she could call her sister, Emma. Zoe new she was frantic. Emma had taken Zoe in after their parents died and Zoe had not made it easy. She was angry and scared most of the time. Angry her parents had died; scared Emma would die, and she would be left alone – or worse – left with Emma's husband. Emma's husband was not mean, and he had never touched her inappropriately, but he was weird. Zoe was pretty sure he didn't like having her around. She would never be able to explain her dislike of him, because she did not quite understand it herself.

Zoe walked around the small room, shivering despite the temperature. There was a small bed with a blanket and pillow and a table with a single lamp. When she first got there, Zoe had picked that lamp up, thinking she would use it as a weapon only to find the lamp was so light it wouldn't hurt a flea. There was a bucket to go to the bathroom and a pump that produced water. She had no food, but at least she had something to drink. The water from the pump was cold and fresh and tasted different than water in the city. It reminded Zoe of water she drank from a mountain creek when she and her parents went hiking.

Zoe had spent the past few days berating herself for talking to the boy online, especially after Emma told her it was probably an adult trying to cause her harm. Zoe was longing for someone to connect with – someone her own age, and upon reflection, someone to love her. She had not made friends easily before her parents died, and when she moved to her sister's house, it was even harder. All the kids in her school had known each other their entire lives, and she was an outsider. They weren't exactly mean, just indifferent. She was the weird kid from the city and didn't have much in common with them. Zoe didn't belong to the Future Farmers of America or the 4-H Club, she wasn't into drugs, wasn't a cheerleader, and was only a mediocre student and athlete. These things put her as somewhat of an outcast in the small farming community.

One night she was browsing Instagram on her computer and Night-Owl816 sent her a direct message. He chatted her up, asking all kinds of questions about her life; her likes, her dislikes, and what she dreamed of for her future. NightOwl816 told Zoe his name was Wes, and he was 16 years old. Wes seemed to like and dislike all the same things. After a few days, the conversations become intimate. Wes started asking Zoe about things related to sex. Zoe had never even kissed a boy, so this was a new realm for her, but she was curious. Zoe thought she was talking to someone her age and by then he had asked her to be his girlfriend. A few more weeks passed, and he asked her to send him photographs. She hesitated but finally sent one wearing her panties and bra. Zoe knew her sister would flip her lid, but Wes was her boyfriend, and she was sure that made it okay. He sent her a few photographs, as well, but Zoe realized now the photographs Wes sent her were of someone else.

Zoe was not sure what made her decide to leave her sister's cute little house and get on a bus to Kansas City, Missouri. Zoe and Emma had fought over the years, but the night she decided to leave, Zoe had decided to push the limits. She was curious and believed the grass would be greener somewhere else. When she got off the bus, a man picked her up and said he was taking her to meet Wesley. He told her Wesley was at work, and Zoe naively believed him. The old man took her to a house in the middle of nowhere and, after a few hours, it was obvious Wes didn't exist.

Zoe was unsure how many days she had been in the house when she decided to try to escape. The first few days, the old man had made her sleep in the same room with him and had stood just outside the bathroom door each time she went inside. The final night in the house, he handed her clothes and told her to shower, explaining he was taking her out to a friend's house and wanted her to look nice. There was a tiny window in the bathroom that appeared to be painted shut. With the shower running, Zoe used her weight to force it open, and then waited. When she was certain he had not heard, Zoe closed the window, with the plan to sneak out when they returned.

Zoe was blindfolded and taken to the friend's house where she was left for hours. She fought the intrusive memories of the violence that had been inflicted upon her. When they returned, the old man told her his friend liked her. Zoe felt bile rising in her throat at the thought of having to return to the "friend's" house. She remembered the window and asked if she could clean up before going to bed. Hearing no dissent she entered the bathroom, turned on the water, opened the window and climbed through the opening. Once through the window Zoe dropped to the ground and ran.

Zoe followed the moonlight to a barn in the woods. She peered in the windows and, not seeing anyone inside, opened the door. The little room attached to the barn was sparsely furnished, but tidy, and smelled of old wood and moisture. Zoe laid on a pallet made of blankets and tried to figure out how she could get back home. The walls were exposed logs, only they were not round like a log cabin, but square like a railroad tie. A small table, child sized, sat in the middle of the room with a jug of water as a centerpiece. There was a window Zoe tried to open to no avail leaving the air stale and still. A large chalkboard hung on the wall. Her mother would have called the space "quaint" and in other situations, Zoe may have agreed.

Once light began to filter inside, Zoe got up from the pallet and looked out the window. She couldn't see anything but trees beyond a small area of cut grass. She thought she heard the sound of moving water but couldn't see it. Sunlight was peeking through the trees, dust floating in the rays. Zoe turned from the window and stared at the chalkboard. It had been erased, but she could see words that had once been written.

Well, I was there, and I saw what you did…. it's all been a pack of lies.

Zoe took the chalk and copied over the shadowed script. When she finished, she stared at the cabinet opposite the window and door. She began opening drawers and cabinet doors slowly, looking for something useful. In the last drawer she found stationary and a pen.

"Oh, please work," Zoe whispered.

She had just signed her name when she heard something outside. Zoe folded the paper and threw it onto the pallet of blankets where she had been sleeping. She sat in one of the small chairs and waited. Zoe didn't have to wait long before the door opened with a creak.

CHAPTER
FORTY-SEVEN

THE OLD MAN looked different this time. His body frame filled the doorway, leaving little room for the vestiges of light to filter through. The salt and pepper gray hair that had previously been well-groomed and tame, was disheveled and gave the appearance of someone who had just rolled out of bed after a restless night and forgot to comb their hair. His face was covered in stubble, but his eyes were what stood out to Zoe the most. They reminded her of a feral cat, wild and searching, and scared Zoe more than the gun pointed at her.

"Did you really think you could get away?" he hissed.

Zoe did not answer and tried to make herself small.

"Did you really think you could hide here? Like this wouldn't be the first place I looked?"

Still Zoe said nothing. In her mind she thought she should plead for mercy, but nothing would come from her lips.

He appeared to stop and take a good look at the room surrounding them, then said, "My daughter used to come here. She had to be taught a lesson…and so will you."

With those words, Zoe snapped and yelled, "No! Please…"

Her screams were met with the meaty palm of his large hand across her face. "You will not yell at me," hitting her a second time with the back of his hand.

Zoe held her face and cried. Quietly, she begged, "Please, I promise I'll be better. I promise I'll do what you say."

The next hour was a blur for Zoe. She felt a needle going into her arm and felt the sensations of the man doing things to her body, but almost as if it were a dream. When he was finished, he half walked, half drug her body back to a dungeon. He left her there with a chain attached to the wall cinched around her waist.

CHAPTER
FORTY-EIGHT

"C'MON TYLER, Uncle Jake is waiting," Frankie said.

Tyler came out of his bedroom with his backpack slung over his shoulder and a piece of toast in his mouth.

"What have I told you about eating in your bedroom? Is there anything else in there?"

Not answering Frankie's question, Tyler said, "I know, but I was in a hurry."

"And why do you have your backpack? You're coming home with me tonight."

"But I want to stay at the farm. Jake said we might be able to camp in the woods or something."

"Another time. You and I are going to spend the day together tomorrow, so you're coming home with me after the bonfire."

"Fine," Tyler groused but made no move to return his backpack to his bedroom.

"Help me take the top off the Jeep, please."

Tyler threw his bag into the floorboard and busied himself helping Frankie remove the top and stow it away. The task was simple, and Frankie could do it by herself, but it made Tyler feel important to think she needed his help. She watched as his lithe frame climbed on the rails and did what he could.

"Thanks, bud. How about a stop at Quick Trip as a reward?"

An hour later, Frankie was driving down the road to the farm, hair windswept, and skin warmed by the sun. A cooler in the back of the Jeep was filled with water and food. She wasn't sure what they expected to find in the woods, but if Mr. Hudson was involved, it may be a good place to start.

When Frankie crossed the creek, she smiled to herself at the site before her. The fields which lined the creek were a lush green and stretched as far as she could see to both sides. The old farmhouse with its wide front porch sat on the hill looking down over the fields like a king sitting on a throne overlooking his domain. The barn Jake and Frank built could be seen off to the side, the doors wide open in welcome.

Patrick was helping Jake check the tanks of the four-wheelers and appeared to be lost in thought. Frankie noticed the side-by-side Jake liked to drive had fishing poles and what looked like a tackle box and cooler in the back. Frankie stopped Tyler before he jumped out of the Jeep and doused him with sunscreen.

"Mom, that's enough. I'll be fine." Tyler jumped out of the Jeep and yelled, "Uncle Jake!"

"Hey, bud," Jake responded.

Tyler slowed down, noticing Patrick for the first time.

"Tyler, this is my old classmate and friend, Mr. Miller," Frankie said. He and I are working on a project together."

Patrick wiped his hands and extended his right hand to shake Tyler's, "You can call me Patrick."

Tyler stood a bit taller, shook Patrick's hand, and then asked, "What kind of project?"

"Your mom and her friend, Jim, are helping me," Patrick caught the look on Frankie's face, "Figure out a puzzle, but today we're going to ride around on the four-wheelers."

Tyler appeared to give the statement some thought. Satisfied, he said, "Nice," and ran to the tire swing hanging from the tree in the back yard.

"Thank you for not saying anything. I don't want him to know what's going on. He sees Mr. Hudson occasionally and, well, he's just a kid."

Jim arrived a few minutes later looking a little tired.

"Must have been a good date," Frankie thought to herself. Aloud she said, "Just in time. Tanks are full."

"Hey, sorry I didn't get here sooner. I got called out last night at 3AM. I wasn't sure I'd even make it today."

Unsure why she was relieved Jim hadn't been out late with a girl, Frankie said, "Not a problem. Seriously, we were just loading up."

Once Jake and Tyler were on their way, and the cooler was strapped to the four-wheeler, Frankie led the men into the woods. As they rode, she narrated the property lines and where they butted up to the Hudson property. When the sun was high overhead, they crossed the creek and circled back to the old barn.

"Let's stop here for a minute."

"I can't believe this thing is still standing," Patrick said.

"My dad knows how to build things to last."

"Are you sure Jake hasn't come out here and made repairs?" Patrick asked.

Frankie gave his idea some thought before saying, "Honestly, I'm not sure Jake remembers it being here. He didn't hang out here as much as Sophie and I did."

Frankie walked up to the door of the little barn, expecting cobwebs and surprised not to see any. She looked around the porch for snakes and finding none, she opened the door slowly. Frankie noticed the floor had been swept and hosted a pallet of blankets.

CHAPTER
FORTY-NINE

FRANKIE SCANNED THE ROOM, looking right to left, taking in every detail. Someone had been there recently. She didn't see any empty food containers or trash, but there were no cobwebs at the ceiling, and she noticed a clean spot on the otherwise dirty windows. Frankie carefully picked up the blankets and a piece of paper fell to the floor.

To whoever finds this,

My name is Zoe Parker, and I'm 14 years old. I was kidnapped by a man pretending to be a 16-year-old boy online. He brought me here, but I don't know where here is. Please call my sister, Emma, she'll be worried about me. Tell her I love her and want to come home.

Frankie read the note twice and sank into one of the chairs at the small table. She stared at the phone number, wondering what to do. She would have to call Emma but was unsure what exactly to tell her. Frankie was certain the woman would want to know where her sister was, but Frankie wouldn't be able to answer or even tell her if Zoe was still alive. Frankie had no idea how long the note had been lying there. A day? A week? Years? She had so many questions and very few logical answers.

Emma may have a few answers, or at least information to help

Frankie figure it out. She would need to do a thorough interview to get as much background as possible, but it wasn't the kind of interview she wanted to do on the phone. Frankie had no idea where Zoe ran from or where Emma was, but she knew any answers Emma could provide might be what would help them find Zoe. Hopefully, alive.

Frankie's head was spinning as she made a mental list of what they would need. They would need to get the computer Zoe used to talk to the "16-year-old boy" but if Emma was not local, she couldn't just stop by. If they weren't local, maybe Jim could send a lead to the field office to get it picked up. That might help figure out who Zoe was really talking to and where they were. Could it have been Warren Hudson? It seemed likely since the note was left so close to his farm, but she doubted it was enough to bring him in for questioning.

Frankie wondered why the note was here. In this barn. Was Zoe close or was this a stop-over point? Was Hudson using this as a place to hold the girls? It didn't make any sense, but neither did a random girl in the barn leaving a note. The barn was way off the beaten path. In fact, only someone familiar with the area would know the space existed. She looked around the room, her eyes stopping on the chalkboard. She remembered seeing those words before but...Frankie shot up like a lightning bolt had struck her backside. She backed out of the space, realizing she was sitting in a crime scene.

"We thought you got lost in there," Jim teased.

Frankie had a serious look on her face and said, "Look at this, but don't touch." Frankie laid the note on the top of the cooler. She was suddenly glad she brought an extra zip lock bag. To herself she thought, *"How the hell am I going to write this up?"*

"Was Zoe Parker on the list of missing girls you found?" Jim asked Frankie.

"Not that I remember, but I don't have the list with me. Patrick, have you heard the name before?"

Patrick shook his head and said, "No, but I was focused on Sasha."

"When we get back where I have decent cell service, I'll call Zoe's sister and see how far away she is. We need to process this scene. At least take photographs," Frankie said.

Jim pulled his work phone from his bag and held it up, "Never leave home without it. I'll snag some good photos and pull up GPS coordinates as well so we can get a sky view."

Frankie walked around the barn, seeing it through different eyes. The area around it had been maintained. Not mowed weekly, but regularly enough that nothing could hide in the grasses within 20 feet of the walls. Frankie would ask Jake if he or their dad had been there recently. The interior of the barn itself still had old pieces of wood and a couple of junk bicycles, but it almost looked staged to be messy. None of it made sense, and the big questions she had were who was Zoe Parker, where was she, and was she still alive?

ONE OF THE things Frankie loved about the farm was that cell service was minimal. When she was trying to take a break from the world, it was a blessing, but when she needed to have a serious phone conversation and didn't want to use the landline, it presented a problem.

Tyler and Jake were still gone when the trio returned to the house. Frankie speculated it would be close to dark before they got back and didn't want to wait for them before calling Emma. She didn't know how long Zoe had been missing but felt an urgency to find out.

"I need to call the sister and can't do it from here. I'm going to drive out to the main road into town and see if I can get in touch with her," Frankie said.

"I'll ride with you," Jim said. "You can use my work phone instead of your personal cell."

"I'll hang back and clean these up before putting them away. I remember Mr. Moretti's rules and assume Jake is the same," Patrick said.

Frankie laughed and said, "Yeah, Jake is definitely a chip off the ole block... he may even be more particular. Everything is in the same place."

After they found the note, the trio had taken a ride through the woods to see what, if anything, they could find. There were trails from the barn, but they looked like the trails they had used as kids and showed signs of overgrowth from lack of use. They walked a few trails on foot but found they could cover more ground, and appear less suspicious if being watched, if they rode. Frankie made a mental note to ask Jake about a couple of places that were not as overgrown, but for the most part she didn't see anything that seemed out of place or different.

Frankie and Jim drove to a convenience store on the main road, and when she pulled into the lot and parked, Frankie asked, "Why'd you come with me?"

"I told you, so you could use my phone. I also wanted to look at my list and see if Zoe was on it, but couldn't access my files from the farm," Jim said.

"That's a nice explanation, but you don't obsess over things like I do, and you don't lie well. Try again."

Jim laughed and said, "You got me. I just wanted to be here when you called. I know making calls like this are difficult." His smile faded. "Especially for the mom of a teenage girl."

Frankie patted Jim on the leg and said, "You're a good man, Jim Craven."

Frankie had been thinking about what she would say during this call since she had found the note. She was still unsure what she would say as she dialed the number and waited for someone to answer.

"Hi, Emma, my name is Detective Frankie Moretti. Can you please call me back at this number?"

"She didn't answer," Jim said.

"No, but to be fair, if I got a call from an unknown number, I wouldn't answer either. I'm going to wait here for a couple of minutes and see if she calls back."

The words were no more out of her mouth when the phone vibrated with an incoming call. Frankie felt her stomach in her throat and her heart felt like it was going to beat out of her chest.

"It's her," Frankie said to Jim. With a steady voice she answered, "Detective Thomas."

"This is Emma. Is this about Zoe? Do you know where she is?"

Frankie explained to Emma about finding the note and then began asking her questions. Zoe had been gone about ten days. She and Emma had gotten into a fight about her talking to a "boy" online. Emma was worried because she found the chats and they went from an innocent chat to sexually aggressive. Emma was unsure but thought Zoe may have sent him photographs of herself naked because the "boy" had asked for them, and there were gaps in the messages she found. After the argument, Emma kept Zoe's phone and she went to bed angry. When Emma woke up, Zoe was gone.

"Zoe was always a bit of a recluse, but it got worse when she came to live with my husband and me. She never really liked living in a small town, but it's where my husband's job is. Momma and Daddy are both gone, and I was the only one left to care for her. She's all the family I have left in the world, Detective Thomas. Can you please bring her home to me?"

CHAPTER
FIFTY-ONE

FRANKIE RESTED her head against the back of the driver's seat of her Jeep, took a deep breath, and slowly exhaled.

"That bad, huh?" Jim asked.

"Just… sad." Frankie didn't say anything more during the ten-minute drive to the farm, and Jim didn't press. She was lost in thought, processing everything Emma had told her about her sister and the messages she found. Zoe was the same age as Danielle and the vulnerability Emma described hit close to home. With Danielle living at her father's house, Frankie could never truly be sure Danielle was not at risk. Danielle lived a different life there – one they kept Frankie out of.

"Based on how long you were gone, can I assume you were able to get in touch with Emma?" Patrick asked.

Frankie nodded, walked over to the cooler, and grabbed a cold Bud Light. She needed a moment to separate her fears and concerns in her personal life with the realities of *this* case. Patrick looked at Jim, who just nodded and followed Frankie to the chairs on the porch.

"Frankie," Jim said, more of a question than a statement.

"I'm sorry, I just needed a moment." Frankie took a long drink of the amber liquid and said, "Emma is Zoe's older sister, but you already knew that. She's only about ten years older, so she's still young herself. Their parents died in a car accident about nine months ago just outside of Chicago, and since they had no other family, Zoe went to live with Emma who lives in a small town just outside of St. Louis. According to her, Zoe was having a real hard time adjusting to small-town life.

"About a month ago, Emma was getting dirty clothes out of Zoe's room and noticed her computer was on and she had a message waiting for her. The message said it was from 'NightOwl816.' Zoe looked at the messages and they were relatively mundane, but it was pretty obvious to her 'NightOwl816' was older than Zoe. Emma thought, based on the comments and questions, he might be in college."

Frankie took another drink of her beer and noticed Patrick's jaw was tightening.

"Emma asked Zoe about it, and she said it was a boy who went to high school in a nearby town. They had 'met' in a soccer group chat Emma had approved her to be in. Emma said there was already a bit of tension because she would not allow Zoe to have Snapchat and of course *everyone* else has it and this just fueled the tension. Zoe got angry with Emma for going through her things and snooping on her computer. Emma said after the argument, she checked Zoe's computer a couple more times and noticed there were fewer and fewer messages. She thought the boy's interest had waned and almost forgot about it.

"Emma wanted the hostility to stop, and since the messages were fading, she let it go. For a week or two, things seemed okay, but then Emma began to notice some changes in Zoe's behavior. She was pushing limits more than before, stopped eating, changed her hair, and started dressing more... and these are Emma's words... like a 'slut.' Zoe became more protective of her phone and was going out of her way to hide it as soon as Emma or her husband walked into the room.

"Emma is not naive and remembered doing the same thing when she was Zoe's age and had an older boyfriend. Emma said her boyfriend started asking her to send him 'sexy' pictures. She never did it but remembered pushing boundaries and trying to look older and "sexier" so he would continue to like her. Emma said the only "boy" she knew Zoe was talking to was 'NightOwl816' and she had not openly dated anyone since moving in with her.

"That brings us to about two weeks ago. Emma said she and Zoe got into a major fight. Zoe had a little money in her account from babysitting and birthday gifts and had taken a rideshare from their small town to downtown St. Louis. Zoe thought she had charged *her* account, and thus wouldn't get caught, but she forgot Emma added her payment information to the app when her phone died, and they needed a ride to the airport after their parents' funeral. Emma was livid because Zoe had gone to the city without permission and the anger swelled when she wouldn't tell her why she went. Words were exchanged, and Zoe was told she wasn't allowed to leave the house for a week except for school and soccer. Regrettably, Emma said she didn't think to look at Zoe's cell phone.

"The next few days were extremely tense. Zoe didn't speak more than one or two words to Emma and the words she spoke were hostile. The night before Zoe left, Emma was at a soccer game and was talking to one of the moms from Zoe's soccer team. She's the one that suggested Emma look at Zoe's phone. Emma waited until Zoe was in the shower because she knew it would be World War III if she asked for it. Figuring out the passcode was pretty easy, but she wasn't prepared for what she saw.

"First thing she noticed were photographs of her sister in various states of dress. Emma looked at Zoe's Insta account and realized it was a different account than the one she followed and there was a series of messages between her, and some guy named Wes-something. The messages were benign at first. Wes referenced Emma 'snooping' on Zoe's computer and the need to move the chats to her 'Finsta' account. They also mentioned Zoe's inability to download SnapChat.

"Emma said she had installed an app and set the security on the phone so Zoe couldn't download anything without her permission, but she never thought Instagram would be a problem. She followed Zoe and knew what was on her page. What she did not account for was Zoe's ability to create a fake account."

Frankie looked out over the field. The sun was beginning to set, sending a shimmer of light across the waving grasses. Unconsciously Frankie began peeling the label of the beer she was holding.

"He repeatedly asked Zoe for pictures, but Emma said she noticed the only pictures on his profile were the profile picture, which she thought was fake, and some other Google downloads. Emma said from the messages she also learned why Zoe went to St. Louis. The 'boy' sent her money for a bus ticket and didn't want it traced to the town Zoe lived in, so he sent it via wire. Of course, he told naive Zoe there were no other places he could wire her the money except the big city.

"Emma was upset with what she found and was waiting for Zoe when she got out of the shower. She confronted her about the boy's age, the photographs, and the money for the bus ticket. The argument became intense, and Emma grounded Zoe from her phone, her computer, and any social activities. She got the typical 'you are ruining my life' screams from Zoe and, though she knew it wasn't over, she thought she had handled it. When she got up the next morning to wake Zoe for soccer practice, Zoe was gone."

THE SUN cast shadows over the trees lining the creek as Frankie let the details sink in. It had been a lot to hear, and she was still trying to process it all herself. Zoe had been here. On her family's farm. In her barn playhouse. What she didn't know was for how long or how she had gone undetected. Of course, she knew the answer to the second question. No one patrolled the woods; that would be unreasonable. Jake worked full time and often had to travel for his job. She doubted her father had ridden through the woods in months, and she and Sophie were rarely there. It would be easy for someone to be in the woods and go unde-tected. They lived in a nice, sleepy county where very little bad happened. Aside from Julia disappearing, Frankie did not know of any other unsolved homicides (because that is what she believed it was) since.

Interrupting the silence, Patrick asked, "Did Emma say if she had heard from Zoe since? Or if she tried to chat with NightOwl816?"

"Emma hasn't heard from Zoe, but she did try to message him, but he had blocked Zoe's account."

"That tracks," Patrick said.

"What do you mean?" Frankie and Jim asked simultaneously.

Patrick sat silent for a couple seconds and then said, "When Sasha disappeared, I tried to chat with the person she was talking to from her computer and her account was blocked, too."

"What was the screenname of the person she was talking to?" Jim asked.

"816Ranger. We thought it was an Army connection at first, but now I wonder. We got nowhere trying to locate the identity of the screenname. When we traced the IP address, it came back to an internet service provider in this county, but we couldn't get the exact location without a warrant."

"Emma said she called the police and made a report, but they tried to pass it off as a typical angry teen who had run away. She has no faith they did anything other than take the information," Frankie said. "I wonder if they even put her name into NCIC as a missing person."

"That's an easy check. Do you think she'd give us access to Zoe's cell-phone and computer?" Jim asked.

"She was ready to drive up here today with everything in tow. I told her I'd call her, and we would arrange to get the electronics. I'm not sure we want the sister up here. We don't know how long it will take to find Zoe... or if she'll be alive when we do. I'm going to ask her to give us something with her hair and a piece of clothing or something with her scent when we get the electronics. Maybe we can use a dog to track her?"

"I'll drive down and grab everything from her," Patrick said. "Any chance we can get an agency to let us use their dog to track the woods?"

"Mia's sister does search and rescue. If our agency won't help, I know she will. Mia is learning so..."

Before Frankie could finish her sentence, she saw Jake and Tyler barreling through the field in their direction. Tyler was driving and sporting a grin from ear to ear. Frankie's initial thought was, *"what the hell,"* but when she saw Tyler's smile, all she could do was laugh. She and her siblings had been about the same age when their dad put them in the driver's seat, so it made since for Jake to follow suit.

Once they were parked, Tyler jumped down and ran to Frankie yelling, "Did you see me, mom? Uncle Jake let me drive. I did really good, too. He says I'm a natural and am a better driver than you and Aunt Sophie. I hope you're hungry. We caught a bunch of fish. I caught more, but Uncle Jake said we had to throw them back because they were too small. We also saw a rattlesnake and a copperhead. I wasn't scared one bit…"

Jake laughed out loud.

"Okay, so I might've been a little scared. But that's okay because they're dangerous. It's okay to be scared when something's dangerous. We moved where we were fishing and gave them some space, so they'd leave us alone."

When Tyler finally stopped to take a breath, Jake asked, "Everyone okay with fish? We did catch a mess, but I can freeze them. I have burgers we can throw on the grill if you'd rather."

Everyone agreed fish was fine, and Frankie watched as Tyler followed Jake to the side of the barn so they could clean the fish.

"He's a good kid, Frankie," Patrick said.

Frankie smiled and said, "He is. Both are, really. I was hoping Danielle would change her mind and come down today, but… her loss, I suppose."

Jim looked at her with compassion, reached over and touched her hand and said, "It really is."

The three sat in silence, watching dark take over the day. They all wanted to scour the woods again and bum rush Warren Hudson's house but knew they had to play it by the book if they had any hope of justice, or more importantly, finding the girls alive.

FIFTY-THREE

THE WEEKEND WENT by in a blur and, before Frankie knew it, it was Monday. Tyler was back in school, and Frankie was back on days. Her shift rotated every 28 days, making her sleep patterns and schedule unpredictable at best. Her squad seemed to see the most interesting cases, and Frankie enjoyed the night shift, but days made things better for her family and gave her some time to catch up on mundane paperwork.

"What's with the suit?" Mia asked.

"Prelim on Blade today. Sam wasn't sure if she was going to need me to testify, so I wore a suit."

"You definitely won't need to testify then. Why didn't they just take the case to the grand jury? Would have been easier on the vic," Mia said.

"I'm not sure. I expect prelims in our other counties, but not here. I plan to ask Sam that very question when I get over there, but knowing her, I'm sure there is a good reason."

"I hope so. Did you bring your workout clothes?" Mia asked.

"Yep. And a change of clothes in case we have a scene."

The department allowed for an hour each day to exercise, which Mia and Frankie tried to use. If they were lucky, they got two to three days out of five when they were on the day shift and one or two when they were on nights. Frankie tried to supplement the days they didn't get to exercise by running. Her best runs being with Jim who would push her a little harder than she would push herself.

"Do you think Blade will make bond?"

"I think he's going to ask for a reduction, and he might get it. If he does, I'm going to ask Sam if we can put a GPS tracker on his vehicle."

Frankie went back to reviewing her notes on the scene and her part of the investigation. Clara would be called to testify about her experience, but Frankie might have to testify to everything else. Frankie was lost in the task when the phone on her desk began to ring.

"Sex Crimes, Thomas."

"Hey Frankie, it's Sam. We're not going to need you after all. Clara did a great job testifying and the judge said he didn't need to hear anything else. Now to build the case for trial."

Frankie looked at the clock, shocked to see it was 10 AM.

"Thank you, Sam. Who's his attorney?"

"Molly Scott. Have you gone up against her before?"

"Yeah. She's good. Did he ask for a bond reduction?"

"Judge Maron didn't give him a chance." Sam laughed. "After Clara testified, she looked straight at him and said he was lucky she didn't hold him without bond."

"Excellent. Let me know if there's anything additional you need from us."

"You know we will."

Frankie stared at the phone for a few seconds after returning it to its cradle.

"Was he bound him over for trial?" Mia asked, breaking Frankie from her thoughts.

"Yep. Judge Maron didn't even give him a chance to request a bond reduction. He has Molly Scott from the public defender's office. I wonder how long it will take her to ask for a plea?"

"My money is on before the next hearing."

FRANKIE FELT her cellphone vibrate in her pocket. Recognizing the caller-id, an involuntary smile lifted her lips. "Hey, Jim, what's up?"

Frankie listened as Jim told her he and Patrick had been out doing knock-and-talks all day and wondered if they could meet up after shift. Mia could hear Jim say, "I know you're on days, but I bet Tyler wouldn't mind pizza for dinner."

"Sure. I should be home by 5. What time do you all want to stop by?" Frankie listened and then said, "Okay. Let's skip pizza. It's a nice night, and I told Tyler I would throw some burgers on the grill."

After Frankie hung up, Mia said, "Dinner with Jim, huh? Holding out on me?"

"It's nothing like that," Frankie protested. "He and Patrick just want to update me on the investigation, and since I have to do it off the clock..."

"I think there's more there than you're ready to admit."

Frankie didn't respond. She was beginning to wonder the same thing.

A few hours later, Frankie, Patrick, and Jim sat on the deck waiting for the grill to heat up. Looking towards the garage apartment, Jim asked, "Where's Sophie?"

"She lives here?" Patrick asked.

"Working late on that reno in Northeast," Frankie said. "Yeah, she and I, with a little help from dad and Jake, turned the loft over the garage into a one-bedroom apartment. It's great having her close by."

"Alright, partner, tell me about Frankie as a kid," Jim said.

Frankie laughed in spite of herself as Patrick and Jim exchanged stories, many of which she was the subject matter. They each wanted to know what she was like without them.

"You were a cheerleader?" Jim asked. "I can totally see that, but somehow it still surprises me."

"She was pretty cute in those little uniforms. I think my favorite was the winter ones though." Patrick winked at Frankie and made curves with his hands as he said. "Sweaters that fit just right."

Frankie was glad Tyler was taking a shower and could not hear this, although instinctively she knew the conversation would be different if he or Danielle were present.

"Still have that uniform, Frankie?" Jim asked. "Wouldn't mind seeing that myself."

Frankie, blushing said, "I need to go get the burgers."

Jim followed her inside, "I'll grab us some beers."

"Thank you," Frankie said, meeting Jim's gaze.

A few minutes later, burgers on the grill, Frankie said, "Are you jokesters going to tell me what you learned today?"

"I would rather talk about you in a cute little cheerleading uniform," Jim teased. "But I suppose we should fill you in."

Frankie threw a towel at Jim, who dodged the hit and laughed.

"We talked to four families today. We still have a handful from this area to visit, and then we'll expand outward. At initial glance, it looks like at least three of the four may be related. All four were similarly aged girls who disappeared, seemingly without a trace. Two of the four had gotten in trouble for talking to an unknown 'boy' online. Both of the families for those girls thought their daughters had stopped talking to the boy, but then they disappeared. The parents of one did not learn their daughter had been talking to a 'boy' online until after she disappeared. The last one is probably not related but..." Patrick's voice trailed off.

Jim said, "It looks like she might have a history of sexual abuse and maybe a bit of mental health problems as a result. Mom didn't say it, but it looks like she may have started using drugs to self-medicate and disappeared into that world."

"Her *mom*," disdain dripped from the word, "did nothing but blame her child for ruining *her* life by getting child protective services involved with their family. Her husband, and wage earner, had to leave the house all because of her '*lying whore*' daughter." Patrick did nothing to hide his disgust. "She went on to say child protective services let him back in the house after he took a lie detector."

Frankie flinched involuntarily, this information striking a chord with her. "Let me guess, the day he came home, she left."

"Yep," Patrick said.

Swallowing a drink of her beer, she said, "Sounds like she might have been a good target for a predator."

"Agreed," Jim said. "But according to her mom, she didn't have any social media accounts or a computer. However, she did have a cell phone, so it's still possible."

"Let's not rule her out as part of this just yet," Frankie said. To herself she thought, "*Even if she is not involved in this, I want to find her. Let her know someone will listen. Someone will believe her.*"

CHAPTER
FIFTY-FIVE

FRANKIE SAT in Sam's small, cramped office filled with trial prep for three cases. File boxes lined the walls, except for a small space in front of the dry erase board on her wall. Assorted legal pads filled with notes littered the desk. Frankie was not sure how Sam found anything, but when asked, she assured Frankie she knew exactly where everything was.

Frankie and Sam had been preparing for an upcoming trial the entire morning and decided to take a quick lunch break before finishing up.

"Frankie, are you listening?" Sam asked.

"What, huh? I'm sorry. I was just…" Frankie's voice trailed off.

"….in another world," Sam finished.

"I'm sorry, this new case has me distracted. Tell me about the latest date. Let me live vicariously through you."

Sam started to laugh. "This last date is one for the books."

Frankie listened as Sam described the man she met on a common dating app.

"He was in the military, clean cut, and super sexy. You know what I'm talking about? Fit, but not so into his body that he was obnoxious. I thought we really connected. Well, the check comes, and I'm prepared to pay for myself, but he picks up the check and I think 'this is a nice surprise' and decide I'm going to suggest we go get a drink somewhere. I had driven out to meet him but figured one more glass of wine would be fine and who knows where it might lead. Before I could say anything, he tells me he has to go back to the barracks, looked at his watch and added he can't be late. I've been around plenty of military guys and thought it was suspect that he lived in barracks at our age but decided not to ask. Well, long story short, I should have. Want to take a wild guess as to why he had to be back by a certain time? And why, as an officer, he was staying in the barracks?"

"I don't have a clue."

"He's on house arrest." Sam paused for effect and then said, "For murder!"

Sam began to laugh uncontrollably.

Frankie joined in the laughter and, as she tried to catch her breath, she asked, "He didn't think to mention that when you two were talking online?"

Sam shook her head.

"Did he tell you the story on how he ended up charged?"

Sam began to laugh again and said, "No, but I looked it up. Apparently, he was involved in a threesome that went bad."

"What?" Frankie exclaimed.

Sam continued to laugh as she described the incident then said, "I don't mean to laugh at someone being murdered, but this was one for the books. His defense is it was accidental."

"Of course, it is. Did he have any idea what you do for a living?"

"Oh, yeah. I told him that was why I moved here."

This made both women laugh a little harder at the stupidity of the man.

"When is your next date?" Frankie asked with a wink.

"Try two weeks from never." Sam's face became more solemn, "Seriously though, I never thought I'd still be single at my age. I wish I knew the secret to meeting a good man."

Frankie smiled. Sam displayed a façade of pure self-confidence. She was a stunning, intelligent, and successful woman with long, raven hair, natural curves, and a smile that disarmed most men with whom she spoke. Frankie was surprised she doubted herself and expressed such vulnerability. To herself she thought, *"I guess all women struggle to some degree. It's not just me."*

Changing the subject Sam asked, "What's the new case that has you so distracted?

"Where do I begin?"

Frankie shared with Sam all that she knew about the missing girls, including Patrick's daughter and Zoe. She explained the possible connection to the farm and maybe her own history.

"You really think it might be related to your friend's disappearance?"

"Maybe. It seems so far-fetched. I mean how would we not know her dad was luring girls, especially if they were at the barn? I'd think we would see signs. We were in the woods all the time as kids and..."

"Frankie, if someone wants to hide something, or someone, they will. You said yourself, you hadn't been to that barn in years. What makes you think your brother is any different?"

"True. I just hope we can find these girls. Before it's too late."

"If you need an extra set of eyes, let me know. I may be able to give a different perspective."

"Thanks, Sam." Frankie pulled out her notepad with questions and notes, grabbed her pen and said, "Now, how about this upcoming trial of ours."

CHAPTER
FIFTY-SIX

IT WAS Zoe's turn to leave the hole where she had been placed with other girls. She had watched the girls come and go with an unknown man, but up to this point, she had only been taken by the old man. He handed her a blindfold, pointed a gun and ordered Zoe to tie it across her eyes. With her eyes covered, he took a pair of zip ties and bound her hands behind her back, then pulled on the tie of the blindfold, making sure it was taught. Then he grabbed Zoe by the arm and led her up and outside to a vehicle. Zoe couldn't see, but based on what she could feel with her feet, she believed she was in the seat by herself. She repeatedly asked him where they were going, but he refused to answer. Zoe continued talking and asking questions. Eventually he turned up the radio to drown out her inquiries.

Zoe wiggled her hands and her head, trying to loosen the ties and maybe get the blindfold to drop so she could see where this man was taking her. The radio was playing country music, but not like the music her sister listened to. This was older, more similar to what her mama had listened to before she died. Zoe kept track of distance by counting songs and focused on the things she couldn't see. The road was bumpy, rocks were hitting the steel of his vehicle, and his driving was slower for one song. Gravel road. Then the road was smooth, no more rocks pinging, but very curvy for three songs. Paved road.

Zoe's wiggling paid off, and she was finally able to glance under the blindfold. Her vantage point was awkward, but she could tell they were still in the country, and she was in an older truck. She wasn't positive but thought it was the one she had ridden in before. Her wrists were starting to hurt from the twisting, but the zip ties were starting to loosen slightly. Zoe thought if she kept moving, she could get them loose enough to slip her wrists out, and when he stopped at a stop sign, traffic light, or whatever, she would open the door and run.

The truck started to slow down. Zoe glanced under the blindfold, and all she could see were cornfields on both sides of the road. The man picked up speed slightly, making jumping from the vehicle impossible. Two more songs and a farm report later, the truck slowed again. Zoe peeked under the blindfold and saw more cornfields on one side of the road and an empty field with an oddly shaped hill in the middle.

Just as the man was turning towards the empty field with the hill, Zoe slipped out of the zip ties, pulled the blindfold off, and tried to open the door. Her attempts were futile. She tried to unlock the door quietly, but it still wouldn't open. Zoe knew she had one chance and if it didn't work, she was afraid he would kill her. She hit the button to lower the window. Just as the man turned to look, her hand was outside the truck, opening the door from the outside. Zoe let herself fall out of the moving truck, rolling away from the road. She glimpsed at the license plate and caught the first three numbers on the plate as it came to an abrupt stop. Before he could get out of the truck and grab her, Zoe was on her feet running through the cornfield.

CHAPTER
FIFTY-SEVEN

ZOE DIDN'T KNOW where she was going but kept running until she saw what appeared to be a clearing. As she got close to the edge of the field, she stopped and looked towards a house and barn. Zoe was pretty sure she wasn't near where she had been kept but couldn't be positive it hadn't been that house or barn, so she stayed hidden and watched both from the refuge of the cornfield.

Zoe saw two kids, who looked like they were in middle school, run out the back door yelling good-bye to someone inside. She hadn't heard the voices of children while she was in the hole. The pair made their way to the end of the driveway to wait for the bus coming down the road. A man, not much younger than her father was when he died, kissed a similarly aged woman at the door, then got in his truck and followed the school bus down the gravel road, a cloud of dust trailing him.

The woman who stood at the door when her family left walked outside to the small deck and looked out over the fields surrounding her house. Zoe thought she may have been seen, but the woman turned and went inside the house. Zoe sat in the field, making herself small, and watched the road and the house. After about ten minutes, she was about to step out of the field when she saw the truck from which she escaped drive by the house slowly. Quickly, Zoe retreated back into the cornfield and watched, holding her breath to see if he stopped at the house. She didn't exhale until she saw the truck pass.

Zoe waited another ten minutes and watched as the truck drove by the house two more times. After the last time, the truck sped up, giving her confidence he was gone for good. Zoe steeled herself to make the walk across the yard and knock on the door. What would she say? Would this woman think she was a crazy runaway? Would she call the police or allow her to call her sister, Emma. The thought of Emma made her pause. She had to be so worried. Zoe was angry with herself for being so selfish and mean. Emma had been so good to her after their parents died, and Zoe had been nothing but unappreciative and difficult.

"Quit stalling," Zoe said. With those words, she left the cornfield and walked up to the back door of the house.

Zoe's taps on the door were answered quickly. The same woman she had seen on the deck stood just inside the storm door.

"Can I help you?" she asked, eyeing the dirty teen with wild, scared eyes.

"Can I please call my sister, Emma? I need her help."

The woman hesitated briefly, wondering if this girl was for real or if she was there to steal from or hurt her.

Zoe's resolve broke, and she began sobbing, her words breaking through in a staccato, "Please… ran away… kidnapped… need help… escaped from truck… need Emma."

"What's her number, honey? I'll get her on the phone." The woman opened the door and let Zoe inside the tidy kitchen. Her husband would later chastise her for being so trusting, but she would always be thankful she listened to her gut and let the child inside.

"Hello, is this Emma?"

"Yes, who's this?"

"My name is Catherine, and I'm here with a young woman who said she's your sister." To Zoe she asked, "What's your name, honey?"

"Zoe."

Emma said, "Zoe's there with you? Is she hurt?"

"She's in one piece but seems pretty scared."

Before Catherine could say more, Emma said, "I need you to call Detective Frankie Thomas."

CHAPTER
FIFTY-EIGHT

FRANKIE FINISHED with Sam and returned to an empty office. Coleman and Wheeler were off doing an area canvas on one of their cases, and Mia had taken files across the street to the prosecutor's office, leaving Frankie alone in the office. She had just put earbuds in and started typing on reports when her phone rang.

"Sex Crimes, Thomas."

"Uhm, is this Detective Frankie Thomas?"

"Yes."

"My name is Catherine Simmons, and I have a girl here who, well her sister said I should call you."

Frankie sat up straight and asked, "What's the girl's name?"

"Zoe."

"Where is she?"

"Right now, she's at my house. I'm just east of town, just outside of Richmond, Missouri. You may not know…."

"I'm familiar," Frankie said. Briefly she wondered if Catherine was related to a guy she graduated with. "Where'd she come from? How did she get there?"

"I don't know. She showed up at my door this morning and asked to call her sister. She looks pretty messed up, Detective. I thought I would let her take a shower and…"

"No," Frankie said abruptly, then softened her voice and continued, "Please don't. Can you give me your phone number and address? I'll arrange for her to get picked up and taken to the hospital."

"Okay. I can probably drive her there if that would be helpful."

Frankie mulled it over, then said, "Can you meet me at the emergency department in North Kansas City?"

Catherine agreed. After a pause she added, "Detective, she seems pretty afraid. What if she won't go?"

"Call me back if she won't get in the car with you, but something tells me if she's still there, she trusts you. Let her know I'm going to call Emma." Frankie had a thought come to mind and added, "If someone comes to the door looking for her before you leave, have her hide and don't let anyone know she's there with you. The faster you can get on the road the better."

"You're scaring me. Should I be worried?"

"Not worried, just smart. How long will it take you to get to the ED?" Frankie asked.

"Give me 40 minutes."

"I'll meet you outside the doors. And Catherine..."

"Yes."

"Thank you. This is a big help."

Frankie briefed Baker and by then Mia was back from the prosecutor's office. Baker was not thrilled with them using department time to interview the girl, but as Frankie pointed out, it was possible she was picked up in their city and transported, which means the case would be theirs. There was no need to muddy the waters by having another agency start something they would just have to finish. They would bring Jim and Patrick in after they developed some rapport and trust and then step back if necessary. The important thing was to get this child back to her sister and hopefully find the other missing girls.

CHAPTER
FIFTY-NINE

CATHERINE HUNG up the phone and looked to Zoe, "Detective Thomas wants us to go to the hospital. Would you be willing to ride with me? She said she'd have Emma meet us there."

Zoe seemed hesitant but nodded her head.

"Let me run a comb through this hair, and then we'll get going." Thinking about what Frankie had said, Catherine added, "Stay away from the windows and don't answer if anyone knocks on the door."

Again, Zoe nodded.

As if on cue, Catherine heard a vehicle turn into the driveway. She looked out the window and said, "Zoe, go into the bathroom. It's the second door on the left. Shut the door and don't come out until I tell you to."

Zoe's eyes filled with fright and her body froze.

"It's okay, honey, it's probably nothing, but I need you to move."

Zoe nodded and scurried down the hall. She could hear the *tap, tap, tap* from outside. After Catherine was sure Zoe was safe, she took a deep breath and opened the back door.

Leaving the storm door shut she smiled and said, "Hi there, can I help you?"

The man standing on the other side of the door was disheveled and his voice trembled as he asked, "I'm looking for my granddaughter. She ran away last night, and I'm just worried sick."

"I haven't seen anyone around my place today. What does she look like so I can keep an eye out for her."

"She's about 16. Pretty little thing. About your height. She was wearing jeans and a tank top, I think."

"What's her name?"

The man stuttered, "Zu… zu… Zoe. Do you mind if I look in your barn to see if she might be in there?"

"My husband keeps the barn locked up, so there's no way she could've gotten in there. Do you want to leave me your name and number? That way if I see her, I can call you?"

The man just shook his head and said, "I'm sure she'll show up. Have a nice day."

Catherine watched as the man walked back to his truck, his shoulders hunched forward. She felt a chill run down her spine. She didn't know what Zoe had been through, but she was certain she had come face to face with evil.

Catherine waited until he had pulled out of the driveway and was out of sight before telling Zoe she could come out of the bathroom. Her hands shook as she grabbed her car keys and purse from the hooks on the wall. Catherine put her arm around Zoe and led her to the car parked near the back door. Once inside, she locked the doors, took another deep breath, and pulled away from her home.

FRANKIE AND MIA WAITED OUTSIDE, next to the doors of the emergency department. If a forensic examination was necessary, they would call in an advocate, but for now, they hoped to get some preliminary information from Zoe and Catherine. Baker did not particularly like them taking the initial report, but it seemed a waste of time to call a radio car out to do something they were more than capable of doing.

"I think this might be them," Mia said.

Frankie watched a young girl with a slight build and a woman about her age walk toward them. The girl, who looked to be about the same age as Danielle, had her head down and watched her feet as she walked. Frankie and Mia both wore their badges around their neck, clearly identifying themselves as law enforcement, even in plain clothes.

"Is one of you Detective Thomas?" the older woman asked.

Frankie stepped forward and said, "Yes. This is my partner, Detective Boden. You must be Catherine."

"Yes. This is Zoe," Catherine said, referencing the girl standing next to her.

"Do you mind if we step inside?" Frankie directed the question to Zoe. "We have a private room where we can talk, if that's okay."

"Okay," was the soft reply.

Frankie led them into one of the rooms the hospital typically used for consultations with families. The room was small, with a round table and a set of chairs that were less than comfortable. Frankie waited for Zoe to sit down before finding a seat across from her. Mia asked Catherine to meet with her in the lobby so she could do a quick interview and then allow her to leave when she was finished.

"Zoe, honey, do you have the piece of paper I gave you?" Catherine asked. To Frankie and Mia, she said, "I gave her my phone number so she could keep in touch. I want to know she is okay."

"Yes, ma'am. Thank you," Zoe said.

After Mia and Catherine left the room, Frankie opened her notebook and started her recorder. She detailed the date, time, and location of the interview, then asked Zoe if she would state her full name and date of birth.

"Zoe Elizabeth Parker. My birthday is January 22, and I am 14 years old."

"*Fourteen,*" Frankie thought. "*She is the same age as Danielle.*" Aloud she said, "Where do you live?"

Zoe provided the name of the town her sister lived in, her cellphone number, and all the relevant biographical information she could remember.

"Thank you, Zoe." Frankie paused and looked at her notes. "You are pretty far from home. Can you tell me how you ended up in Kansas City, Missouri?"

"You mean like today when Catherine brought me here to meet you?"

"How about you start when you were with your sister. Tell me what you remember about how you left and ended up here."

CHAPTER
SIXTY-ONE

ZOE THOUGHT for a minute and said, "I guess it all started when my mama and daddy died. They were driving, and a drunk driver ran a stoplight and hit them. Daddy died right away, but mama held on for a few days. After she died, Emma said we had to sell the house and I had to move in with her. She's married and her husband works in the small town where they live, so I had to leave everything. My friends, my school...."

"I moved in with Emma and her husband because I had to, but it was hard, you know? The town is small, so everyone there has known each other, like forever. I did finally make friends with one girl, and we hung out sometimes. One night we were playing around on Insta, and this guy started messaging me," Zoe got quiet, placed her hands in her lap, and began clasping and unclasping her fingers.

"Tell me what you remember about the messages," Frankie prompted.

"He said he was sixteen, played soccer, and liked the same music we did. Eventually he asked if we could talk on Snap. My sister made it so I couldn't download the app, so I told him I didn't have it. He suggested I set up a Finsta..." Zoe stopped and looked at Frankie with question. "Do you know what that is?"

Frankie smiled and said, "Yes." She knew sometimes teenagers set up a fake Instagram account so parents would think they were looking at their child's profile, not realizing there was a fake one, hence a Finsta, account.

"I set one up and gave him my username, and he immediately DM'd me."

Zoe told Frankie she began chatting with Wesley, also known as NightOwl816. She said her friend had Snap and added him, but her parents found out and made her delete the app. Emma tried to stop Zoe from talking to Wesley, too, but she didn't know about the Finsta account, at least not at first.

Zoe said she complained to Wesley about how much she hated living at her sister's and the school she went to. Wesley listened to her complaints then began to send her photographs and asked her to send photographs of herself. Eventually Wesley's requests became bolder, and he asked her to send nude photographs. Zoe said she sent a couple and instantly regretted it. After a couple of weeks, Wesley started asking her to come to him. He told her to go to St. Louis, and he would send her a bus ticket.

"I took an Uber to the bus station, but there was no ticket, so I went back home. I thought I was careful, but my sister found out and took my phone and my computer. I was so mad. She told me I was grounded and lost all privileges, but right before she went to bed, I convinced her I had to turn in a school assignment and needed my computer. She had to work the next morning and after a while she fell asleep on the couch. I started talking to Wesley on my Finsta, and he said he sent the ticket to the wrong station. He said to go back to St. Louis, and it would be there by morning. I took cash from my sister's purse and did what he said. He told me he would pick me up, but instead some old dude was there. The old guy told me Wesley was at work, but he would take me to him."

"Zoe, do you remember the destination for the bus ticket?"

"Kansas City."

That was what Frankie needed. Zoe was lured to Kansas City by a man pretending to be a similarly aged boy. Once she was in Kansas City, it was kidnapping. She thought about calling Sam to run the facts by her to make sure the kidnapping did not belong to the town where she was taken, but she decided against it. She wanted to see what, if any, connection there was to the farm. And to Julia.

CHAPTER
SIXTY-TWO

MIA ENTERED THE ROOM QUIETLY, sitting next to Frankie, who wrote a note which read, *It's ours.*

The pair sat quietly listening as Zoe continued to tell her story. An older man picked her up and said Wesley was at work. She was unsure what the man's name was, he only told her once. Zoe said initially everything was fine. The man got her McDonald's and told her Wesley talked about her all the time and was excited for her to be there. Wesley worked at a place where they would not let him take his phone, so the man said he couldn't call him, but he'd be at the house in a couple of hours.

"Things didn't get weird until we got to the house…." Zoe's voice trailed off.

Frankie and Mia sat in the silence, giving Zoe time to process her experience. She stared past them to the wall, her eyes welling up with tears but not falling onto her cheeks.

"We walked inside the house and even though it was dirty and dark, it was normal. I think there was a kitchen, too, but I never saw it. I asked to use the bathroom, and that's when he flipped. He pointed to the hallway but then came up behind me and grabbed me. That is the last thing I remember until I was in a dungeon or something."

"Were you alone?" Frankie asked, pretty sure she knew the answer.

"No. There were three other girls, and they were pretty messed up."

"What do you mean messed up?" Mia asked.

Zoe thought carefully then said, "They looked scared, and their clothes were dirty. One of the girls seemed younger and cried a lot and one of them seemed like she was on drugs or something."

"What happened next?"

"I started looking around the room, trying to find a way out," Zoe looked down at her hands and began picking at her cuticles.

"Tell me more about the room." Frankie said.

"It was dark, but there was a light bulb hanging from the ceiling, so it wasn't pitch black. The walls were blocks, kind of like concrete. The floor was dirt."

"Tell me more about the girls."

"I mostly just talked to Nikki. The other girls were quiet and seemed more scared, but Nikki showed no emotion. She'd been there the longest and appeared to be the leader. She left with the man a couple of times and when she came back, she always said the same thing. 'Just do what they say, and it'll be over fast.' I was afraid to ask what they told her to do."

Frankie ran through the names of the missing girls whose families Patrick and Jim talked to. The one they thought was not related. The *lying whore daughter*. Her name was Nikki.

"The other girls only left one time each. When they came back, it was different. They wouldn't speak to anyone and cried themselves to sleep. I decided I had to get out of there before they came for me. So, the night the last one came back…I'm not sure how many nights it had been by then…I found a way out."

CHAPTER
SIXTY-THREE

IT WAS apparent to Frankie the girls were being removed from the room for the purposes of engaging in sex acts, even if Zoe did not seem to realize it. She listened intently as Zoe explained her escape.

"I paid attention to what the man did when he picked up the girls and when he brought them back. He was super careful when he knew we were all awake. He shut the door behind him and after he locked it, he pulled it to make sure the lock caught. The first couple of nights when he brought the others back, he did that, and I started to think there must be a problem with the door. Or at least he must have thought so. One night when he brought the last girl back, I pretended to be asleep. He shut the door and locked it but didn't pull on it like he had before. I waited until it was super quiet, and I was pretty sure everyone was asleep. That's when I tried the door. It was loose but it I couldn't get it to open."

Frankie and Mia sat quietly waiting for Zoe to continue.

"When he would bring us food, he always brought us that plasticware you get with fast food orders and collected it when he left. The next day he brought us food and he missed me slipping a plastic knife into my pocket. That night, after Nikki got back, I used the knife on the door and this time it opened."

After a several minutes of silence Frankie asked, "Did you wake the other girls?"

Tears began to well in Zoe's eyes. Before she answered, they spilled onto her cheeks. As she wiped them away, she said, "No. I was afraid. I didn't want to get caught and thought if I took them with me, he would catch us.

"I was careful. And quiet. I pushed the door open quickly and when I shut it, I didn't pull it tight. I thought if they heard me, they would see they could get out and I was going to tell someone so they could be rescued. I didn't know where I was going, but I took off running. It was so dark, and there were woods everywhere. I found a house with outside lights, but I didn't know whose it was. It might have been *his,* so I went away from that house into the dark woods. I'm not sure how long or how far I ran, but it felt like a long time. There was no moon when I left but then I started seeing light filter through the trees and that was when I found this old barn. There were no lights anywhere but where it sat, the moon shown right overhead, and lit up the porch."

Frankie knew what she was talking about. The barn she described. The way the moon shown on the front, spotlighting the porch of the apartment. She had sat on that porch and watched the moon rise many times. First with her father, then with her siblings, and finally with her friends.

"There was no lock on the door, and the moonlight let me see inside through the windows. No one was inside, just a little table and chairs. Like kid-size. I went inside and started going through the cabinets, looking for…something. Anything. I found a little flashlight in the drawer with some pens and paper. I used the light to check inside the other cabinets and found some old board games, and then I found a couple of sleeping bags and a pillow. There was also some water. It was almost like someone had stayed there before." Zoe abruptly added, "I really need to use the bathroom. Do you think we can take a break?"

Mia said, "I need to stretch my legs. How about you and I go find Courtney. She's the forensic nurse here, and she'll take you to a private bathroom."

As Mia escorted Zoe from the room, Frankie thought about the last time she and Julia made plans to stay in the barn. It was just a couple of weeks before Julia disappeared.

CHAPTER
SIXTY-FOUR

Twenty-eight years earlier

FRANKIE UNLOADED the sleeping bags and pillow from her four-wheeler. The cooler was already inside with water, sodas, and enough snacks to get them through the next 24 hours. She couldn't believe she and Julia had both convinced their parents to let them sleep in the barn. It was not that they had never done it, they had slept out there routinely as young girls. But now they were 16 and dating boys. Julia even had a steady boyfriend. Frankie was not sure what Julia told her parents, but she had promised hers there would be no boys and no parties. The penalty for breaking that promise would be her dad locking them out of the barn for good.

Frankie turned on the radio she had brought and checked her bags for extra batteries and cassette tapes. She and Julia had planned the entire evening. They were going to build a fire in the pit between their houses and roast hot dogs and marshmallows. They would listen to their newest tapes and maybe throw in a few oldies for fun. The girls planned to swim in the creek under the light of a full moon and stay up all night talking like they did when they were in middle school.

Frankie looked at her watch. They agreed to meet at the barn at 8, but

Julia was late. Frankie knew she was planning to have dinner with her parents, but they usually finished by 7. Even with clean-up she should have been there by now. Another 30 minutes passed before Frankie began to think she was getting stood up.

Frankie was about to pack up and leave when something told her to go by Julia's house. Tree coverage made it difficult, but she could see Julia's property from the barn, especially when they were burning trash in the pit, but the house itself was barely visible from the porch of the barn. Leaving the four-wheeler parked by the barn, Frankie grabbed her little flashlight and walked quietly through the woods just before the house. She was about 100 feet from the back door when she froze.

"You ungrateful bitch," the yell of the angry man was followed by the sound of skin hitting skin and then a loud clatter. Frankie couldn't be sure, but it sounded like furniture crashing.

"Dad. Stop it," Julia screamed. "Leave mom alone. It's not her fault."

"Who the hell do you think you're speaking to, you little whore?"

"Do not talk to her like that," shouted Julia's mother.

Another sound of skin hitting skin and more crashing. Frankie wanted to run down to the house. She wanted to stop whatever was happening inside, but she couldn't move. All she could do was stand there and listen to the screams of her friend and her friend's mother. Frankie had never heard a man speak to a woman or child like that. Her own father rarely raised his voice, even though she knew there were times he had gotten angry.

When she could finally unroot herself from the spot in which she was standing, Frankie ran back to the barn, grabbed the cooler and the four-wheeler and left – vowing never again to freeze like that when someone was in trouble.

The next day, Julia called and asked Frankie to meet her at the barn. Frankie gasped when she saw her friend, but both were careful not to speak of the bruises developing on her face and arms. Julia confided in Frankie how scared she was of her dad. She had never seen him as angry as he was the night before. She was afraid what he would do the next time her mother made him mad. Frankie wanted to tell her parents, but Julia begged her not to.

"It'll only make it worse. Please don't say anything. Please."

Reluctantly, Frankie agreed, then said, "I left the sleeping bags and pillow in the cabinet with some moth balls. There's a jug of water in the other cabinet, a radio and a flashlight with extra batteries. If it gets bad again, you can come here."

Two weeks later, Julia and her mother were gone.

CHAPTER
SIXTY-FIVE

MIA OPENED THE DOOR, startling Frankie out of her memories. Frankie noticed again how young and tiny Zoe appeared, but her eyes told a different story. She held a bottle of water and some crackers in her hand.

Mia nodded at Frankie signaling it was okay and said, "Courtney took a swab of her mouth so she could have a snack."

"That's great," Frankie said as Zoe settled into her chair. "Tell me more about what happened at the barn?"

"I snooped around the cabinets. There was paper and a pen, so I wrote a note just in case I disappeared. I wanted someone to know I was there. There was a radio, but I didn't turn it on because I was afraid any sound would give my location away. I pulled the sleeping bags out and laid them out on the floor to try and sleep. It was nice laying there. For the first time in a while, I felt… safe. I know it sounds crazy but there was something about the place that made me think I was going to be okay."

It didn't sound crazy to Frankie. She felt the same way when she went there.

"The sun was starting to come up when he came into the little room. I don't know how he knew I was gone or how he knew where I was. He usually didn't come to the dungeon in the morning, but I guess he did that day. I must not have been far from where he held us, because he found me.

"He was so mad. His face was red and twisted. He told me I was stupid and never should've left. He told me he was going to teach me a lesson about running away, a lesson I would never forget. He had a gun in his hand, grabbed me by my hair, and pulled me up off the floor. Then I felt a needle in my arm… and…" her voice trailed off.

"What happened next?" Frankie gently asked.

Zoe picked at imaginary pieces of lint on her pants before saying, "I don't know what was in the needle, but it felt like I was outside my body. He did…. stuff… to me then took me back. I can't really remember much about how I got back to the dungeon."

Frankie asked, "Did he ever say how he found you?"

"He mumbled something about me being stupid because this was the first place he thought to look. It's where his daughter used to run to when she tried to get away from him. He said he taught her a lesson and was going to teach me one, too."

Frankie felt like she had been punched in the stomach. She had long thought Julia and her mom were dead. She had even assumed Mr. Hudson had killed them but hearing this made it more *real*.

"Eventually he dragged me back to the dungeon and left me chained to a wall. A couple of days later, or at least I think it was a couple days, it was my turn to go with him like the other girls did. He unchained me and put a blindfold on me, then took me back to that house he took me to the first night. He made me get into the shower while he stood and watched me wash myself. Then, when I was dried off and in clean clothes, he made me put the blindfold back on and put plastic ties on my wrists.

"He drove around for a while. I'm not sure exactly how long, but I tried to keep track of songs. Eventually we ended up on a gravel road, and he started to slow down. I'd been moving around and could sort of see under the blindfold. I could see a field with a mound of grass, almost a small hill, and it seemed like he was going there. I didn't want to go to another dungeon. I had seen a house before we got there, so when he slowed down enough, I opened the door and rolled out of the vehicle."

"HE SLAMMED on the brakes when he realized what I had done, but by the time he got out, I had started running through the corn field. I didn't stop until I got to the edge, where the house was. I hid in the corn-field and watched the road in front of the house. I saw the truck drive back and forth, back and forth. I watched as Catherine's kids got on the bus and her husband left. By then, the truck was gone, and I decided I had to knock on her door."

Frankie was not sure, but she was pretty sure she knew where the man was taking Zoe. Based on the location of Catherine's house, and her knowledge of the area, she was somewhat confident he was taking her to an old, abandoned coal mine. Likely to dispose of her body after he ended her life. Was that where he took Julia? *To teach her a lesson?*

"I did get part of the license plate number."

Frankie's eyebrows lifted in surprise as she asked, "What was it?"

"EJ4B."

"That's great Zoe." Remembering the chalkboard, Frankie said, "I need to ask you a few follow-up questions, okay?"

Zoe nodded.

"Do you remember anything else about the inside of the barn?"

Zoe closed her eyes and when she opened them, she said, "There was a big chalkboard. Like the ones they used to have in schools. When the sky started to get light, I noticed there had been words at one time. I found a piece of chalk and traced over them… I wasn't sure what they meant but I figured if no one found my note they would see the words and maybe look around."

Frankie nodded. A memory stuck in her mind, but she couldn't retrieve it. She made a note on the side of her paper which said, *Chalkboard?*

Frankie began asking the more difficult questions about the "stuff" the man did to Zoe. When she had written her last note, she felt her phone vibrate with a text from Sergeant Baker.

The sister called and is parking at the hospital now.

"Zoe, I think I have all I need right now. I'm going to go check and see if the forensic nurse is ready for you."

Zoe's sister showed up to the hospital just as the forensic nurse was preparing to take her to the examination room. Frankie wasn't sure who cried harder, Emma or Zoe.

"I thought we'd lost you," sobbed Emma. "I thought you were gone like mama and daddy."

Zoe clenched her sister and through breakthrough sobs said, "I'm so sorry, Emma. I promise I won't ever run away again."

Frankie and Mia turned away, overcome with the emotion of the moment. They both had younger sisters, and the same thought went through their minds, *"What would I do if it was my sister?"*

Courtney coughed softly. Getting the attention of Emma and Zoe, she asked, "Ladies, how about we take this into the examination room?"

Zoe clung to her sister, suddenly seeming even younger than her 14 years, and asked, "Can Emma come with me."

Courtney looked at Frankie with question in her eyes.

"Yes, I think that would be okay," Frankie said. To Courtney she asked, "Can I talk to you for just a second before you get started?"

Courtney took Emma and Zoe into the room and told them she would be right back.

"What do you need, Frankie?" Courtney asked. She and Frankie had known each other for long enough the formalities of 'Detective Thomas' were long gone.

"She disclosed some details of her sexual assault, but I think she's holding something back. I didn't want to push too hard today. I'm hoping maybe she'll tell you more. There are at least three or four other girls who are still being held. Will you let me know if she discloses anything additional?"

"Of course. Have you talked to the sister yet?"

"Only on the phone. I need to do a formal with her, but Zoe is pretty shaken, so we should probably let her stay with her." Frankie thought for a moment then asked, "Did you call MOCSA when you got paged?"

"You know I always do. The advocate should be here any minute."

"Great. Maybe we can try and figure out where this man was holding her. I know two places she was at already, but the third is where we'll find the other girls."

After Courtney went inside the exam room, Mia asked, "Are you thinking about taking her out there today?"

"Maybe. There are young girls missing, Mia, what are we supposed to do? She was at my family's farm. Hell, for all I know, she wasn't the first to have been there."

"As harsh as this is going to sound Frankie, that poor kid has been through hell. Let her and her sister rest tonight. We can go try and find those girls tomorrow. I know this is hard for you. She's Danielle's age, and when you look at her, you see *your* little girl, but she's *not* Danielle. And neither are those other girls. You told me this morning Tyler is expecting you for dinner, and he'll be upset if you don't come home. *Your son* needs you as much as those girls."

Frankie did not like hearing it, but she knew Mia was right. She turned away to wipe the tears filling her eyes, nodding slightly. With her back to Mia she quietly said, "You're right. Let me at least get Emma's statement. Can you go call Sarge and see if he can get funding to put these two up for the night? Or maybe we can see if Synergy or Rose Brooks will take them in for one night? I get the impression money might be tight."

Mia put her hand on Frankie's shoulder and said, "You got it, partner" then left Frankie alone to wait for Emma.

SIXTY-SEVEN

DANIELLE SAT in her room alone, like she did most nights. Her dad had married a woman with kids, but most of the time she felt alone. It felt like they ignored her – until it was time for her to go see her mom and Tyler. A few days before her visit, Frankie's stepmother and dad would start talking about what they were going to do for the weekend. The stepsiblings would taunt her and say it was too bad she was going to see her mother. Danielle did not want to miss out on the fun, so she almost always stayed.

Danielle had only been there a few months but moving in with her dad had its perks. One of the things they told her was that if she chose to live there, they would give her a cellphone. Her mother had refused to get her one, saying she was too young and irresponsible to handle having a phone, but after she moved Danielle pacified her mom's concerns by saying she needed the phone so they could communicate. Most of the time it seemed like her mom was the one calling her, but Danielle always intended to send a text message or call, she just got busy. Her mother just didn't understand how much she had to do every day and lately, there had been someone else she was focused on.

A couple of weeks earlier, Danielle got a message on Insta from a boy named Wes. She was pretty sure he didn't go to her school, but he looked familiar to her, so she accepted the message. Since then, they talked almost every day. Wes really understood how lonely she was in a house so full of people. He also understood how scared she was something would happen to her mom. She didn't tell him her mother was a police detective, after all she didn't want to scare him off. Instead, she lied and said her mom was in the military and was deployed. She figured she would tell him the truth when they met. Wes was pretty great, and she knew he would understand why she had lied.

Lately Wes had been getting a little pushy, though. Even though he knew Danielle didn't have a car, she wasn't even 16, he was trying hard to get her to meet him. When she reminded him of her age, he told her he could come pick her up in his truck if she wanted him to. He tried to get her to skip school, but she chickened out at the last minute. Then he started asking for photographs of her…without any clothes. Danielle had pushed him off, but he was getting more forceful and making veiled threats. When she didn't comply, he blocked her for a couple of days, which really upset Danielle. Tonight, Danielle noticed he had unblocked her and sent a message. She sat on the bed, chewing her fingernails, waiting to see if he replied.

"Have you changed your mind? I can't talk to a baby."

"I'm scared. What if someone sees them?"

"No one will see them but me… I promise. You trust me, don't you?"

"Yes. Okay give me a minute."

Danielle hopped off her bed and locked her bedroom door. She removed her t-shirt and bra then grabbed her phone. Turning the camera towards her body, she struck a pose she hoped was sexy. She looked at the photograph, added it to their chats and hit send before quickly deleting the image from her phone.

"Nice. Now send me one completely naked."

"My dad is calling me. I have to go. Night."

Danielle quickly signed off and turned off her phone. She had a sick feeling in the pit of her stomach. Something didn't feel right. For a brief moment, she wondered if she should tell her mom.

SIXTY-EIGHT

"WHAT DO you mean she got away?"

"It isn't a big deal. I have another one on the hook. She sent me this today," said Warren Hudson, showing Hank a photograph of a partially naked teen.

"You stupid old man. What makes you think the girl who ran won't be able to bring the cops to the girls?" shouted Hank.

"I already moved them. There's nothing left but an old, abandoned, overgrown mine with no identifiable road. It was dark when I brought her to the house, and she was blindfolded when I took her from here. There is no way that girl is going to take them anywhere."

Hank seemed slightly mollified but didn't say anything.

To fill in the silence, Warren asked, "Do you want me to set it on fire? You know, to cover all traces?"

Hank seemed to give it some thought but never answered the question. Instead, he asked, "Where's this girl in the photograph?"

Warren began to get excited, "That's the best part. She's close by. I was looking at her Instagram page and it looks like she's in a neighboring town. She has been complaining about...."

Before Hudson could finish his sentence, he felt the back of Hank's hand hard across his cheek.

"Are you really that fucking stupid, old man? What have I told you about luring girls close to home? You are becoming a liability." Hank began to pace, clenching and unclenching his fists. "You know what I do with liabilities? I eliminate them. Find another girl. One that won't be missed."

Before Warren could respond, Hank walked out the door, slamming it behind him. Warren stood and stared at the door, considering what Hank had said. He knew Hank had a point about not picking up any girls close to home, but this one fit *his* desires. Maybe he would just see if he could get her to send him more pictures. Maybe chat with her a little more. What harm could that do? If he was really nice, maybe she would meet him. If she did, he would do to her what he had done with the others Hank didn't know about.

Warren chuckled. Hank thought he knew everything. Hank thought *he* was in control. Warren had been in business for a long time and had been luring girls long before the internet. That just made it easier. He didn't need Hank for places to hold or dispose of the girls. There were mine entrances and abandoned cellars in the area Hank knew about and there were others he didn't. Those were where Warren took the girls he found and didn't want to share. He took good care of those girls until they became a problem. When that happened, he took measures to make sure they would never be found.

CHAPTER
SIXTY-NINE

"THIS IS the house where you met Catherine. Is that the cornfield you ran through?" Frankie asked, pointing to the field behind the house. She noted Zoe seemed more at ease and rested after spending the night with her sister.

"Yes," Zoe pointed at a spot in the field at the corner of the barn. "I hid there. I just watched the house and him driving back and forth."

Frankie used to know the area like the back of her hand, but she hadn't lived there for more than 20 years, and a lot had changed. Jim drove them out of Catherine's driveway back to the road. Patrick sat in the backseat with a map that showed property boundaries and areas of interest.

"Take a right and it should take you to a road behind the field," Patrick directed.

When they reached the turn, Frankie said, "Hold up a minute. Let me see that map."

Frankie thought about what Zoe had said about there being a small hill in the middle of a field. She scanned the area, looked at the map, and made some notes in her notebook before telling Jim to go.

Patrick leaned over and asked, "What is it?"

Whispering, Frankie said, "She said something about a hill, and I am pretty sure there's an abandoned mine over there."

Patrick nodded in understanding. There were a lot of abandoned coal mines in the county. He made a note to get a map from the historical society.

"Do you recognize anything here?" Jim asked Zoe.

Zoe let her gaze wander before saying, "This is probably where I jumped out of the truck, but I can't be sure. All the fields kind of look alike, but I didn't cross any roads to get to Catherine's, so this is probably it."

Satisfied with what they had up to that point, Jim began driving on the road to the barn. As they wound their way up the hills, Zoe began to tense and sit straighter. The closer they got to the barn, the more she fidgeted.

About a mile out, Frankie said, "We aren't going to stop, but I need for you to tell us if you recognize anything."

Jim turned onto a gravel road and drove slowly past an old, two-story house that had been abandoned since Frankie was a kid.

Zoe jumped and said, "That's where he took me first."

Frankie tried to hide her surprise at learning Zoe had been taken to the old house. Evenly, she said, "Can you tell me more about that?"

"That first night. He took me to that house. I remember thinking it was weird that he was using kerosene lamps, but he told me he liked to conserve energy. The house was pretty dirty too, but Wes said he lived alone with his dad, so I figured they didn't clean much."

"What happened next?"

"I asked to use the bathroom, and he flipped. He grabbed me from behind and that was the last thing I remember until I woke up in the dungeon. It had rock walls with cots and buckets for us to go to the bathroom. The other girls were there too."

Frankie needed to look at a topographical map of the area around the farm. It sounded to her like Hudson was smart enough not to take her to his house and moved Zoe to one of the old mines. She grabbed her phone.

"Hey dad. Do you still have that old map of the farm and the areas around it? You know the one that shows the abandoned mines?"

Frankie and her siblings had been given carte blanche to ride their four-wheelers in the woods, but not until after Frank took the map and showed them where the dangers were. Old mines and abandoned cellars could sink. Frankie waited impatiently as she watched the three dots indicating her father was replying. Luckily, she didn't have to wait long.

"Yes. What do you need them for?"

"An investigation. Are they in the barn office?"

"Yes. Make sure you put them back when you're done."

"Thanks, dad. Love you."

"Be careful. Love you, too."

Frankie smiled at the text from her dad before putting the phone back in her pocket.

Jim turned away from the farm, having agreed with Frankie earlier that they didn't need to take Zoe to the barn. He drove them to the church parking lot where Emma was waiting for them, but before Zoe got out of the SUV, Frankie asked her to wait.

Pulling a manilla folder from her bag and turning on her digital recorder, Frankie said, "I would like for you to look at some photographs and see if you recognize anyone. If you do, I need you to sign the photograph and tell me how you know the person. Do you understand?"

Zoe nodded. Frankie handed her the manilla folder and Zoe took the 8 ½ by 11 photographs and looked at each one carefully. When she got to the fourth photograph, she put it aside but did not say anything. Instead, she took her time and looked at the remaining two. After looking at each one, Zoe placed the photograph with the number four in the corner on top of the file and said, "That's him. That's the man who kidnapped me."

Her hand shaking, Zoe signed the photograph, shoved them back towards Frankie, then jumped out of the vehicle. Frankie followed, taking a few minutes to explain to her and Emma what they could expect next.

After they were gone, Jim asked, "What do you want to do now?"

"What I *want* to do and what we *should* do are two different things."

"Do you think the girls are still in the same place they were when Zoe saw them?" Patrick asked.

Simultaneously, Frankie and Jim said, "No."

"I suspect he moved them as soon as Zoe got away, but we should see if we can find it anyway," Frankie said. "When I was a kid, dad took Sophie, Jake, and I out on the four-wheelers with an old map and pointed out a couple old wells and a few other places where abandoned cellars or mines had been. We didn't go onto the Hudson's property, but the map covered the farms around us. It's in the barn office. I want to run down and get. Jake, Sophie, Julia, and I have covered every inch of that place. I would have thought we would have noticed an entrance to a mine."

"The entrances to those old mines got overgrown pretty quickly. You could have driven past it and never seen a thing," Patrick said. "It may have looked like nothing more than an overgrown hill."

Ten minutes later, Jim, Patrick, and Frankie stood around a table with a yellowed map laid out in front of them. Frankie thought about what Patrick said as she studied the map. She narrowed in on places close to the barn and panned out... away from her family's farm. Frankie was about to give up but then stopped, her finger on the map. She grabbed her cellphone and took a photograph of the area by her finger, then zoomed in to the thing that caught her eye.

"I think I know where she was being held. We need to go back to the abandoned house Zoe pointed out. It should be about a half mile from the back of that house."

CHAPTER
SEVENTY

GIVEN THE DENSE OVERGROWTH, they jumped in the side-by-side at Jake's and drove to the spot on the map. Jim threw a first-aid kit in the back with some bottled water and snacks, just in case they found the girls.

Frankie saw the smoke before they found the entrance. She knew either the girls were gone, or they could be on a recovery, not rescue mission. Frankie and Patrick held on as Jim increased their speed, slowing down only when they were within feet of the opening. Frankie and Patrick jumped off before the side-by-side came to a full stop. They ran towards the smoke and the smoldering ash billowing from what they would learn later was an entrance to an old storm shelter and cellar.

"Can you see anything?" Jim called.

Frankie and Patrick shook their heads, the feeling of defeat heavy on their shoulders. There was still a chance someone was inside, but the entrance was buried in rubble.

"Is anyone in there?" Frankie began to yell.

Patrick and Jim joined in. "Hello? Can you hear me?"

A voice, barely audible, answered, "He... help... me."

Without thinking, Frankie began grabbing the boards and throwing them aside, an urgency driving her to act. She wouldn't walk away from someone who needed help.

Patrick put his hand on Frankie's shoulder and said, "Wait." When she wouldn't stop, he said with more urgency, "Frankie! Wait. You could make it worse if you're not careful. We don't know how deep this goes. One wrong move and it could cave in, and you could fall in with the rubble."

Frankie fell back dejected, and said, "Someone is in that pit. We can't leave her there."

"We aren't going to leave her there. I simply want us to be strategic about how we get this open." Patrick said. "We *will* get her out Frankie. I promise."

Jim had the topographical map and was studying the area. He looked at the mound by Catherine's farm and then looked back at the structure in front of them.

"I don't think this is a mine. There used to be a house here at some point. I bet it's either part of the house or…"

"It could be an old storm shelter. A lot of the old houses around here didn't have basements, so they built storm shelters they could use as cellars. It's a great way to keep canned goods from spoiling," Frankie said. "I remember dad telling me stories about them when I was a kid. His family had one and when storms blew in, he was mesmerized and wanted to sit on the porch and watch, but his mom would make him go to the shelter."

"What is the entrance supposed to look like?"

"Stone stairs down to a room. Zoe said there were beds where she was kept but didn't mention much else."

"We still need to be intentional. Something has collapsed and closed off the entrance and there was a fire. There is no telling what we will find inside. I'm going to call for the fire department to come just in case."

Frankie, Patrick, and Jim began pulling boards and stones away, slowly and methodically, one at a time. Periodically Frankie would say, "We're going to get you out of there. Hang on."

Five minutes turned into ten which turned into 15. The work was painstakingly slow, and every time there was a shift under their feet, they slowed more. When the fire department got there, the chief confirmed it was a storm shelter from a house that had burned down around the time Julia had disappeared. Frankie had forgotten about that house. It was on the other side of Julia's and had been abandoned for as long as she could remember. Frankie vaguely remembered when the house burned down because it always seemed a little odd to her. Amid all the rumors being passed by the neighbors, Frankie's dad told her the most likely cause was a lightning strike, so she had filed it away as not important. Now she wondered if there was more to the story.

The extra hands from the volunteer firefighters made the work go more quickly. The fire chief had an ambulance dispatched, just in case, and it arrived just as the final board was removed. Frankie was the first to see the small girl beneath the rubble. She moved carefully, but quickly in the direction of the girl. Fearing the worst, she gently touched her neck for a pulse, careful not to move the body's position, lest she had a spinal injury.

"She has a pulse," Frankie shouted. To the unconscious girl she said, "I told you we'd get you out."

FRANKIE WAS grateful for the weekend. It had been a long week, and she was going to finally get some quality time with Danielle and Tyler. The young girl they had found was taken to the hospital and, as of the end of her shift, she had not regained consciousness. The hospital said they would call her when she did. Based on the photographs Jim and Patrick had gotten for the missing girls, they were pretty certain they had found the girl Zoe called Nikki. If they were right, her full name was Nikki Green. Frankie had called child protective services and told them they had a Jane Doe on the way to the hospital. She told them it was possible she was a runaway named Nikki Green, but until she woke up, they couldn't be certain. The worker told Frankie, based on what she said, even if it was Nikki she would likely be placed in foster care. As sad as she was, Frankie was also relieved. She didn't think she could stand the thought of Nikki being with the woman who referred to her daughter as a "lying whore."

Frankie and Tyler picked Danielle up after school, and the kids prattled on about their day, their friends, and all their favorite things. Frankie listened, trying not to let her mind drift to her cases. She did not get time like this often and wanted to enjoy and appreciate it. She noticed Danielle was a little more reserved than normal, but she assumed it was because she had not been to visit in so long. Danielle lived in a house full of people, which meant lots of noise and activity. Comparatively things were quiet here. Even though it had only been a summer, Frankie considered Danielle might be more accustomed to the hustle and bustle of a full house.

After dinner, Tyler disappeared to his room for his one hour of game time. In spite, or perhaps because of Danielle's visit, Tyler was not about to give up his coveted hour. When he was done, Frankie planned for the three of them to watch movies and eat popcorn. It was something she and her dad used to do and something she liked to do with her kids.

As soon as Tyler turned on his game, Danielle announced, "I'm going to my room."

"I thought you and I could hang out and talk for a bit. Just the two of us."

"I need to study for Bible Quiz Team. We have a competition next week."

"Okay. When Tyler's game time is up, I thought we could watch a movie. Maybe have some popcorn," Frankie tried.

"Maybe. I need to get these verses memorized."

Frankie tried not to feel rejected by Danielle. She was a teenage girl once. Of course, Danielle had things she wanted to do that did not involve her mother, even if she hadn't seen her in almost a month.

CHAPTER
SEVENTY-TWO

ONCE INSIDE THE ROOM, Danielle carefully shut and locked the door, hoping her mother did not hear the click. That would be hard to explain. She pulled out her cellphone and got online to see if Wes was on. She scrolled for a few minutes, looking at photographs her classmates had posted, then saw a message pop up.

"I was hoping you would be online tonight. I really liked your pics, but I want more."

"Promise you won't show anyone?"

"Of course."

Danielle removed her clothing and tried to hold her camera and take a photograph, but her arms were not long enough to capture a full body shot. She sat on the bed and took a photograph that showed a glimpse of her breasts and the side of her buttocks and sent it to Wes.

"Cute. I want to see more. Spread your legs and show me what you have."

Danielle did not immediately answer.

"C'mon baby. I love you and want to see all of you."

Before Danielle could take a photograph or respond, Frankie knocked on her door.

"Hey Angel-girl, Tyler and I are going to watch a movie. Why don't you take a break and come out?"

Saved by the knock, Danielle thought. "Okay, mom. Give me a second. I'm getting my pajamas on."

"Okay."

Danielle quickly typed, *"My step-monster is calling. I have to go"* and closed her phone.

CHAPTER
SEVENTY-THREE

FRANKIE DIDN'T MAKE it a practice to snoop in Danielle's phone, but after the week she had, she felt the need. She waited until Danielle was asleep, then removed it from the desk in her small room. She had been very clear with her daughter; if Danielle was going to have a phone, Frankie must have all access to include the password for the device and for any apps.

Frankie sat on the sofa and stared at the phone, feeling a wave of guilt for violating her daughter's privacy. Danielle was 14 and, like all teenagers, needed room to complain about her parents without fear of someone seeing or hearing what she said. She was about to call Jim and get his advice when an alert popped up on Danielle's phone which caused her to catch her breath.

"What did your stepmonster want?"

The message was from someone who identified themselves as "Wes." Frankie felt a pit in her stomach. Zoe said the man who messaged her used the name "Wes." She stared at the alert then grabbed her phone and took a photograph of the screen before calling Jim.

"Hey, Frankie. I'm surprised to hear from you tonight. Kids asleep?"

"Yeah. Shit, I'm sorry. I didn't realize how late it was. Am I interrupting something?"

Jim chuckled, "It's fine. I'm actually up on a wire, and nothing's happening. Are you okay?"

Frankie's voice trembled, "No, actually I'm not. I think the same man who was talking to Zoe is talking to Danielle."

"Frankie, hold on a second," Jim said. "Hey, can you handle this for a bit? I need to follow-up on another case. It's kind of urgent. Okay, great. I'll let you know when I'm headed back. Frankie, have you opened the message yet?

"No."

"Good. Wait until I get there. Do you know her password?"

"Yes. Unless she changed it. If she did, I'll get her up so we can get into the phone." Frankie hesitated before saying, "Jim…I'm scared."

"I know, Frankie. Maybe it's just a kid from school."

Frankie thought about what he said. It could be a kid from Danielle's school. Or maybe a kid from Bible Quiz. Maybe she was freaking out for nothing. While she waited for Jim, she grabbed her laptop and pulled up the yearbook for Danielle's small school. She looked through her class and the classes ahead of hers and behind, but no one by the name of "Wes" or "Wesley" showed up. She did the same for a couple of neighboring communities and found three possible matches, but it seemed unlikely they were the right ones.

Jim pulled in just as Frankie wrote down the final possible match. She had left the front door slightly ajar so he could walk in without knocking. Jim closed the door and walked over to where Frankie sat, finding a spot next to her on the sofa.

"How are you doing, kid?"

"I thought about what you said and started researching the name against kids in her and neighboring schools. I only found three possible boys, but based on their activities and club involvement, I would be surprised if it was them."

Jim looked at the phone before grabbing a device from his duty bag. He grabbed the phone from Frankie and began making an image of the content. Frankie was familiar with the process but had never seen it done away from the office.

"This may take a minute. Got another one of those?" referencing the beer in Frankie's hand.

CHAPTER
SEVENTY-FOUR

FRANKIE AND JIM talked while they waited for the phone to finish being imaged. Frankie asked about the wire and the case it was for. Jim could not tell her everything but shared what he could.

"What is going on with you and that cute waitress you went out with a few weeks ago?" Frankie asked.

"Damn girl, that's out of left field."

Not letting Jim deflect, Frankie said, "It looked like she was really into you."

"She's a nice girl. We've been out a few times, but you know my schedule and how crazy it is, so…" Jim trailed off when the machine imaging the phone made a sound. Saved by the bell, so to speak. "This is done."

Jim pulled out his laptop and looked at the content from the phone. Frankie looked over his shoulder as he maneuvered the content.

"You know the drill, Frankie. We'll be able to get anything that is saved on her phone but may still have to go in and dig through her social media accounts. If she has taken any photographs or saved any chats, they'll be on here. If we're lucky, she saved the passwords to her social accounts, and we can access them on my computer. What accounts does she have?"

"She has Facebook, I think, but I don't think she posts. Mostly she's on Instagram. I'm pretty sure she doesn't have SnapChat. Her dad and I don't agree often, but not letting Danielle have Snap is one thing we do."

Jim looked through the apps and found the ones Frankie mentioned but no others. "Frankie, do you want to look at the photographs first? Just in case?"

Frankie faltered before clicking the photo icon. She scrolled through the photographs, seeing images of Danielle, Tyler, Danielle's father, her stepmother, and her stepsiblings. She made her way to the bottom of the folder and saw 13 images in the recently deleted folder. Frankie held her breath as she clicked to see what was in the folder.

A couple of images looked like accidental shots of pavement. There were a couple photographs that were out of focus, but the final images were the ones Frankie was afraid would be there. Thankfully, there were no images in which Danielle was completely nude, but the progression of photographs indicated that was next. The date of the final photo was that day, and the background of the image was Danielle's room in Frankie's house. With that, the tears Frankie had been holding back began to flow down her cheeks.

Jim put his hand on Frankie's shoulder, giving her time to process what she had seen then said, "Frankie, we need to look at the messages. I have the password if you're up for looking now."

Frankie nodded her head. Jim pulled up Instagram and logged in using Danielle's screen name and password. The icon showed a message waiting. Frankie had seen the message Zoe received and knew what "Wes" looked like. This was her chance to see if it was the same. She clicked on the message and there were three messages from Wes. One click and Frankie's worst fear was confirmed.

SEVENTY-FIVE

FRANKIE LOOKED through the messages from Wes, grateful the photographs her daughter shared, although risqué, were not completely nude.

"It looks like she was nervous and trying to be…" Frankie stopped.

"Sexy?" Jim finished.

Frankie nodded and continued to read through the messages in silence. Danielle told the "boy" her mother was overseas in the military, and she was living with her father, stepmother, and stepsiblings. Frankie had never told her children not to say what she did for a living, but as Danielle got older, she noticed it was no longer "cool" to say her mother was in law enforcement. In this case, Frankie was glad she had left that detail out. Her heart broke as she read the messages her daughter wrote about being lonely in a house full of people, never feeling like she fully belonged. She never talked about missing her mom but did say she was angry and felt like her mother chose her career over her. Some of the words she read were typical teenage angst, but Frankie knew much of it was Danielle's reality. Sharing those feelings created a vulnerability predators looked for. The person responding fed on the words Danielle said and encouraged her disgruntled feelings and anger. The "boy" didn't suggest she speak to her parents or seek help from the guidance counselor. He just added fuel to fire up the resentment growing in her daughter.

Finished with the messages, Frankie stood up, stretched, and said, "Do you want another beer?"

"Sure. I'm going to check in with Scott and let him know I won't be back tonight."

"Crap, Jim, I'm sorry. I got so wrapped up in what was going on here, I forgot you were on a wire tonight."

"Frankie, this is more important than sitting and hoping for a target to talk."

Frankie grabbed two beers from the refrigerator and took her dog, Isabelle, outside to the deck. After making his phone call, Jim joined her at the railing overlooking her tidy yard. Frankie surveyed the yard and couldn't help but think how much she had let her children down. She owned the old bungalow and she and Sophie were slowly renovating it one room at a time, but Frankie's schedule meant she was gone a lot.

Frankie thought about what Danielle said, that she chose her career over her children. Although the words weren't true, they stung, nonetheless. She *was* devoted to her work, but if she had to choose between it and her kids, the choice was simple. Danielle and Tyler always came first. Danielle had her dad and his family to fall back on, but she was the only parent Tyler had left.

Jim broke the silence, "Frankie, I know what you're thinking, and this isn't your fault. You're a good mom. Your kids know you love them and would do anything for them."

Frankie didn't answer. She appreciated Jim's kind words, but he was wrong. This *was* her fault. The move into this house was from a loft downtown and was supposed to create a sense of stability but then Danielle chose to go live with her dad and shook things up again. It had taken all summer for Tyler, and for her, to get over being angry. If Frankie were honest with herself, she was still angry. She could not help but wonder if she had just rolled with things, not pushed Danielle to visit more, would she have talked to some stranger online? Or better yet, if she had put her foot down and refused to let Danielle move in with her dad, would she have been better protected? Frankie recognized it was because of *her*, and her choices, Danielle had experienced things most her peers had not. She was old enough to remember the knock on the door when Tyler was a baby. Old enough to remember Sergeant Blake's face when he told them Tyler's father had died while serving a warrant. It was something she never truly got over. All this was *her* fault and now she needed to find a way to fix it.

SEVENTY-SIX

"FRANKIE. Frankie? What do you want to do?"

Frankie shook her head and said, "I'm sorry. I don't know. What are the options again?"

Jim had spent a lot of time with Frankie's kids and knew this was hard for her. He wanted to be patient and give her space, but there was a window of opportunity he didn't want them to miss.

"What are my options again?" Frankie asked.

"We can always do nothing. You can wait until the morning and talk to Danielle. See what she says. I can get one of our people to set up a sting and try to lure him out without using Danielle's account. Or we can start chatting with him from my computer, where all the messages can be saved, and see what he says."

Normally Frankie didn't struggle with decisions when it came to cases, but this was different. This was her 14-year-old daughter.

"What would you do?"

"He's online now. It's late, and he'll probably take the bait."

Frankie considered the options, then said, "Do it."

Jim opened his computer and pulled up the page and set it to show Danielle was online. They didn't have to wait long for "Wes" to send a message.

"Not used to you being online so late. Need help getting to sleep?"

"Not tired."

"Want company?"

Jim and Wes exchanged messages for a few minutes. Frankie was getting impatient and paced the living room floor, but Jim paced the messages to seem aloof but still keep Wes interested.

"Send me a photo."

Jim did not immediately respond.

"C'mon Danielle. I want to see you."

"I can't."

"Give me a glimpse…"

"What do you want to see?"

Jim did not get an immediate response. He was beginning to think he wasn't going to get one. When he was about to close the computer, the text appeared.

"Your naked body."

CHAPTER
SEVENTY-SEVEN

A WAVE of nausea swept over Frankie. A grown man was asking her 14-year-old daughter for naked photographs. This was new territory for Frankie. She normally dealt with adult victims, not juveniles. And this was not just any victim. This was *her* daughter. Her thoughts were racing. Should she call Danielle's father? Should she call the Crimes Against Children unit? Should she call Baker? Or could she keep it between her and Jim and just handle it herself.

Jim knew what Frankie was thinking because he was thinking it too. They could go rogue and find this guy and ensure he never hurt another girl. Or they could do it by the book and find any other girls that might be missing. That was what he needed to stress to Frankie. They needed to do this right. There were *other* girls and going rogue put the lives of other children at risk.

Before Jim could say anything, Frankie asked, "Do you think we have enough to get a search warrant?"

Relieved, Jim answered, "I'm not sure. I'll reach out to one of the cyber detectives at the RCFL and see what they say. They may want to keep him chatting and set up a meet. In the meantime, we need to disable the app on Danielle's phone. Does she have access to a computer?"

"I think she has one for school, but they should have it locked down pretty tight."

"You need to talk to her, Frankie."

"I don't know what to say."

Jim put his hand on Frankie's and said, "The words will come. Start by telling her you love her and take it from there. We have to change the password to her account just in case."

"Thank you, Jim." Frankie offered a weak smile. "I…"

"I know," Jim replied.

He always seemed to know just what to say to try to make her feel better. Jim had become a solid rock for her and tonight was no different. The two sat and continued to talk into the early morning hours. They discussed next steps with Danielle, the missing girls, and other cases they were both working. Eventually the conversation returned to the waitress, Holly.

"What's holding you back?" Frankie asked.

Jim didn't immediately answer. He wasn't sure he had the answer to her question. Holly was intelligent, beautiful, had a good sense of humor, and was sexy as hell. The only answer that came to mind was she wasn't Frankie.

Jim stared into Frankie's intense, blue eyes and eventually said, "Holly is great, but…" Jim didn't finish his sentence. He leaned in slightly and just before he could kiss her, his phone buzzed, breaking the moment.

SEVENTY-EIGHT

DAWN CAME SOONER than Frankie wanted. Tyler tried to stay quiet, but eventually ended up sitting on the end of her bed bouncing up and down while he watched cartoons.

Before Frankie could tell Tyler to stop bouncing, Danielle stormed into the room, and yelled, "What the hell, mom? Where's my phone?"

Frankie sat up and calmly said, "Danielle, language. Tyler…"

Her voice escalating, "Where's my phone?"

"Tyler, please take Isabelle out and get her some food."

"Okay mom." To the dog he said, "Come on, Iz. Let's get breakfast."

Danielle stood in the doorway with her arms crossed and jaw squared. Frankie pulled her knees into her chest trying to find words to assuage Danielle's anger and yet stay firm and resolute.

Through gritted teeth, Danielle asked again, "Where's. My. Phone?"

"Close the door, Danielle Elizabeth and watch your tone of voice with me. I'm still your mother, and you will not speak to me that way."

Huffing again, Danielle slammed the door and looked at Frankie in expectation.

"You *may* get your phone back after we speak about what was on it, and there *will* be rules and restrictions to go with its use."

Danielle's face paled at the realization her mother had viewed the content of her phone. She leaned against the wall and looked down at the floor, preparing for Frankie to yell at her.

Frankie kept her voice soft, patted the bed, and said, "Have a seat."

Reluctantly, Danielle sat on the edge of the bed, trying to make herself small. She stared at her socked feet and folded and unfolded her hands in her lap.

"When did you start talking to Wes?"

Danielle sat quietly, and after a gentle nudge from Frankie, she said, "About a month ago."

Frankie had read the messages but still asked, "How did the conversation start?"

Danielle considered lying, telling her mother she met him at the pool or something like that, but then thought better of it. Her mother had a way of knowing when she was lying, and it was always worse when she got caught.

CHAPTER
SEVENTY-NINE

"HE CONTACTED ME ON INSTA. He said he went to school in Excelsior and saw me after Bible Quiz when we went for tacos. I thought his picture looked familiar, so I believed him."

"What happened next?"

Frankie held her body still and her voice soft to offset Danielle's fidgeting, in hopes it would help calm her.

"He asked me a lot of questions and seemed really interested in what I had to say. He told me how pretty I was and said he would like to get to know me better. Then he…"

Danielle started crying, her sobs wracking her small frame. Frankie scooted next to her daughter, wrapped her arms around her and held her while she cried. She remembered what it felt like to be a teenager and to want to be liked by a boy. When Danielle stopped crying, she let her go, but stayed close.

"Danielle, I need you to tell me what he asked you to do."

"He, uh, he, uh, wanted pictures."

"How many did you send him?" Frankie asked, not giving her a chance to say she had not sent any.

"Five or six."

Frankie had only seen three. "What were the pictures of?"

Danielle hesitated before saying, "Mostly of my face, but a couple were with my sports bra and shorts."

"And the others?"

Danielle did not respond.

"Danielle, did you send him any photographs of you naked?"

Danielle shook her head then said, "Just the side. I covered everything up." She paused and then added, "I deleted those pictures."

"Okay. Did he tell you anything about himself?"

Danielle thought for a moment. "Not really. Just that he went to school and lived with his dad. Seemed to like the same things I do."

"What did you tell him about yourself?"

"That I lived with my dad, stepmom, and her kids. I told him you were in the Army and overseas."

"Why did you tell him that?"

Danielle didn't immediately answer, afraid it would hurt Frankie's feelings. Finally, she said, "Sometimes when I tell people you're a cop they change the way they are around me. I didn't want him to change so I didn't tell him what you do."

Frankie gave her a slight smile. "Did you tell him where you lived?"

"He already knew what school I went to. But I didn't tell him my address or anything."

"Okay. Good."

"Mom, why are you so worried?"

Frankie considered not telling Danielle the truth but then thought better of it. After a moment she said, "Because this boy you've been talking to is really an adult."

CHAPTER
EIGHTY

FRANKIE AND DANIELLE talked more openly and honestly that morning than they had in months. Eventually Tyler found his way back into the room and plopped himself on the end of the bed where he watched cartoons, oblivious to the world around him. Frankie looked around the room at her children, pets, the laundry that needed washing, and thought, *"This is what life is about."*

The rest of the weekend went by in a blur, and when it was time for Danielle to go home, Frankie felt a pit in her stomach. She had talked to Jim, and he was getting a search warrant to confirm where "Wes" was located. Or at least where he was sending messages from.

"Why do you have to tell dad?" Danielle whined.

"Because I want to make sure you're safe."

"Why can't I just block the jerk and move on? Why do you always have to be a cop?

"Danielle, my first job is as your mother. And since I can't be with you 24/7, I need to make sure there are others who will look out for you."

"You realize you're ruining my life, right? Dad will never let me do anything ever again."

Frankie knew to Danielle, the fear of being grounded or losing her phone equated to "ruining her life," but she stood her ground.

The conversation with Danielle's father was difficult, and when it was over, Frankie was less than confident her daughter would not incur punishment, despite all her requests. Before Danielle got her phone back, an app had been installed that would alert Frankie when certain words popped up in text or if Danielle attempted to download any new apps. Danielle would be locked out of Instagram until Jim was finished trying to lure Wes out, but Frankie wasn't sure Danielle would ever get it back.

Sophie stayed with Tyler while Frankie took Danielle home, so on the drive back, she was left to silence. Her mind raced and her thoughts finally drifted back to the girl they found in the rubble of the storm cellar entry. In her gut, Frankie knew who it was, but the girl had lost consciousness before they removed her from the scene and, as of this morning, had not woken up. She made a decision.

"Hey, Soph, what're you guys doing?"

"Hey, sis. Tyler is whooping my butt in this videogame of his. Are you on your way back?"

"That's why I'm calling. I am, but I need to take a quick detour first. It shouldn't take long. I can bring dinner home if you want."

"No problem. I don't have anywhere to be. The boy toy is working."

In the background Frankie could hear Tyler ask, "What's a boy toy?"

Frankie tried not to laugh as she quickly said, "Do not answer that! I'll be home in about an hour."

Frankie parked her Jeep and slowly walked into the hospital. She stopped at the front desk, showed her credentials and asked for the room number for their "Jane Doe." She was not surprised to find they had placed her in the pediatric wing.

The door to the room was closed and, as she started to walk in, the charge nurse quickly asked who she was and why she was going into the girl's room. Frankie quickly identified herself, showed her credentials and asked if the girl had regained consciousness or if they had been able to confirm her name.

"She's stable but still hasn't woken up. Or if she has, she has pretended to sleep when we've checked on her. We have her on a low dose of pain meds for her broken bones but are gradually reducing them. She's pretty banged up."

"Has a forensic nurse examined her?" Frankie asked.

"Our peds forensic nurse took photographs but hasn't done a full examination. You think that's going to be necessary?"

"Unfortunately, yes."

Frankie walked into the small room, the only light coming from the wall above the bed. Someone had left a television on the Disney channel, the sound barely audible, likely in hopes the child would be less afraid if there was noise when she woke up. Frankie moved to the side of the bed and gently took the child's hand in hers. The girl looked so tiny and young as she lay ashen against the sheets.

Softly she said, "Hey there. You may not remember me, but I'm one of the ones who found you. I know it's probably nicer and less scary where you are right now, but I would really like you to wake up. If you're not ready to open your eyes, at least give my hand a squeeze."

Frankie felt a slight squeeze from the girl's hand.

"That's it. That's it."

Frankie saw the child's eyes flutter but not open. Then a small voice whispered, "I… remember… you."

Frankie knew she should alert the nurse, but before she did, she asked, "What's your name, sweety."

Barely audible, the girl replied, "Ni...kki."

CHAPTER
EIGHTY-ONE

FRANKIE SAT with Nikki long enough to confirm she was the daughter of the woman Jim and Patrick interviewed. She was 15 years old and had been missing for about six months. Because of her mother's choices, she had been forced to grow up quicker than most. Over time she had developed a strong defense mechanism and independence.

As she walked to her Jeep, Frankie thought about Nikki, the one Patrick and Jim thought was not connected to the other missing girls. The girl everyone assumed was just an insolent teen who had run away. Frankie empathized with this girl and had held her hand and assured her she would do everything she could to keep her safe.

Before Frankie had left the floor, she told the nurses Nikki was awake but not to call her mother. She wasn't safe at home. Frankie assured the charge nurse she would call and update the Division of Family Services and have a worker meet her at the hospital first thing in the morning.

Frankie kept her word and was home with dinner just over an hour after she called Sophie. For the next few hours Frankie enjoyed the simpleness of life. Tyler regaled her with stories about beating Sophie at his videogames and his plans for recess and soccer practice the following week. Sophie was a master carpenter and supervised a team who renovated old homes. She talked about her latest work project, piquing Tyler's attention when she said they found relics the previous week. The house they were renovating was more than 100 years old and located in the northeast part of Kansas City. It had all the drama in real life, as one of the HGTV shows Frankie and Sophie loved to watch. Sophie promised to take both on a tour one day that week.

"Tyler, it's time for you to you take a shower."

Tyler grumbled as he scooted his chair back. He loved sitting at the table with the adults and knew bedtime soon followed his shower.

"And don't stay in there all night or use all the hot water. I need a shower, too."

Frankie and Sophie got up with Tyler and took their beers to the deck. Once they had the citronella candles going and were settled in their chairs, Sophie asked, "How bad was it?"

Even though there was over a decade age difference between the two, Frankie and Sophie were close. Frankie loved being a big sister. As a child Sophie was like having a living doll to play with, but now that they were both adults, she was Frankie's best friend.

"Which part?" Frankie asked. "Danielle's dad or the girl in the hospital?"

"Both."

Frankie explained the conversation she had with her ex-husband and his wife. Sophie knew it wasn't easy for Frankie to speak to either of them. She felt betrayed by Danielle's father and attributed his betrayal to his wife. He had once promised Frankie he would never try to take Danielle, saying "a girl belongs with her mother," but this past summer they manipulated Danielle into wanting to live with them. And to make matters worse, they influenced her to routinely miss visits.

"I think Danielle is going to be on an even tighter leash. What's worse is, they didn't want to hear how sad and lonely she is. Instead, they blame her for always staying in her room. I'm at a loss, Soph. She knows she can come home anytime, but I think she's afraid to do it. Or maybe she just doesn't want to. Did I tell you what her stepsister told her?"

Sophie shook her head.

Frankie took another long drink from her beer bottle before saying, "She told her she might as well call her mom 'mom' because I was going to get shot and killed anyway, like..."

Sophie sat up straight and said, "What the..."

"Yeah. Real nice, huh? As if Danielle isn't scared enough after..." Frankie left the words fall into the silence. After a breath she continued, "Then...the girl today. Sophie, I can't let her go back to her mother. It'll kill her. Or at the very least, damage her soul. The other victim we talked to said Nikki was the toughest of the group. But in that hospital bed she was so...so...young and fragile. Her eyes... she's the same age as Danielle, but her eyes have lost their brightness. They were dull, and she seemed so sad and lost."

CHAPTER
EIGHTY-TWO

SOPHIE DID what sisters do and let Frankie be vulnerable. Frankie did not let her guard down often or show many people that side. Sophie knew Frankie did not need her to "fix" things, she just needed to talk so she could refocus, raise her kids, and continue to solve cases. She couldn't do that if she didn't let it out once in a while.

To lighten the mood, Sophie asked, "What's up with you and Jim?"

Frankie smiled slightly before saying, "Did I tell you he almost kissed me the other night?"

"What?" Sophie exclaimed. "You are holding out on me sis."

"It was nothing, really. I asked him about the waitress he had gone on a few dates with and next thing I knew he was leaning in."

"What stopped him?"

"Danielle. Well, her phone. Then the moment was gone. Don't you think it's weird?" Frankie asked. "I mean it's Jim. With all our history and Tyler's dad…"

Sophie carefully considered what Frankie said and then softly said, "Brad's been gone more than five years. He loved you and he would have loved Jim. You know Brad would want you to be happy."

"But…"

"I know. Jim is one hell of a good guy and he's really been there for you."

"I know Sophie, but what if he leaves like...."

Sophie nudged Frankie with her shoulder and asked, "That boy's not going anywhere. Have you seen the way he looks at you? Because I have."

The color rose in Frankie's face as she playfully shoved Sophie back.

The sisters stayed up late into the night talking, knowing full well they would both regret it the following morning. Frankie loved those nights, reminiscent of when they were younger. Between the sisters, there were no topics that were off limits. And no matter where the evening started, they always ended up with cold beer, Doritos, and chewy chocolate chip cookies.

"For the life of me I cannot figure out why these are so good together," Sophie said.

To herself Frankie thought, *It's the memories attached to them that make them so good.* Aloud she said, "What's not to love? Ice cold beer with just the right amount of frost. Chocolate, I mean it fixes all things. And Doritos for the salt and cheesy add-on."

"The order matters," Sophie announced. "The Doritos must come first, followed by the cookies, then wash it down with the cold beverage."

"The order *does* matter," Frankie started, "but it should be Doritos, followed by a long swig from the bottle, then finished up with chewy goodness."

The ridiculousness of the banter was just what the mood needed. Frankie and Sophie let the conversation evolve into stories that kept them holding their sides from laughing so hard. When they had sufficiently covered everything, and were having trouble keeping their eyes open, Frankie stood up and started to walk down the hall then stopped, looked back and said, "Love you, Soph."

"Love you too, little big sis."

CHAPTER
EIGHTY-THREE

MORNING CAME TOO EARLY for Frankie. She had a slight hangover and was a bit cloudy–headed. She left Sophie asleep on the sofa with a bottle of ibuprofen and a glass of water on the side table. Hustling Tyler out the door quietly, she managed to drop him off and make it to the parking lot on time.

"Hey, Frankie, how was your weekend?" Mia asked.

"Insane. Want to run to the hospital with me?"

"You get a call this morning?" Mia knew Frankie was not on call, but some of the forensic nurses called her directly, especially if the case facts matched a pattern they knew she had been working, or if it was close to shift change and knew she was coming in.

"No. Remember that girl we found in the rubble of the storm cellar entrance?"

"Yeah."

"She's awake. It's the girl Patrick and Jim didn't think was connected. Nikki."

"Did the hospital call you?"

Frankie explained she had stopped by after dropping Danielle off at her father's house. She didn't tell her what she had found on Danielle's computer, but she would when they had more time alone.

"If there's no one in custody, I say let's go to Quick Trip to grab a diet

Coke and run by and see if we can get her statement before they have to notify that bitch of a mother," Frankie suggested.

Mia agreed, dropping her things on her desk. Before Frankie could go in and talk to Baker, she asked, "Do you ever have a *normal* weekend?"

"Mia, you have no idea."

Thirty minutes later, the pair were standing outside of Quick Trip, sipping their diet sodas. Frankie told Mia about Danielle's computer and how Jim thought he could lure Wes out far enough they could snatch him.

"You really think this guy will bite?"

"You should have seen his messages, Mia. He really wants to meet up with my daughter. I'm just hoping he hasn't figured out where she lives. If he tried to grab her…"

"It won't happen, Frankie. Was her father receptive at locking down her phone?"

"He claims he never wanted her to have all the apps on her phone to begin with. He's so…spineless. I think his wife wears the pants in that house. She said she would monitor her, but based on the things Danielle was saying to this guy, it sounds like she pretty much ignores my girl."

"Are you sure Danielle isn't just saying that to get more attention?"

Frankie thought about what Mia said and then responded, "I don't know. Maybe."

"Are you sure she doesn't hole herself up in her room on her own accord? You said when she was still living with you, she had taken to shutting herself off from you and Tyler. I mean, we didn't exactly hang out with our parents when we were her age."

Frankie considered what Mia said, "Yeah, she could be. I can only go off what she said in her messages. Her dad paints a perfect *Leave it to Beaver* picture, and I know that's not true. Of course, she told this dude *I* was in the military and overseas, so who the hell knows what's true and what's exaggerated."

Mia laughed loudly and, with a mock salute, said, "Let's go, ma'am."

Frankie laughed with her, thankful for the moment of levity imposed.

CHAPTER
EIGHTY-FOUR

NIKKI WAS ALONE in the room when they arrived, sitting up in the bed, watching the Disney channel. Frankie smiled at the movie Nikki chose to watch. It was one she had watched many times with her own children. In the light of day, Nikki didn't appear quite as young or vulnerable, but Frankie suspected most of that was because of the front she felt she needed to keep up.

"Hi, Nikki, do you remember me?" Frankie asked.

Not looking away from the television, she said, "You were here last night. And you were out *there* the other day."

"That's right. I'm Detective Thomas, and this is Detective Boden, but you can call me Frankie and her Mia. We want to talk to you about how you ended up in the storm cellar."

"What if I don't want to talk about it?" Nikki asked.

"Then we'll call social services and leave, but we'll come back and try again tomorrow and the day after that."

Mia looked sideways at Frankie who simply nodded. Frankie would not pester a child, but she also knew there were other missing girls, and information Nikki had was key to finding them.

"Fine," Nikki said, still not looking away from the television.

Frankie walked closer to the bed and Mia walked to the other side.

Frankie asked, "Do you mind if we turn the television off so I can record our conversation?"

With a huff, Nikki turned the television off, but still wouldn't look at Frankie or Mia.

"Do you mind if we sit?"

Nikki shrugged. Frankie and Mia looked at one another and then sat in the chairs on either side of the bed. To herself Frankie thought, *"I doubt she's used to having a choice."*

"What's your full name?"

"Are you going to call my mother?"

"Not yet, but eventually someone will contact her," Frankie said. There was no point in lying to her, it wouldn't do anything but destroy any trust she built. "We called the Division of Family Services, and they'll call her."

"I won't go back there."

"Is that why you ran away?"

With that, Nikki laughed wryly, "You think I ran away? She put me out because I told my teacher what her husband was doing to me. If she said I ran away, she's a liar."

Frankie made notes, then asked, "Where did you go when she put you out?"

"I roamed the streets for a couple of days. I tried to go to a friend's house, but she lives kind of far away, and I didn't have any money. I finally ended up at the bus station. There were a lot of people, and I thought I might be able to sleep. Instead, I sat on the bench all night looking at all the places I could go. I considered what it would be like to be somewhere else. I didn't even have enough money for a bag of chips but thought I would be able to get on a bus. How stupid is that?"

Frankie and Mia sat quietly while Nikki spoke.

"It was almost sunrise when this dude came up to me and started talking. He wasn't like the others hanging around. He was clean and seemed like he was my grandpa's age. He offered me a Coke and some chips. I probably should have said no, but I was *so* hungry. I watched him get them out of the machine, and then he just sat down next to me. He asked me where I was going and if I had family around. I told him I didn't have any family or money, but I wanted to go somewhere warm, like California.

"We talked for a while and then he told me I could work for him for a few weeks, and he would buy me a ticket to San Diego as a payment. He said he had a friend out there that I could stay with. He told me he would work it all out. Next thing I knew, I was getting into his truck, and we were driving away from the city."

"Did he tell you *his* name?" Frankie asked.

"Warren."

Frankie asked, "Are you sure?"

"Yeah. He said his name was Warren."

FRANKIE AND MIA looked at one another. He didn't tell Zoe his name, or if he did, she didn't remember it.

"What happened next?" Frankie asked.

"We drove to the middle of nowhere. I had never been in the country before, and this was *coun-try*," Nikki said, exaggerating the last word. "He took me to this big old house and said I could choose the bedroom I wanted. There was a really cool room with purple walls and lots of books. I like to read, so that was the room I picked."

Frankie knew that room. She had spent countless hours there. Julia's mother surprised her on her 14th birthday by painting the room a light purple with bookshelves along one entire wall. Over the next year and a half, Julia filled the shelves with books, vinyl albums, trinkets, and photographs of herself and Craig.

"Did he ever tell you whose room that was?"

Nikki looked at Frankie curiously and then said, "He told me it was his daughter's room, but she didn't live there anymore. He said I could look in her closet for clothes if I wanted, but there wasn't much, and they were super old. Like from when my mom was a kid."

"Did he tell you anything about his daughter?"

"Not then, but later…later, when he was angry, he threatened all of us. He said his daughter had disrespected him, and she and her mother tried to run away, but he taught them a lesson. He said if we disrespected him or tried to run away, he would teach us a lesson, too."

Frankie contemplated what Nikki said and how it mimicked what Zoe had told them. She knew she should move on, but she had one more question. "Did he give you any details about the lesson he taught his daughter and her mother? Like what or where?"

"All he really said was he knew places a person could disappear and never be found. That he had done it before."

Frankie felt her stomach in her throat. Mia saw the look on her face and steered the conversation back to Nikki. "Tell us more about what happened after he showed you the room?"

"Warren asked me if I wanted to shower and showed me where the bathroom was. He gave me some old clothes to wear and, when I got out, he gave me some food and told me to rest. He said I could start working the next day. I never really asked him what he was going to have me do. I guess I should have done that." Nikki started coughing and took a drink of water before continuing. "I laid down in the bed and before I knew it, he was waking me up the next day. It was barely light outside, and he said he wanted to show me what he had in mind for me to do to make money.

"The first day he drove me around the land near his house. He took me to an old, abandoned house that he said was his. He told me I was going to clean it up and help him do some repairs so he could sell or rent it out. The house was creepy, but I figured it was worth it to be able to get some money. Then he drove me by an old barn with a porch on the front and told me that was the edge of the property and forbid me from going into the barn. What an idiot, all that did was make me want to go there more. Anyway, then he took me to the worst place of all."

Nikki erupted into a fit of coughs. Frankie handed Nikki a cup of water which she emptied before continuing.

"Warren said it was an old storm shelter, but we called it a dungeon. There were trees around the entrance, but the weeds and grass were cut down so the door could open. He led me into the dark and told me to follow him because he wanted to show me where the light string was. He took a few steps inside and shut the door. He walked me further into the cavern to a big room. The room was barely lit, but I could see a tiny bed against the wall and shelves with water and food. That was when I realized I was in trouble. I tried to back away and go back towards the doorway, but he grabbed my arm and made it so I couldn't move. It was the first time Warren actually scared me. Before I could say anything, he had me on the small bed. He…" Nikki's voice started to break up. "He… did… things… to me. When he finished, he told me it was a 'good audition, but next time, don't cry. My clients don't like it when the girls cry.' I immediately threw up.

"I don't know why I thought he was going to take me back to the house with the pretty room, but I did. While I was throwing up, he took off and locked me inside. Alone."

CHAPTER
EIGHTY-SIX

NIKKI ASKED FOR A BREAK, so Mia went to get the nurse to help her get out of the bed without pulling out her IV. Frankie and Mia stepped into the hall while Nikki took a moment.

"We need to get an advocate here," Mia said.

"I agree. To be honest, I'm not even sure we should even be doing this interview. She is so young. Do you think we need to get her an appointment with the Child Advocacy Center?" Frankie asked.

Mia gave the question some thought before responding, "She really seems to like and trust *you*, Frankie. I'm afraid if we pull someone else in, she may shut down."

"What if…"

"Frankie, stop with the what ifs. What does your gut tell you."

"To listen to you and keep going."

Mia smiled, "I *am* very wise."

Frankie elbowed her partner and said, "Yes, yes you are."

The nurse had a sour look on her face when she exited the room. She started to walk past without talking to either Frankie or Mia, but they caught the look.

"Is everything okay," Frankie asked.

Turning back the nurse said, "Huh? Oh, yeah. I think we need to get a forensic nurse in here as soon as possible. She has some pretty significant marks below her waist, and I don't think they're related to her being in the rubble."

"Did she say anything to you while she was taking care of business?"

"No, not really. Do you want me to call the nurse on call?"

"If you could. Would you mind asking them to call MOCSA for an advocate too?"

The nurse nodded and walked back to the nurses' station. Frankie and Mia took a deep breath and walked inside the hospital room. Nikki was sitting up a little straighter.

"Can I tell you what happened after he locked me in the storm shelter?"

"Of course. Let me start the recorder again," Frankie said.

"I think it was a couple hours after he left when he came back. He brought my backpack, a couple of books, a radio, and a blanket. I didn't say anything, and I think that pissed him off. What did he want me to do? Thank him for bringing me books and leaving me locked in a dark hole? He tried to talk to me, to make things seem okay, but I wasn't having it. I just glared at him. He told me he would be back the next day and to be ready. He said he had a special day planned, and it would get me closer to having enough money to get away.

"His idea of a special day, Detective... Frankie, was to take me to meet this other guy who took me for a 'test drive,' as he put it. I don't know what his name was, but he became a regular face. I must have passed, because he didn't kill me. The guy didn't talk to me much, but I listened as he talked to Warren. I think he was Warren's boss because a few times I could hear him yelling at Warren just outside the shelter door, especially after the other girls got there."

Frankie thought about what Nikki said. Warren had a *boss*? She wondered if he always did.

"Every night when I got back from whatever hell experience Warren had planned for me, I looked for ways to get out of the hole. I thought with as old as it was there had to be a way to escape but.... anyway, I think a week passed before Warren brought more girls in. At one time, there were seven of us down there."

Frankie felt her stomach lurch. Seven? Zoe only talked about three besides herself. What happened to the other three?

"Did you say there were seven of you?" Frankie asked.

"Yeah. There was me, Sasha, Kaitlin, Wendi, Meg, Nica, and Zoe."

Frankie quickly wrote all the names on her notepad and then asked, "What happened to the other girls?"

Nikki didn't immediately answer. Her face paled and, for the first time since they started talking, tears filled her eyes. She looked away from Frankie, stared out the window and tried to collect herself.

"Nica was the baby. I think she was only ten or eleven. I'm not sure how he got her. All she did was cry. I heard they were using her for movies, but then the place where they were filming got raided, and Nica never came back."

Frankie and Mia shared a knowing glance. They knew about the raid. A few months earlier, they served a warrant and discovered a sex trafficking ring that was also producing child pornography. Several young girls and boys were rescued. She would ask Jim to double check the names of the children found and see if Nica was one of them. If so, it would help narrow down how long Nikki had been in the storm shelter.

"I tried to ask Warren one time where Nica was, and all he would say is not to worry about it. Meggie left to go on a job and never came back. They didn't tell us what happened to her, either. The night before the fire, Zoe got away. I don't know how, but she did. After that, Warren freaked out. He took Sasha, Wendi, and Kaitlin out the next day and left me there asleep. When I woke up, there were flames all around me. I tried to claw my way out, but the entrance crumbled…and then you found me."

FRANKIE AND MIA took notes as Nikki provided descriptions of all the girls. Frankie recognized the names of all the girls Nikki mentioned. All, that is, except Nica. She was not one of the girls on Patrick and Jim's list. When they got back to Police Headquarters, she would look at the list Jim emailed of kids from the warehouse. Maybe Nica had already been rescued. Maybe she was back with her family.

"Tell me more about Meg," Frankie said.

"She was the first girl who got there after me. She was a year younger than me but a lot smaller. Wendi was a foster kid, and her foster parents were mean to her, so she ran away to meet some guy she met on Insta. I don't remember the town she came from, but she ended up here. She was pretty developed for her age and was one of the favorites. Warren and that other man took her out a lot."

"Tell me about Sasha," Frankie said.

"She was probably the quietest of all the girls that came through, but she was so pretty. And smart. When she talked, she had this cute accent. I liked to listen when she told Nica stories. She got there the same way as the rest of the girls. Some guy was talking to her on Insta, and she ran off to meet him. Sometimes she cried and said she missed her dad and his boyfriend Patrick. Warren liked her, but I heard the other man yelling a few times when they brought her back because she had started crying on the job."

"How about Kaitlin?" Frankie asked.

"Kaitlin had just gotten there. She wouldn't talk to any of us. Warren took her out a few times and when she came back, she usually had scratches and bruises. Sometimes I would hear her crying at night."

Nikki gave Frankie and Mia as much information as she could about Warren, the girls, where they'd been kept, and where they'd been taken. Nikki described two different cellars and the occasional girl that was only with them for a night before Warren took her away. She had just answered their last question when the orderly knocked to see if she could bring in her lunch.

Frankie looked at her watch and said, "I didn't realize how long we'd been here."

Nikki asked, "What happens to me now?"

Frankie looked at Nikki, whose tough façade was replaced with a look of fear and vulnerability. "A forensic nurse will give you a thorough examination. She will explain everything and get your permission before she does anything. Later today, a social worker will come talk to you. Tell the truth about your homelife, Nikki... about everything." Frankie hesitated, then pulled a card from her pocket, writing her cellphone number on the back. "Here's my number. If you need anything, you can call me."

It made Frankie's stomach roll knowing this girl may end up in a situation just as bad as the storm cellar, only this time the abuse would be at the hands of someone who was supposed to care about her. The laws were made to protect the parents, not the child. It was the exact reason Frankie didn't work in the Crimes Against Children unit. She didn't think she could handle the heartache.

Frankie and Mia stood by the car, breathing in the fresh air and letting the sun warm their faces. They were back where they started, Quick Trip, getting a fresh drink and a much-needed break.

"What now, Frankie? Are you going to turn this over to the CAC? Or the FBI?"

Frankie thought for a second and then said, "Only if Sarge forces me to. The first thing I'm going to do is call Patrick and tell him his daughter was alive within the last few days. Then we are going to hatch a plan to catch this son of a bitch."

THE CONFERENCE ROOM off the squad room was full of people. Along with Frankie's full squad were Jim, his Sergeant, two analysts with their computers, brass from the police department, and Patrick. Frankie didn't have to try as hard to convince Baker as she had feared. Passing this case off held the risk of something being missed or forgotten, and that could lead to the loss of two more kids. Baker didn't need to hear anything more than that. The compromise was to bring the FBI in, in a limited capacity. Baker also insisted they contact the local sheriff's department and read them in, just in case things went south.

"An undercover detective has been talking to Warren," Jim began. "The UC is using the handle of someone Warren made contact with a fairly recently." Jim was careful not to out Danielle.

"Are you planning to set up a meet?" Baker asked.

"No. We considered that, but there are at least two young girls missing, and we don't believe he's holding them at his house..." Baker started to interrupt, but Jim continued. "He lives in a rural area, and we have access to a place where we can watch the house unobserved. We're going to sit up on his house and see where he goes."

"What if he has her on his property. Do you have a way to follow him there?" Coleman asked.

Jim and Frankie exchanged a look, then Frankie said, "We have every reason to believe Warren is a neighbor to property owned by my family; the farm where my little brother lives. We have access to a side-by-side and three four-wheelers, and I know those woods like the back of my hand. If he has the girls on his property, we'll be able to find them."

Coleman nodded, noticeably surprised at this revelation.

"Jim and I will park at the farm and take the ATVs up to a barn that's adjacent to the Hudson farm where we can watch from inside. Jake is going to bring the side-by-side to Mrs. Longneck's house, which is close to the highway. Patrick and Mia will wait there and, depending on where or how he goes, they will either grab the side-by-side to help us or follow in an undercover car. Coleman, you and Wheeler will post up in an undercover car at a church down the road just in case he spots a tail, and we need to hand off."

"How far is this church and will we be obvious?" Wheeler asked.

"Great question," Frankie began. "There are actually two churches. You'll be at the small one, which is about a mile away from the road that leads to the farm. The church is on a curve, so hopefully he'll be paying attention to the road and not the parking lot."

After a few more tactical questions, the group grabbed their bags and vests and made their way to their cars. The local sheriff's department said they would send a couple of deputies to meet them before they headed into the property and their assigned positions.

"What are you thinking, Frankie?" Mia asked, noticing a look of concern on her partner's face.

Frankie didn't immediately answer. She had a strange feeling in the pit of her stomach but couldn't articulate why. Something felt *off*. When she finally spoke, all she said was, "Just hoping this feeling in my gut is nerves and not a warning."

CHAPTER
EIGHTY-NINE

THE GROUP'S first rally point was at an elementary school several miles away from the Hudson and Moretti farms. Three deputies from the local county sheriff's office were the last to arrive. Frankie immediately recognized one of them as someone she and Patrick had gone to school with. Greg Cantor had been a year behind her and two behind Patrick. Frankie didn't know him well but remembered he had been kind of a jerk to the girls.

"Greg, I didn't know you were a deputy," Frankie said, shaking hands with her former classmate. "Do you remember Patrick?"

"Sure. How've you been, man?" Greg asked, extending his hand to shake Patrick's. Looking back at Frankie, he continued, "I've been with the County for… I guess going on ten years now." He gestured in the direction of the two other deputies with him and said, "This is Nix and Millsap."

Frankie and Patrick shook the hand of each of the deputies Greg introduced and thought to herself they had to be fresh out of the academy. Neither looked more than 22 or 23 years old. Frankie finished introducing her squad and Jim.

"What's your plan, Frankie? And what do you need *us* to do?" Greg asked, just a hint of disdain in his voice.

"We are heading down to Moonglow Road to do a stakeout." Frankie wasn't sure why but she decided not to give the deputies their exact location and decided to minimize their reasons for what they were doing. "We've been looking for a girl and got word she might be somewhere down there. We need you guys to stay in the area and be ready to jump in if something goes sideways."

"Are you planning to serve a warrant?" Greg inquired.

"No," Frankie said and couldn't help but wonder if Greg had been listening. Repeating herself, she explained, "We're going to scout the area and follow the target. We're hoping he leads us to a missing girl."

"What makes you think he has girls out there against their will?"

Jim noticed Greg made 'girl' plural and added 'against their will.' Before Frankie could say anything, he said, "We aren't sure the *girl* we're looking for is in the area. This is kind of a hail Mary at this point."

"Seems like a waste of a perfectly good day, but we'll hang around the area in case you need back up," Greg added, "I know these roads better than anyone."

Frankie, Jim, and Patrick got into Jim's SUV and before they were out of the parking lot Frankie asked, "What was that all about?"

"I'm not sure, but I didn't like the way Cantor was asking questions. It felt…"

"Off," Frankie said, finishing his sentence.

"Yeah. What do you know about him?" Jim asked.

"Not much really. He's lived around here as long as I can remember. He was a year younger than me in school, but we didn't hang out or anything. He has an older brother. Hank, I think. He was already out of high school by the time I was a freshman. I think Hank was in the same class as Danielle's dad. I met him a few times, but he creeped me out, so if he was around, I found an excuse to leave. Did you know Greg or Hank, Patrick?"

Patrick ran his hand through his short hair then said, "I didn't know either of them well, but was around Greg more than Hank. Hank was two or three years older than me and ran with a rough crowd. He and his friends did a lot more than smoke weed. I don't remember their mom being around, and their dad was a real piece of work. I saw both of them with black eyes more times than I can count."

"I didn't realize that," Frankie said. "He sure gave me a weird vibe today."

"I'm probably being paranoid, but something says to keep the details of this case close to the vest," Jim said. "Let's stay off the radio as much as possible."

CHAPTER
NINETY

AT THE LAST MINUTE, Frankie and Patrick decided to jump in the side-by-side together. Mia and Baker went to Mrs. Longneck's house, and Jim took the four-wheeler into the woods to watch from a different vantage point. They drove to the barn in silence, parking the side-by-side behind the building where it wouldn't be seen from Hudson's house.

Once inside, Frankie said, "Feels a little like old times. We were so… fearless."

Patrick smiled and said, "Or at least pretended to be."

Twenty-eight years earlier

There was a nip in the air, but the sun filtered through the trees, keeping the chill down. Frankie and Patrick were at the farm and told Frank they were going to take the four-wheelers on the trails by the old barn. They *were* going to ride the trails, but they were also going to snoop around and see if they could figure out what happened to Julia and her mother. Frankie didn't think her dad needed to know that.

"Keep an eye on the time, Francesca," Frank said. Wiping his hands with a red oil rag he added, "You know when the sun begins to set, it's going to get dark in the woods."

"I know dad. I'll keep an eye on it." Frankie put her arm around her dad, giving him a side hug.

Frank ruffled her hair, "No need to be in that barn either. Michael and I need to do some work on the roof."

Frankie knew that wasn't the reason her dad didn't want her and Patrick in the barn, but just smiled, "Yes, sir."

Frank dropped the rag onto his work bench and began walking towards the house. He called back, "Be careful."

As she and Patrick walked towards the four-wheelers, Frankie said softly, "Love you too, dad."

Frankie and Patrick rolled the ATVs out of the shed, checked the tanks, and started down the hill toward Shack Creek.

"Come on, Patrick," Frankie yelled, taking the lead in the race they were not running.

Patrick laughed, accelerating slightly. The path into the woods had been worn down from years of trail riding, so it wasn't hard to follow. When they got to the barn, they stopped and looked towards the Hudson farm.

"Where do you want to start?" Patrick asked.

Frankie grabbed the notebook from her backpack and reviewed the notes she had taken the past week.

"Mr. Hudson usually gets home around 5 o'clock during the week, but I think he's gone this weekend. I watched him put a suitcase in his truck last night. After he burned the mattresses, I started watching the house and keeping notes. He ripped out the carpets about a week ago and took big trash bags to the burn pit. I thought we might start there and see what we could find."

"Lead the way."

Frankie and Patrick poked around the rubble for more than an hour and were about ready to give up when something caught Frankie's eye.

"Frankie, we need to head back. It's almost five and the sun is going to set soon."

"I know, but I think I found something." Frankie continued to rummage through the debris and stopped only when she found what had caught her eye. The edges were charred, but underneath one of the trash bags was Julia's journal. "He's been in the barn."

"What?"

"He's been in the barn. This book was inside the night of the fire."

CHAPTER
NINETY-ONE

The Journal

FRANKIE AND PATRICK made it back to the Moretti farm just as the sun made its last appearance behind the trees. They made a show of adding gas to the four-wheelers, even though they had barely used any, before putting them away. If Frankie's father noticed, he opted not to say anything. Once they finished, they went to the front porch to sit, journal in hand.

Frankie sat with the leather book in her lap as fields in front of her began to darken. The light from the porch was just bright enough she would be able to read her friend's words as easily as one of the many novels she had consumed in that very spot.

"This feels like such a betrayal," Frankie said, breaking the silence. "She wrote her personal feelings, hopes, fears, frustrations. I mean, these words were never intended to be read or heard."

Patrick touched Frankie's hand, "It might help us figure out what happened to her. I think she'd want that."

Frankie opened the journal, scanning past the entries about Craig and school. The entries the month leading up to Julia's disappearance were about her dad and caused Frankie to read a little slower.

June 15

Dad is at it again. I wish he would leave mom alone. So what if dinner was cold when he got home. He was the one who was late. I snuck out of my room and went to the barn, so I didn't have to listen to him yelling. When I came home, she had an icepack on her cheek. I should have stayed behind and helped her.

June 16

Mom put makeup on to cover the bruises on her face, but it didn't really help any. She ended up calling off work so no one would ask questions. I offered to stay home with her, but she said that would make dad even more angry. I wish we could just leave.

June 20

Dad was acting really weird today. I was coming back from work, and he was pulling out of the field near the Jenkins mine. When I asked him about it, he told me to mind my business and gave me a slap across the face. It stung but more than that it surprised me and made me... angry. Why does my mom stay?

June 25

Craig and I went out to the Jenkins mine and snooped around today. I thought I heard someone inside. Craig said I was hearing things, but I know what I heard. Someone was inside. The door was padlocked so we couldn't get in. Craig said to let it go, but I can't. I need to find a key to that lock and see what my dad is hiding.

June 30

After school I went back to the mine. This time without Craig. I had to walk in from the road, and it was a good thing because dad showed up while I was snooping around. I heard the voices from inside again but before I could do anything I heard his truck and hid in the brush. Dad went inside the mine! He used a key from the same ring as his truck keys. Thank God, he didn't see me because I don't know what he would have done if he had. He lost it on mom again last night. Frankie and I were supposed to meet at the barn and have a sleepover, but I couldn't leave mom alone. He might have killed her. I tried to help, and it got really bad. I have to come up with a story about the bruises on my face before I go back to work. There isn't enough make-up to cover what he did.

July 3

Dad was at it again. I don't know what set him off, but he was yelling and then started slapping mom. When he started strangling her, I ran to my room and called the sheriff. I thought he was going to kill her. What a waste that was. Dad stood outside talking to the sheriff for ten minutes, then slapped him on the back as he walked back to his car. When dad came inside, he told me if I ever did anything like that again it would be the last thing I ever did. And I believe him. I want to leave but am afraid if I do, he'll kill mom. I'm the only one who can help her.

July 5

Mom said she's finally had enough, and we're going to leave dad. She hasn't told my sister yet, but we think she'll be okay with it. She hates dad and since she moved away, she doesn't really come home anyway. Mom said she's not sure where we'll go but it's going to be far from here. She told me to start taking things out of the house a little bit at a time. I suggested taking stuff to the Moretti barn, but she said dad'll find it there. She told me she has seen him snooping around up there at night, so it's not safe. I told mom about the mine and the voices I heard. She freaked out and told me to stay away from the mine and to never tell anyone else about it. I didn't tell her Craig already knew and thought I was hearing things. Maybe I'll tell Frankie before we leave.

July 10

Mom said we're leaving day after tomorrow and I can't tell anyone — not even Craig. She won't tell me where we're going. Honestly, I don't know if she knows. I'm scared to leave but even more scared to stay. I think dad broke mom's arm during their fight last night and if we stay dad is going to kill her. Maybe me too. He's never been a great dad, but this is.... it's like he is someone else. Tonight, is my last chance to figure out who, or what, is in the mine. I'm going to take his keys after he goes to bed and go out there. If there is any chance there is a person in the mine, I need to get them out before we leave.

"The last entry was the same week rumors started about Julia. Did Craig ever say anything to you about going to the Jenkins mine?"

"Maybe. If he did, it was in passing. Like a joke. Do you think she went back out there?"

Frankie gave the question some thought, "Knowing Julia, yes. Want to check it out tomorrow?"

"You sure her and her mom didn't just run away? Sounds like that was the plan."

"Maybe, but neither of their cars are gone, so how did they go? And why would she leave her journal behind?"

"Maybe they had someone take them to the bus or train station. Or maybe her mom had a car stashed somewhere. Sounds like she may have been planning it for a while."

"Maybe," Frankie acquiesced. She looked out over the dark field and hoped beyond hope that Julia was somewhere safe with her mom. "So tomorrow?"

"I have a better idea. Let's turn the journal over to the sheriff's department and let them handle it."

Frankie didn't like that idea as much as playing detective like in her Nancy Drew and Hardy Boys books, but she ultimately gave in and the following day they took the journal to the sheriff's office. Within a week, there was a fire at the Jenkins mine, leaving a pile of rubble where the entrance used to be.

CHAPTER
NINETY-TWO

Present day

SOMETHING WAS BOTHERING FRANKIE, but it was just below the surface of her memory leaving her unable to articulate it to Patrick, so she sat in silence. Time moved slowly as they watched Warren Hudson go about his daily chores. He took the trash out to the firepit, fed his chickens and meandered around his yard stopping occasionally to look at his cell phone. An hour passed before Hudson got into his truck and started to move. At first, it appeared he was going to leave. He pulled the truck out and headed towards the road, but then he quickly turned and headed into the woods.

"He's on the move," Patrick said. As an afterthought, he added, "Don't put it on the radio."

Frankie texted her team in a group text. *"He's heading south-southeast into the woods. Patrick and I are following."*

Jim responded, *"He's heading my direction."*

Frankie and Patrick took the same trail they had taken from the farm, but before they got to the empty field in front of the house, they made a sharp right, taking the trail that went up the hill.

"Something's off," Frankie finally said aloud.

"What do you mean?"

"I'm not sure I can explain it, but it's almost like he knows we're here and is leading us into the woods."

"There's no way he would have seen us."

"No, but it doesn't make sense that he would drive up the hill. There's nothing out that way."

Frankie had no more gotten the words out of her mouth when the truck veered right onto a different trail, heading back towards his farm.

Frankie called Jim who said, "I see him. Looks like he's taking a trail back west."

The phone on speaker, Frankie asked, "Where the hell is he going?"

Hudson slammed the brakes on the truck and sat, not moving. Jim responded quickly,

pulling the ATV over with brush for cover.

The color drained from Frankie's face. "…. Oh damn! Stop!" Frankie yelled, "Get out of there, Jim!"

Frankie immediately texted the group to go back to their original positions and stay off the radios.

"What the hell, Frankie?" Patrick had stopped but was noticeably confused.

"It's an ambush. I'll explain later, but we need to get the hell out of here."

Suddenly they heard the gunfire through the phone, but instead of retreating, they headed towards the sound. Shots were coming in bursts, providing cover fire for Hudson to retreat into the woods, back to his house.

Frankie was out of the side-by-side before Patrick could bring it to a stop. Her gun drawn; she scanned the area trying to determine the source of the gunshots. As soon as the truck carrying Hudson was gone, the gunfire stopped. Frankie looked for Jim, but he and the ATV were nowhere to be seen.

Frankie grabbed her cellphone and yelled, "Jim, where are you?"

She could hear her voice coming from the woods, but Jim didn't answer. She yelled again. Frankie heard her own voice and, again, no answer. She and Patrick moved cautiously towards the sound. One hundred feet into the woods, Frankie began to run.

CHAPTER
NINETY-THREE

JIM WAS LYING, unmoving, on the ground less than five feet from the ATV. Frankie felt the fear well up inside her but fought the urge to release a guttural scream. Instead, she focused on what was in front of her and let her training take over.

"Jim," Frankie knelt beside his still body, scanning for an obvious cause of injury. She checked and found a pulse. "Jim. Jim… dammit! Wake up!"

"It's… okay… Frankie," Jim softly responded.

"Are you okay?" Frankie asked.

Jim sat up slowly and rubbed the back of his head. He met Frankie's look with, "I'm okay, Frankie. I took a couple to the vest, but nothing major."

Frankie dropped back onto her butt and said, "I was afraid we lost you like…"

"You can't get rid of me that easy," Jim said. "I'm going to have a hell of a headache though. I tripped over something and hit my head when I dove for cover."

Frankie let out a sigh that became a laugh. Patrick and Jim looked at one another, then back at Frankie, and joined in her laughter.

"Cause of injury? A 100 – year – old tree that jumped up and tripped me, sir," Jim said in between guffaws.

After the nervous laughter subsided, Frankie said, "Thank God you had your vest on. I mean, if you hadn't…. if I lost you…" Frankie could not bring herself to finish her thought.

Jim gently lifted Frankie's chin and said, "But I did, and you didn't."

Patrick stood on the sidelines watching the brief interaction with curiosity. He thought Jim was interested in being more than Frankie's friend, but just as she had in high school, Frankie held things close to the vest.

"I'll take the ATV back to the barn. Frankie, why don't you drive Jim in the side-by-side."

Jim started to object, but Frankie stopped him with, "Don't say a word. Get in the passenger seat."

"Yes ma'am," letting the twang of his southern accent drip from the words.

Fifteen minutes later, the entire team, sans the deputies, were at the barn. Hudson had left but Coleman and Wheeler lost him. Frankie was pacing and noticeably angry.

"What the hell happened out there?" Baker shouted. He rarely raised his voice, but he had to answer for this mission and didn't like being in the dark. "First, you tell us to pull out, then next thing I know there's gunfire coming from your location."

Frankie didn't like Baker being angry, especially at her, but she needed to answer carefully, and she knew her story would make little sense.

"There was a journal…"

"You found a journal?"

"No. Yes. I mean, yes, I found a journal. No, it wasn't today. Patrick and I were reminiscing about when Julia, Hudson's daughter, went missing, and I remembered we found a journal and took it to the sheriff's office and gave it to Deputy…"

"Cantor." Patrick finished. "Oh shit, now I understand."

CHAPTER
NINETY-FOUR

"CAN someone please explain it to the rest of us," Baker said, frustrated by the shorthand.

"Roger Cantor is Deputy Greg *Cantor's* uncle," Frankie explained. "We found a journal Julia had kept, and she mentioned calling the sheriff when her dad was strangling her mom and when he got there, the two of them talked, shook hands, and he left. Roger Cantor patrolled this area, and he would stop by to visit dad and Hudson pretty regularly. I'm pretty sure he would have been the one who responded. A week or two after Julia went missing, Patrick and I found a journal down at the burn pit. It was laying on the outer edges of the pit, the pages barely singed. The journal detailed abuse she and her mom..." Frankie looked away from the crowd, "Sorry, I haven't thought about this in years. The day after we found it, we took it to the sheriff's office and gave it to Roger Cantor. Anyway, that wasn't what made me pull everyone back." Frankie looked at Patrick and said, "Remember the Jenkins mine?"

Patrick nodded.

"Julia wrote in her journal that she heard voices in the Jenkins mine. A week after we gave the journal to Roger, the mine burned and the investigation into Julia's disappearance screeched to a halt."

"You think Cantor tipped Hudson off?" Patrick asked.

"I think it's possible. Hudson was driving around the woods in circles. It wasn't making sense. In all the years I've known Hudson, I've never known him to take his truck into the woods. Dad and Jake told me he had become even more strange over the years, barely keeping the house up but today he was out doing chores. When I saw him driving into the woods, it seemed odd. Then he started driving in this weird path – like he was leading us somewhere."

"Or into something. Like an ambush," Jim said, rubbing his chest where the bullets hit his vest.

"Did you get a look at the shooter or shooters?" Baker asked.

"All I saw was muzzle flash."

"The woods are dense. It would've been easy for someone to hide," Patrick added. "Especially if they came in on foot or on an ATV."

"Let's get the dogs out there," Baker said.

"Let's wait, Sarge. I think there might be another way to get this guy."

"What are you thinking Frankie?"

Frankie's stomach rolled at the thought, but she said, "Let's lure him out using Danielle."

"You sure about this, Frankie?" Jim asked.

"Well, you aren't going to use my daughter per se, but let's use her profile. We know he's interested. Maybe we can find an undercover that's similar to her. We have to plan this because if something happens to Danielle…"

"It won't, Frankie," Jim said. "You have my word."

"Then let's do it. Time is running out, and there may still be young girls out there."

CHAPTER
NINETY-FIVE

FRANKIE DROVE BACK to the City of Fountains in silence. Baker wisely sent her and Mia back with Jim in tow, while he and Coleman updated Cantor and his deputies. He called after to let them know Cantor was full of questions but didn't push when Baker told him it was just another dead end. Neither he nor Cantor mentioned the gunfire.

Ten minutes from headquarters, Mia broke the silence, "Are you sure about this, Frankie?"

Frankie did not take her eyes off the road.

When it appeared she wasn't going to answer, Jim said, "It's not too late to change your mind, Frankie. We can find another way."

Pulling the car off the highway on to the side street leading to headquarters, Frankie finally said, "No, I'm not sure, but I know there's no other way. I just have to figure out how to make sure Danielle doesn't actually get caught up in this."

Jim put his hand on Frankie's shoulder and said, "We're not really using Danielle, Frankie. We're just using her account."

Frankie parked the car and turned to face Mia and Jim. "You're using her account from here. She lives in a town less than 15 minutes from this creep's house. He may already know where she is and may already be watching her. What if he gets to the real Danielle before you all can swoop in and get him? What if *my* Danielle gets put in an old cellar or old mine? What if…" Frankie turned away, not wanting her fear and vulnerability to show, the stress of the day catching up with her.

Neither Jim nor Mia jumped to answer, knowing Frankie made a good point and they couldn't make any promises or guarantees. The trio gathered their equipment and walked to headquarters in silence. Jim walked them to the door, then turned to go back to the SUV Patrick had driven.

Before he got inside, he said, "Frankie?"

"Yeah?"

"Do you trust me?"

"Why would you ask me that?" Frankie asked.

"That's not an answer."

"Of course, I do," Frankie stressed.

Jim nodded his head and got inside the vehicle, never taking his eyes off Frankie as they drove away.

Mia, never missed anything and said, "Okay, he's gone. Talk to me. Are you okay?"

Frankie leaned against the wall near the stairway door. "When I saw Jim on the ground today, it was just like…"

"Brad?"

Frankie leaned forward, her hands on her knees, sucking air into her lungs. "What the hell is wrong with me?"

"Frankie, your husband, the father of your child and love of your life was shot and killed while serving a warrant. You and Jim are close. Why *wouldn't* it bother you to see him on the ground after taking fire? Contrary to what you may think, you are, in fact, human." Mia stepped closer to Frankie, put her hand on her shoulder and said, "I'm sorry for being so harsh."

"Your brutal honesty is one of the things I love most about you," Frankie smiled.

After a brief pause, Mia softly asked, "Are you sure there isn't something more between you and Jim?"

Frankie looked up, meeting Mia's gaze and said, "Honestly, if you would have asked me that a week ago, I would have said no, but now I just don't know. When I thought he'd been shot, I…" Frankie didn't finish her thought. Wiping the tears from her eyes, she said, "I can't lose him too. I can't go through that again."

"You know there are no guarantees in this life Frankie."

"I know and that's what scares me," Frankie said. "And you know I trust Jim, but I am terrified Hudson is going to get to Danielle before *we* can get to *him*."

Mia nodded, knowing nothing she said would ease Frankie's worry. Instead of filling space with empty words, she said, "Let's go print a couple of pictures of Hudson, change our clothes, and go put the pics on the heavy bag. Might feel good to beat the hell out of something."

Frankie laughed, put her arm around Mia and said, "Good plan, partner."

"WHAT'S NEXT?" Frankie asked. Her neighbors, Keith and Bruce had started the process of adoption. Tyler had just gone to bed, and they were raising a drink to celebrate the official notice they were approved to foster-to-adopt.

"We have to get full physicals, take some classes, get a safety assessment of the house, then we go on a call-out list," Keith replied.

"We requested elementary school or older," Bruce said.

"What, no babies?" Frankie laughed.

Bruce and Keith, in unison, said, "No."

Before Frankie could say anything more her phone rang. Looking down, she sent a quick text, *"Can I call you in a bit?"*

"No. This is urgent."

To Bruce and Keith, she said, "Sorry, Bobby said it can't wait." Frankie stepped into the kitchen and asked, "Hey Bobby, what's up?"

"Are you still working that case with the missing girls?" Bobby asked.

"Yeah, why?"

"It may be nothing, but we got called out to a house in Brookside. Their 15-year-old daughter is missing."

"Are they sure she isn't at a friend's house?"

"Frankie, you aren't dealing with a rookie here. I'm calling because this girl was talking to some guy online and is now missing. The parents are willing to let us search her computer, but I think you need to come talk to them."

Frankie got more details from Bobby and told him she'd call him back. Keith recognized the look on her face when she returned to the table.

"I guess the celebration is over," Keith said.

"I hate to ask, but can you all hang here until Sophie gets home? I'll text her so she knows you are waiting."

Bruce quickly stepped in and said, "Of course."

"I'm sorry guys. It's another…"

"Don't worry about a thing, Frankie. Go do what you need to do. Tyler will never even know you're gone."

Frankie quickly changed her clothes, sent Bobby and Sophie texts, grabbed her bag, and headed for the door.

"Thank you," Frankie said. Before walking out she turned around, hugged each man, and added, "Congratulations! You are going to be great dads."

"Thanks, Frankie. Be safe."

Frankie made a quick stop at headquarters to get a car, thankful she kept a set of keys in her go-bag, so she didn't have to go inside. She tried to focus on the things Bobby told her, but her thoughts kept returning to Danielle and how easily this could have been her.

Frankie sent Jim a message, *"We may have another one."*

Within seconds he responded, *"Let me know if I need to come out."*

CHAPTER
NINETY-SEVEN

FRANKIE PULLED up to a Tudor-style home with a carefully manicured lawn. It was obvious to her the homeowners took great pride in appearances. One step inside the residence and her opinion was confirmed. The phrase, "a place for everything and everything in its place" ran through her mind as she stepped inside the front door and scanned the space. The home could have appeared in one of the home decorating magazines Frankie liked to read. It didn't look…lived in.

Bobby led Frankie towards the parents but stopped before making the introductions.

"Mom has not said a lot, but we've been able to establish dad is actually the girl's stepfather. The girl's name is Kaitlin, and she's been missing for about a week."

"A *week*?" Frankie hissed. "How old is she?"

"14."

"And no one thought to call the police?" Frankie asked, gritting her teeth as she tried to maintain a whisper.

Bobby nodded, "They thought she was at her dad's house, and he thought she was with mom. It wasn't until the school called and asked why she didn't show up before anyone even realized she was gone. Mom said things had been tense the last few weeks at the house, but she thought Kaitlin was just rebelling. They had a fight before school the last day they saw her. Before she stormed out, Kaitlin said she was going to her dad's house after school. Mom didn't think anything of it. Apparently, he lives nearby, and Kaitlin can spend time at either house as long as she lets the other parent know."

"How did you connect this to my case?" Frankie asked, growing impatient.

"After the school called and mom learned Kaitlin was missing, she searched her bedroom. Her iPad was lying on her bed with an old notification waiting. The message alarmed her and that is when she called her husband, then us."

"What did the message say?"

"I'll meet you at the bus stop. Wes."

"Did you say Wes?"

Bobby didn't say a word, but simply nodded his head.

A man with graying hair paced the floor, his mouth twisted, with a scarlet neck and cheeks. A similarly aged woman sat at the table, her face cradled in her palms. Any makeup she had been wearing had washed away with the tears, and her eyes were red-rimmed and bloodshot.

"Mrs," Frankie looked to Bobby.

"Copeland," Bobby said.

"Mrs. Copeland, I'm Detective Frankie Thomas. Do you mind if I ask you a few questions?"

Looking up she said, "Anything if it will help find my Kaiti-bug."

"Did you say Kaiti?" Frankie asked, thinking about the list of names Nikki had given her.

"Yes, her name is Kaitlin, but I've called her Kaiti-bug since she was born."

"Have you noticed any changes in Kath…I mean Kaiti's behavior lately?" Frankie asked.

Before his wife could answer Mr. Copland said, "She's a teenager, Detective. She was moody, sullen, and prone to pushing limits."

Frankie, annoyed Mr. Copeland wouldn't let his wife speak, said, "What about you Mrs. Copeland, had you noticed anything different?"

The distraught woman looked at her hands, then said, "She had started staying at her father's house more and when she was home, she stayed in her room a lot. She also stopped having friends over here."

"Officer LeGrande said you and Kaiti had a fight the last time you saw her. Do you mind telling me what it was about?"

Mrs. Copeland did not immediately answer, instead looked at her husband, who continued to pace.

"Kaiti said she wanted to go live with her dad, and I didn't respond very well."

Frankie understood the pain of your child telling you she wanted to live with her dad. "Did she tell you why?"

Again Mrs. Copeland looked at her husband, but this time he stopped and stared at his wife.

"No," was her soft answer.

"Did Kaiti get along with you and your husband?"

"What does this have to do with anything?" Mr. Copeland asked, his voice elevated.

Frankie was startled at the man's abruptness but calmly said, "Maybe nothing. Did you and your stepdaughter get along?"

"My *daughter* and I got along fine."

Softly Mrs. Copeland said, "They were very close."

FRANKIE SUSPECTED there was more to the Copelands' story than they cared to share, but she didn't have the time or energy to push. She asked for a recent photograph, the iPad, and all the passwords the parents knew. With their permission, Frankie and Bobby went to Kaiti's room to search for anything that could direct them to her.

The ornate door opened into a large room with polished wood floors and a plush area rug centered in the space. The bedroom furniture was a delicate antique distressed with a softy cream to look shabby chic. A handstitched quilt adorned the bed, with pillows of various sizes carefully placed at the head. A light pink chenille blanket laid at the end, carefully placed to look like it had been tossed without care. The closet was well-organized and color-coded. Frankie suspected that was the doing of Mrs. Copeland, not 14-year-old Kaiti.

A matching dresser sat on one wall with a gilded mirror adorned with necklaces and snapshots of Kaiti and her friends. Frankie looked at the teens in the photographs, all seemingly happy. Under the window sat a matching desk with a lamp. On either side were open shelves with dance trophies and ribbons and tiny animals on display. There were no stuffed animals or reminders of childhood beyond the items on the shelves and the snapshots. Frankie did not know why, but this struck her as odd. She glanced back at the photographs and realized one looked like it had been printed on paper and the boy wasn't in any of the other snapshots.

Frankie captured photographs of the space and began to walk out of the room when something told her to turn back. Again, her eyes gravitated to the white desk. Frankie rummaged through the drawers but found nothing beyond extra school supplies. She looked around the room, trying to think like a teenager. She looked in the side tables and under the bed. As she stood up, she noticed something sticking out from between the mattress and box springs. She got closer and pulled out a leather-bound notebook and laid it on the perfectly made bed. Feeling intrusive, she reminded herself, *"This may hold the key to where Kaiti is. Or at least why she ran away."*

With a gloved hand, Frankie opened the book and saw there were only a few entries, and the last one was from a few days before the fight with her mom. Frankie took photographs of the pages, scanning each entry.

July 11

I have been talking to this guy on Insta. He says he goes to Rockhurst and lives in Waldo. That isn't far. He's really cute and totally gets me. Right now, his messages are the only thing I have to look forward to at night.

I felt his presence in my room before I saw him. I felt the weight on the bed but kept my eyes closed, hoping he would leave. This is not the first time he has done this. I don't know how long he sat there, but he finally left when mom got home.

July 13

Wes and I've been messaging every day. It's nice to have someone who understands and doesn't judge me. We've exchanged a few pics and he is so cute. He asked me to send some sexy pics, but I don't think I'm ready for that.

Mom is working super late again tonight. I tried locking my bedroom door, but it won't lock. He came in my room again. I kept my eyes closed and laid very still. He sat on my bed and…eventually he left. I want to tell mom, but what do I tell her?

September 5

Wes and I are still talking. I swear he's the only thing keeping me sane right now. I finally sent him a couple pics, but he wants more. And he wants me naked. I finally sent one of my boobs.

I've been staying at dad's house, but mom made me come home today. I don't know what time it was, but he came in my room again. This time he laid next to me. I kept my eyes closed but this time it didn't stop him from doing things. I don't want to hurt mom, but I can't stay here anymore.

September 10

I told mom I want to live with dad. That I'll visit. She lost her mind. She told me if I left, I could never come back, not even to visit. She said she wouldn't have it. I didn't know what to do so I told her I'd stay. I took a knife from the kitchen. If he touches me again…

I told Wes what was going on and he said he'd help me. He's meeting me at Minsky's in Waldo after school.

Frankie felt sick to her stomach. She knew the way the stepfather acted was strange but had hoped she was wrong. She let the book close and placed it in her bag with Kaiti's iPad. She looked under the mattress and pillows but was unable to find the knife Kaiti referenced. Satisfied she had not missed anything, Frankie turned off the light then made her way back to the kitchen.

The Copelands wanted an Amber alert issued, demanded it, but Frankie gently explained there was criteria for issuing an Amber alert, and this case did not fit. She assured them she would get Kaiti's photograph on the news and in social media once she had the approval from her chain of command. She did not tell them she would be calling Division of Family Services as soon as she got into her car. Frankie looked at Kaiti's mother and wondered if she had read her daughter's journal. Did she know about the abuse and do nothing about it? Had Kaiti left the journal behind intentionally or had it been an oversight? Whichever it was, she vowed to find the girl and get answers.

Once outside the house, Frankie felt like she could breathe again.

CHAPTER
NINETY-NINE

THE MORNING FLEW by as Frankie focused on writing her reports. She had not checked her cellphone since she got to the office. She was surprised to see missed text messages from Jim asking her to call.

Before Frankie could respond to the text her phone rang.

"Are you busy?" Jim asked.

"Well, hello to you, too. I'm just working on a report from last night and was going to call. It's a missing girl who was talking to..."

"I'm coming to your office," Jim interrupted. "I've already called Patrick. He's on his way. I think I know where the girls are, and if we wait, it may be too late to save them."

When she disconnected the call, Frankie pulled Mia into Baker's office and said, "We have a break on the missing girls. Jim has been up on a wire the last few days, and overnight he started hearing some interesting chatter. His target was talking to some guy who only identified himself as Hank. It didn't mean much until he heard him say he needed help moving some girls." Frankie took a breath. "He remembered me telling him that Nikki mentioned some guy named Hank. Long and short of it, the girls that are still missing are about to be delivered to a man Jim believes is part of the cartel. He couldn't tell me much but said the guys he's been listening to are pretty hardcore. They grab people they don't think will be missed, mostly girls, and use them for trafficking. Some drugs, but mostly sex. Some stay in the states, but others get sent out of the country – specifically, the ones that could cause them trouble. Jim believes if we don't intercept these girls today, we may never see them again."

"Frankie, don't you think the tactical unit should be called out?" Baker asked.

Frankie stifled the frustration building in her chest, recognizing Baker had to answer for the manpower and possible overtime. Finally, she said, "Jim is calling in TAC for the extraction, but Mia and I should talk to the girls. And Jim wants my help talking to Hudson. I need to see this through, Sarge." Frankie paused, then added, "On or off the clock."

Jim briefed the team on what he knew, then explained his plan. The Tactical Response Team was watching the Port of Kansas City and had eyes on the container they believed would house the girls. They couldn't get eyes on Hudson but knew the vehicle he would likely be using for transportation and had lookouts along the route to the Port.

Frankie and Mia followed close behind Jim, with Baker and Patrick bringing up the rear. They intended to post close enough to the Port that they could respond once the suspects were in custody and the girls had been rescued.

"Penny for your thoughts," Frankie said to Mia.

"Hmm?" Mia turned away from the window and said, "Huh? Oh, nothing really. I have a weird feeling in my gut. I'm sure it's nothing. I can't really explain it. It's probably just adrenaline." Mia tried to laugh it off, but before she could say anything more, Frankie's cellphone began to ring.

DANIELLE WALKED the few blocks home from school, alone and angry. She had math club after school and had asked her stepsister to wait for her, but she didn't. Even though her dad had asked her stepsiblings to make sure she got to and from school okay, she was walking alone. Again. Maybe her stepsister would get grounded for not waiting.

"Yeah, right," Danielle said aloud. "Little miss perfect probably won't even get yelled at."

Danielle kicked at the rock on the sidewalk as she slowly walked through town. She was frustrated, confused, and didn't understand why her dad seemed to favor her stepsister over her. Danielle was two blocks from the driveway when she noticed an old man in a pickup truck slowly pulling up behind her. She glanced back briefly but continued walking. Nothing about the man seeming unusual.

"Hey, sweety, can I ask you a question?" the old man asked.

Danielle hesitated, then said, "I guess."

"I can't find my dog and wondered if you might be able to help me." The man got out of the truck and walked towards Danielle with a curved back and a halting gait.

Danielle felt the hair on the back of her neck rise, but then looked at the infirm man, and disregarded the eerie feeling she had. "What does your dog look like?"

"He's a little sheltie mix. His name is Jax."

To herself Danielle thought, *"that's my favorite kind of dog."* Aloud she asked, "Where'd you last see him?"

"Over by the school. I just moved here, and we were walking at the track. He got off his leash and started running. I couldn't chase him," the old man said, nodding towards his bent leg. "I thought maybe you might have seen him run by."

Again, the hair on the back of Danielle's neck tingled. Shelties don't typically run away from their person when they walk. They herd their person like they would sheep. Danielle started to question him, but instead she asked, "Do you have a picture?"

The man walked in Danielle's direction with a phone in hand. He walked slow and unassuming, furthering the image of a frail old man. When the man got next to her, he put his arm around Danielle's shoulder and brought the phone down presumably to show her a photograph of his little dog Jax. Before she could respond, he squeezed Danielle's shoulder and started to drag her to his truck with a strength belied by his appearance.

A quiet voice said, *"Fight."*

Danielle hesitated for a moment, but then she remembered the self-defense training her mother and Tyler's dad forced her to learn. She raised her head and made contact with his jaw then used her elbow to hit him in the gut. She kicked ferociously and screamed as loud as her lungs would allow. When he tried to cover her mouth, Danielle bit him, clamping her teeth into his arm with as much force as she could muster. When the arm dropped, Danielle began to run towards her house, but the man started to chase after her. Danielle leapt over the broken sidewalk where an errant tree root had lifted the stone. The man, focused on her, didn't see the broken path, tripped and fell face first. Before he could get up, Danielle was inside the garage of her house dialing Frankie's number.

ONE HUNDRED ONE

FRANKIE ANSWERED the call on the first ring, "Hey angel-girl I'm out on a… wait a second, what? Where are you? Are you okay? Is he still there? No! Don't go outside. Is your dad home? Are you sure? Okay, okay. You did good, Danielle. You did good. It's okay, you're safe now. He's gone? Are you sure? Did you see the truck drive away? Okay. Yes, let me talk to her."

Mia looked at Frankie, whose face had drained of color. Quietly she asked, "Are you okay?"

Frankie shook her head, then in the phone she said, "Hey. Bring her up to the city to the hospital. We need her to get a medical exam and be processed for evidence. What? No, it can't wait until tomorrow. We need her to be brought up today. Don't let her change her clothes. Yes, you get her here, and I'll make sure she gets home. You won't have to wait for her." Frankie took a deep breath in an effort not to curse at Danielle's stepmother. "Okay, I'll let the nurse know she's coming and will meet you all there in forty-five minutes."

Frankie disconnected the call and, when she was certain she would not be heard on the other end, she yelled, "You stupid, fucking, lazy, piece of shit, selfish bitch."

"Don't hold back, tell me how you really feel."

Frankie looked at Mia then let out a laugh. "I'm sorry, but that woman is a special kind of stupid."

"What happened, Frankie?"

Frankie explained what Danielle had told her and asked if she would take a formal statement from her daughter. She knew Mia would get what was necessary but in a way that was trauma-informed and respectful. She did not trust many people with her kids, but Mia was one.

"Of course, I will. You think it was Hudson?"

"Not a doubt in my mind."

Frankie and Mia sat in a companionable silence for almost 10 minutes before Jim texted.

Hudson just arrived. Looks like he's alone, but he's being followed by someone in a white panel van.

Aloud Frankie said, "Could that be any more stereotypical? A white panel van? Do these creeps have a manual or what?"

Another ten minutes passed before Frankie got another message.

Warren Hudson and Hank Cantor are in custody. Three girls were recovered. Sasha is not one of them.

He.is.MINE!

Frankie had the car in drive and was pulling out of the parking lot before the message had fully sent. Minutes later, she was out of the car and running to the van where the two men were being detained.

Mia was hot on her heels and grabbed Frankie before the punch she was throwing could land on Hudson's jaw.

"Frankie, what the hell do you think you're doing?" yelled Jim.

Frankie was seeing red, and all rational thought was gone. "That son of a bitch just tried to kidnap my daughter as she walked home from school. He's lucky if all I do is punch him in the face."

The TAC officers holding the men watched with bemused expressions as Mia and Jim pulled Frankie back, pushing her back to the car she had jumped from.

"What the hell, Frankie? You punch him and he walks. Is that what you want?" Jim yelled.

"You can let go of me," Frankie said, jerking her arm. "You want to know why he didn't have any girls in the truck with him? Because he was too busy cruising the streets of the little town where my daughter lives. He grabbed her, Jim…" Frankie doubled over, choking on the words she had said, turning away so no one could see the anguish in her face.

Jim put his hand on Frankie's shoulder and said, "Tell me what happened."

Frankie composed herself, then stated, "He was driving through town and asked if she could help him find a dog. He got out to show her a picture, and he grabbed her." Frankie laughed sardonically, "He shouldn't have messed with a cop's kid. Especially one who taught her how to fight. He should have some bruises and scratches. She bit his right arm, and when they were running, he tripped over a tree root and face planted into broken concrete."

Mia joined the pair and said, "His face is pretty scratched up, and I had him lift his sleeve. There are, what appear to be, teeth marks. Danielle did good. And she's safe, Frankie."

Frankie mumbled, "My girl did good."

ONE HUNDRED TWO

MIA TOOK the keys from Frankie and didn't give her the option of driving to the hospital. Jim and Baker waited for the patrol wagon to take Hank and Hudson to police headquarters for booking, while Patrick followed the ambulance that took the rescued girls to the hospital. He buried the disappointment at not finding Sasha, holding onto the hope she was still out there, and they would find her. Alive.

Mia put the car in park, but before Frankie got out, she said, "Thank you, Mia. You and Jim really saved my bacon out there."

"You would have done the same for us," Mia said.

"I don't know what I would have done if he'd gotten her." Frankie stared out the window, unable to see anything but fear.

"But he didn't," Mia said.

"I'm worried about Patrick. This has to be really hard on him."

"It's not over," Mia said. "Now let's go get the information we need to convince him to give up Sasha's location and put him away for a very long time."

The ambulance pulled in at the same moment Frankie and Mia were walking up to the Emergency Department door. The back of the bus opened, but before anyone could step out, Mia saw muzzle flash, pushed Frankie aside, and yelled, "Gun! Down!"

Frankie and Mia found cover just as gunshots began to rain on the area. A plethora of bullets hit the ambulance, but stray bullets kept them from being able to advance towards the shooter. They needed to move the ambulance, but the EMT who had been driving was lying on the mezzanine.

Patrick was within shouting distance and yelled, "Lay down cover fire."

Frankie and Mia advanced to a place that yielded them better visual on their target. Patrick ran near the passenger door of the ambulance, keeping as low a profile as possible. Once at the door, he climbed in across the seat and put the bus in drive. Patrick was not sure where he was going to take the ambulance, but he knew he needed to get the gunfire away from the entrance to the Emergency Department where innocent civilians were at risk.

The movement of the ambulance provided Frankie and Mia just the opening they needed to advance on the shooter. There was a wooded area near the hospital property, and that was where the shooter appeared to be lying in wait. With the ambulance moved, the gunfire stopped and, as they carefully advanced, they could see the back of the shooter running away.

Frankie and Mia ran after, dodging the occasional shot fired in their direction, but the shooter had too much of a lead. They reached the road just as a dark SUV pulled away.

ONE HUNDRED THREE

FRANKIE AND MIA walked back quietly, the intensity of the last few minutes catching up with them. Patrick brought the ambulance back, the girls still inside, as they were walking up. The EMT was being loaded onto a gurney and rushed into the Emergency Department for treatment.

Baker was out of the car the second it was parked and yelled, "What the hell happened here?"

Jim was close behind, concern obvious on his face.

"It was an ambush, Sarge," Mia started. "They had someone in the woods waiting for us. The EMT opened the back of the bus and before anyone could get out shots were fired. Patrick… oh crap, how are the girls?"

Mia and Frankie ran to the ambulance. The back of the ambulance was littered with bullet holes. It didn't seem possible to either of them that someone was not hurt. Patrick jerked the back door open, and they watched as two of the girls, clinging to one another, stepped down onto the pavement. Blood spatter highlighted their clothing, skin, and hair. Tears streamed down their faces. Mia took action and guided them into the Emergency Department. Frankie and Patrick climbed into the ambulance where the third girl lay on the floor next to the gurney, unconscious and covered in blood.

"Get a doctor!" Frankie shouted. "I have a pulse, but it's faint. She appears to be breathing." Frankie stuck her head out of the back of the ambulance and did not see anyone heading their way. She looked at Patrick and said, "Let's take her!"

Patrick lifted the waif of a girl into his arms and climbed out of the ambulance. He ran inside, Frankie and Jim behind them. Baker remained outside, guarded the crime scene and made all the necessary calls to get assistance.

Frankie was so focused on the child Patrick was carrying she didn't initially see Danielle sitting in the waiting room. Jim noticed her sitting in the lobby and grabbed Frankie's arm. Looking back, she saw her child sitting in a chair, shock written on her face.

Frankie and Jim stopped. Looking at him, she asked, "Can you ask Mia if she'll talk to Danielle now? I can start talking to the other girls."

Jim nodded, then said, "Your mom is a hero, Danielle. She saved a bunch of girls today."

Danielle's eyes welled with tears as she nodded. Her stepmother and stepsister looked around the chaos that had taken over the Emergency Department waiting room. They stood up and went to take their leave.

"We're going to go now. You'll see that Danielle gets *home*, won't you?"

"I'll make sure my daughter is taken care of. I'll have her call her father when we leave here," Frankie said, refusing to acknowledge the smugness with which the woman said 'home.'

Frankie knew the likelihood of her being able to return Danielle had gone down exponentially with the shooting that had just occurred. She needed her sister's help.

Hey Soph. Danielle is with me at the hospital. It'll probably be another hour or two, but do you think you can pick her up and take her back to her dad's when we're done?

…Is she okay? Are you?

We are both okay. Hudson tried to grab her off the street and her stepmonster refused to wait for her. There was a shooting here at the hospital and I'm going to be stuck working for… God knows how long.

I got you sis. Text me when you have an update. Tyler is busy whipping my butt in Sorry.

Frankie smiled. Sorry was a new game for Tyler, and he reveled in beating anyone who would play it with him. She exhaled, knowing he was in good hands with his Aunt Sophie.

Love you sis. XO

Love you too.

Frankie kept her seat with Danielle until Jim returned to the lobby and let them know Mia had secured a room to meet. Danielle didn't have any injuries that required immediate medical attention, but they did want to collect her clothing and take photographs of any visible scratches or bruises. Frankie would gather supplies from their car after Mia began her interview.

"Danielle, Miss Mia is going to ask you a lot of questions. It's very important you tell her the truth… even if you think it'll get you in trouble," Frankie said.

"Frankie, I've got this," Mia gently chastened. "Why don't you go get the stuff from the car and then talk to the other girls."

Frankie nodded, opened the door, but then stopped and turned around. "I love you, Angel-girl."

"I love you too, mom."

Frankie closed the door, closed her eyes, and said a silent prayer of thanks that her daughter was safe.

ONE HUNDRED FOUR

FRANKIE MOVED SWIFTLY through the double doors to the inner sanctum of the Emergency Room. The doctors and nurses moved with purpose throughout the space, navigating the people in need of their help. Frankie found Patrick talking to the charge nurse amidst the chaos.

"They just took her to the OR for surgery. She never regained consciousness," Patrick said.

"Did we get an ID on her?"

"Not yet. I haven't gone in to talk to the other two yet. They are pretty shaken up and I'm not sure…"

Frankie put her hand on Patrick's arm and said, "We're going to find her, Patrick."

"We have to, Frankie. I can't go home without her."

Frankie squeezed Patrick's arm gently then walked towards the room where the two girls sat on the bed, still holding onto one another. Before closing the curtain, she asked the nurse to page the forensic nurse and a victim advocate.

"My name is Detective Thomas, but you can call me Frankie." Offering a slight smile, she pointed at the stool next to the bed and asked, "Do you mind if I sit on this stool?"

Both girls nodded.

"What are your names?"

The girls looked at one another, hesitating slightly. A couple of seconds passed before one of them said, "I'm Kaiti. Well, Kaitlin, but everyone calls me Kaiti."

Frankie recognized the name. This was the girl who wanted to live with her dad and was missing for a week before the police were called.

"Thank you, Kaiti. How old are you?"

"I'm almost 15."

Frankie smiled. If she remembered her birthday correctly, she would not be 15 for eight more months. Someday she would not be in a hurry to make herself older.

Frankie made eye contact with the doe-eyed girl holding onto Kaiti's left hand. "What's your name?"

"Enya," was the soft response. Frankie thought she detected a slight accent.

"How old are you?

"I just turned 13."

Frankie definitely heard an accent. Possibly eastern European, but she couldn't be sure.

"What's the name of the girl who was with you?"

Again, the girls looked to one another, hesitant to answer.

"It's okay. You all aren't in trouble. We want to help you."

Kaiti sat up a little straighter on the bed and said, "Wendi. Her name is Wendi."

Over the next two hours, Frankie listened as the two girls gave a description of what had brought them there that day. Kaiti's story was similar to Zoe and Nikki. She had left home to meet a "boy" she was talking to on social media. Just like with the other two girls, the boy ended up being Hudson. Enya's story was slightly different. She hadn't been talking online, she had been grabbed off the street in New York City.

CHAPTER
ONE HUNDRED FIVE

ENYA WAS BORN IN SARAJEVO, Bosnia to Daris and Amina Muratovic. Her parents had grown up together in a small town but moved to Sarajevo after the war. Shortly after they relocated, Enya was born and, two years later, they welcomed her sister, Ema. Daris and Amina had spent their entire life together and subsequently died together in a traffic accident, leaving the girls orphaned. Their only living relative, Daris' mother, took the girls in, and within a few months she decided they needed a fresh start away from the constant reminders of their loss.

They sold their worldly possessions and immigrated to America. They had very limited means, and her grandmother worked two jobs to support her and her little sister. Enya helped as much as she could and watched her little sister while her grandmother worked her second job at night. One evening after feeding and bathing her sister, she realized they did not have milk, and the girls would be without breakfast. She didn't have a way to call her grandmother at work, so she left her sister at home to go to the neighborhood bodega for milk. She never made it home. The man who snatched her off the street moved her to a couple of different places and had just recently brought her here. Enya wasn't even sure where *here* was.

Kaiti and Enya's stories re-aligned when they both ended up with

Hudson, who kept them behind a padlocked door in a dark hole with no light. They had a limited amount of food and water, but he made sure they had access to a shower so they could work to earn their keep. The work was also similar. Some men paid Hudson to have sex with the girls, and others paid for him to send them photographs of their naked bodies. If they refused or tried to fight back in any way, they were threatened and sometimes severely punished. Enya told Frankie that Hudson and the other men frequently told her if she did not do what they told her they would send videos and photographs of her engaging in sex acts to her grandmother or go back to New York and take her sister like they took her. Both threats earned her compliance.

Neither girl knew Wendi's story, but they knew she was a fighter. She often had scratches and bruises on her body when Hudson brought her back. Wendi had kept to herself, rarely spoke, and was often heard crying at night.

"But she saved us," Enya said. "When the shooting started, she shoved us to the floor to make sure we were safe. She covered our bodies with hers."

Kaiti and Enya both had tears flowing down their cheeks. Frankie sat patiently, giving them space to release some of their sadness and fear.

After a few moments, Enya said, "There were other girls, too. Every week or two, Mr. Hudson would bring in a new girl. He would send the girl out with Mr. Hank or one of the other guys. Sometimes they would come back and… and sometimes they would not. Mr. Hudson never told us what happened to them.

"We were moved around a lot, too. The places always looked the same inside. They were dark and pljesniv… what is it you call it? Musty, like wet dog."

Kaiti added, "And only one way in and out. He would lock the door from the outside. Warren just moved Enya, Wendi, and me this morning. There were six of us at the last place, but this morning, before Hank came, he divided us. There are still girls out there."

FRANKIE STEPPED OUTSIDE of the examination room, leaving the girls with a forensic nurse and advocate. Jim and Patrick were standing at the nurse's station, a grim look on their faces.

"She didn't make it," Patrick said.

"Enya and Kaiti said Wendi was a hero," Frankie said. "That was her name, Wendi. They said she pushed them to the floor of the ambulance and covered them with her body when the shooting started." She let the information sink in, then said, "Kaiti and Enya said there are other girls being held somewhere. I think Hudson was keeping some for himself. We need to find them."

"Did they have any idea where?" Jim asked.

"No. He mostly moved them in the dark or used blindfolds so they wouldn't be able to see. Dark, musty, and one way in and out was the best description they could provide. He made sure they had access to a shower and food but kept them locked away when he wasn't selling their bodies."

Their conversation was interrupted by the advocate who had been sitting with Enya and Kaiti. "Detective Thomas? Kaiti said she remembered something that might help you. Can you come back inside?"

Frankie followed the advocate to the private room where the girls had been moved for their forensic examinations. Frankie noticed the girls were starting to relax. Enya was no longer clinging to Kaiti, but instead was sitting on the end of the bed as they waited for the nurse to start the examination.

"Alex mentioned you may have remembered something, Kaiti?"

"Warren sometimes talked when he was driving. It wasn't really like he was talking to *me* but more like to someone I reminded him of. When he moved us the last time, he moved me last and by myself. I had been out with…" Kaiti hesitated then said, "Hank had taken me out. When I got back, Hank told him I had done good, and I heard him tell Hudson he would get a lot of money for me. I don't know what he meant by that, but Hudson decided I couldn't stay there because he was afraid Hank would come and get me like he had the others and cut him out of the money. He and Hank moved the other girls, and when Hank left, he took me.

"At first, he was mumbling while he drove. Something about they wouldn't steal from him, and we were *his* girls, not *theirs.* He had found us, and he wasn't going to give us up. Then he started talking a little louder. Right before he got to the last place, he started asking if I remembered the Halloween corn maze we went to when I was a kid. He was talking about how much fun it was, and then he called me a different name."

Frankie felt a chill run up her spine. She knew what Hudson was talking about. She knew who he thought he was talking to. Frankie was surprised she had not seen the resemblance before. Kaiti didn't look exactly like Julia, but she had similar characteristics. Frankie kept her voice steady as she asked, "What name did he use?"

"Julia. We've never had anyone with that name since I've been there. When I asked him about it, he told me to shut up and made it seem like I'd heard things. But I know what I heard, Detective Thomas."

"You did good, Kaiti. This is very helpful, thank you."

Frankie stepped out of the room into the hallway. She was headed for the entrance of the hospital when she heard her name and turned, concealing the look of surprise at seeing her daughter standing with Mia.

"Sorry, I was just going outside for a little air. Are you all about done?" Frankie asked.

Mia looked at her partner and friend, "We are. Danielle was going to change her clothes so we could get some photographs and take these as evidence, but I need to get some paper bags out of the car first."

"Dang it. I'm sorry, Mia. Kaiti called me back in before I could get to the car."

"Why don't you and Danielle wait here, and I'll go grab the bags."

Frankie nodded and when Danielle turned her head away, she mouthed, "Thank you."

CHAPTER
ONE HUNDRED SEVEN

FRANKIE TOOK Danielle to a quiet corner of the waiting room and nodded her head towards and empty chair. Her little girl suddenly looked much older. Frankie asked, "Are you okay, Danielle?"

"Does this mean I can get my phone back?" Danielle asked, avoiding the question her mother presented.

Frankie looked at her daughter who desperately wanted to be grown but still had so much to learn. She was the same age as Kaiti, but Frankie hoped, at least, she was more innocent, and that the innocence could be preserved a bit longer.

"Mom?"

"Hmm? I don't know, Danielle. I need to talk to your dad. Maybe, but it'll be with some pretty tight restrictions."

Danielle seemed to give Frankie's answer some thought before leaning into her mother and resting her head on her shoulder. Frankie stroked her daughter's hair, resting her cheek on her head. Sitting there she almost forgot the horror that delivered them to that spot.

The brief moment of peace was broken by the sound of Mia's voice yelling demands at the hospital staff.

"Get me some help over here," Mia demanded.

Frankie jumped up, looked at Danielle and said, "Wait here."

Running towards Mia she asked, "What the hell is going on? Where did this girl come from?"

Mia didn't answer, fire in her eyes.

Hospital staff took the girl from Mia's arms, rushing her back into an examination room. Mia was breathing heavily, not quite out of breath, but feeling the exertion from carrying the girl.

"Mia, where'd you find her?" Frankie asked again.

"Not here," Mia said, vitriol dripping from her words.

Frankie looked over at Danielle and said, "Let me get her in a room to change. Go. Sit with her." Frankie found a nurse and said, "I need at least two bags to use for temporary evidence collection. Please."

The nurse provided Frankie with the bags and led her and Danielle to a room with a bathroom. "You can use this room."

"Thank you." Frankie waited until the nurse was gone and said to Danielle, "I need you to go into the bathroom and take your shirt off and put it in this bag. Then take your pants off and put them in this bag. You can leave your underwear, bra, and socks on. I'm going to be right outside the door. I need to talk to Mia."

Danielle looked at Frankie with question in her eyes. She had never seen Mia angry and was curious about what she had seen.

"Danielle, do you understand?"

"Yes, mom. Pants in one bag and shirt in another. I got it."

Danielle went into the bathroom just as Mia walked into the room. Frankie looked at her and said, "What happened."

"Those mother fuckers left her by our car. And by our car, I mean on the trunk of our car. They left her there to die. More accurately, they wanted us to find her dead. She was tossed aside like a piece of garbage." Mia was speaking softly but her words were impassioned. "They. Have. To. Be. Stopped."

Frankie texted Sophie to pick Danielle up and then said, "We *are* going to rescue these girls. I think I know where they are."

ONE HUNDRED EIGHT

SOPHIE ARRIVED with Tyler in tow, and he was full of questions about why there was crime scene tape and wanted to know why Frankie and Mia both had blood on their clothes. He was very concerned they were hurt. Frankie chastised herself for not telling Sophie to meet them at the main hospital entrance to spare Tyler the scene.

"We are both okay, Tyler. This isn't my blood or Mia's blood."

Tyler's lower lip quivered as he asked, "Are you sure you aren't hurt?"

Frankie thought Tyler was too young to remember his father's blood on the officer's shirt when he came to the house, but she knew he felt the absence every day. She knelt down and to herself Frankie thought, *not physically*, but aloud she said, "I'm sure baby. I promise. We are all okay."

Frankie kicked herself for not asking Sophie to bring her a change of clothes, as she worked to give Tyler answers that were age appropriate. Danielle was spirited in her responses when he asked her why she was there and received more than one sideways look from Frankie.

"Danielle, that's enough."

Just before they left, Frankie messaged Danielle's father and told him she thought it would be best if Danielle stayed at her house for the night. For once, he didn't push back, but simply agreed.

"Call your dad, Danielle. Let him hear your voice and know you're okay."

"I don't have a phone, mom," Danielle challenged back.

"Use the landline when you get to the house." Anticipating an argument, she added, "Sophie has his number."

Frankie hugged both of her children, squeezing them a little tighter and holding them a little longer. Once they were gone, she looked at Mia and said, "Let's get Patrick and Jim. Is Erik on tonight or do you think he can join us?"

Mia got on the phone to her husband, following Frankie outside. Looking around at the ordered chaos, she saw at least two news trucks on the perimeter. She didn't see the boom mics, but she knew they were there. They would need to find somewhere more private to talk.

Baker was the first face Frankie saw. She waited until they were within a whisper's distance before she said, "They dumped a girl on our car, Sarge. Mia took her inside. We don't have an ID, and I don't know how bad her injuries are, but we have four rescued." Baker nodded. Before he could ask any questions, she added, "And I'm pretty sure I know where at least two more are, but we have to move fast."

Jim and Patrick arrived in time to hear Frankie's last comment. Patrick asked, "Are you serious, Frankie?"

"Yes, but not here. There's a lot of media skulking around, so we need to go somewhere else, and I'll explain."

Frankie wondered if Patrick would have the same memories she did or if too many years had passed. When they had found a private place to talk, Frankie looked at him and asked, "Do you remember the corn maze?"

Patrick looked at her with a puzzled expression, the memory taking a moment to register.

"Halloween. 5th or 6th Grade. The corn maze and haunted house on the edge of town?" Frankie maintained eye contact with him.

A few more moments passed before he said, "Wait, you mean down in Camden?" Patrick smiled in realization. "The one out by the Master Key Coal Mine."

ONE HUNDRED NINE

Twenty-eight years earlier

"COME ON YOU GUYS, quit being such chickens," Julia yelled, flashlight in hand. "They are just old corn fields. No ghosts or goblins for miles…unless you count the ghosts of the dead coal miners." Laughter filled the air as the teenagers wandered through the fields just weeks from harvest.

Craig, Beth and Brent followed Julia with Patrick and Frankie bringing up the tail at a safe distance. None of them believed in ghosts or goblins, they were in high school after all, but Frankie and Patrick were more interested in watching their friends then being in the middle of the scare fest.

The further they went into the field, the sillier Julia and Beth acted, and the wilder the stories got. On the far side of the field, before the old mine, was a section of open space big enough to spread out a few blankets and look at the stars and full moon rising from the east.

"You know, I've heard the ghosts of the old coal miners out here," Julia said. "Isn't that right, Craig?"

Craig didn't answer, but instead put his arm around Julia's waist and gave the rest of the teens a bemused look.

"I'm serious. We were out here the other night, and I heard screaming. And it sounded like it was coming from over there." Julia pointed at a mound with an old wooden door that didn't look like it had been opened in years.

Julia was no longer laughing. Frankie heard a hint of fear in her friend's voice. Not wanting the perfect night to end she said, "Maybe if we all lay here quietly, we'll hear it, too."

Julia tacitly agreed.

Frankie laid on the blanket with her friends watching the stars fill the dark sky. Beth and Brent were the first to leave, quickly bored with the quiet stargazing. Craig and Patrick wanted to leave as well, but Julia was insistent they stay a little longer. Craig went home, but Patrick stayed, not wanting to leave the girls alone in the field.

Filling the silence Patrick asked, "Do you know what that door leads to?"

"It's the old entrance to the Master Key Coal Mine," Julia quickly answered. "My great grandfather used to work there. Remember when they had that corn maze out here a few Halloweens ago?"

Frankie and Patrick nodded.

"My dad brought me and my sister. He told us how he used to pick his grandpa up here when he was a little boy. He said he used to watch all the coal miners come out after a long day, covered in black soot. But one day, one of the miners didn't make it out. He said as a little boy he couldn't understand why no one went back in to get the miner. Then his grandmother told him they couldn't because the section the miner had been working collapsed, and it was too dangerous to go in after him. He told my sister and me if he ever wanted to get rid of someone, that's how he'd do it. Put them in a mine and make sure the section they were in collapsed or got blocked off somehow.

"Dad's story scared the devil out of me, and that night I went into my sister's room because I couldn't sleep. She said it was Halloween, and he was just trying to scare us. After the last few weeks, I'm not sure that's true."

Frankie and Patrick listened intently, neither sure how to respond. Frankie reached over, placed her hand on Julia's, and squeezed gently.

Breaking the spell, Julia jumped up and said, "Last one to the car has to buy the limeade." Julia didn't wait for Frankie or Patrick to respond, but instead grabbed her blanket and took off running.

Present day

"I had forgotten about that night. And that conversation," Patrick said. "I remember now thinking how weird her comment was, but…"

"I know, me, too. It wasn't until Kaiti said Hudson brought up the corn maze and called her Julia that I remembered. I think that's where he's keeping the girls. That old mine has been abandoned for years. I vaguely remember my mom talking about the land surrounding the mine going into the Conservation Reserve Program after the flood in '93, so no one is farming it anymore."

"Makes it a pretty good place to go unnoticed," Jim said.

"Yes, it does," Frankie said. "What do you think, Sarge? I know it's outside city limits, but I don't trust Cantor. His brother's name is all over this, so I think we need to keep this tight."

Baker, normally strait-laced and by the book, nodded and said, "Let's go save some girls."

CHAPTER
ONE HUNDRED TEN

DECIDING THE FEWER CARS, the better Frankie and Patrick climbed in with Jim, while Mia and Erik jumped in with Baker. Jim led the way to the rally point, half a mile from the Master Key Mine. A third car, with a pair of FBI SWAT agents and their medic, followed close behind.

The sun had fallen, giving them the advantage of darkness as they planned their approach. Jim and Frankie did a quick drive by of the area, returning a few minutes later to confirm no one was around the property. Best case scenario, they would get in there and rescue some missing girls. Worst case scenario…Frankie couldn't let herself think of the worst case.

"Let's keep our heads about us," Baker said. "We don't fully know what we're going to find. There could be guards. And there could be nothing. Let's plan for the worst."

"Got it, Sarge," they all said in unison.

They caravanned to the field and, with vests on, and flashlights and guns at the ready, Jim led the team into the dark night. They crossed the field, careful to approach quietly. The closer they got to the old wooden door, the more they fanned out. Jim and Patrick approached from one side, Frankie and Mia from the other. Erik and the others scanned the area, taking note of the 55-gallon drums positioned along both sides of the mound of earth that covered the door.

At the door, Frankie whispered, "The door looks new. And the lock definitely is."

Jim said, "Stand back." He grabbed a mini crowbar from his pocket and popped the cheap lock from the latch, then eased the door open. Patrick grabbed an oversized log to prop against the door.

Frankie flashed the light into the silent darkness and yelled, "Kansas City Missouri Police. Anyone in there?"

Jim flashed his light into the darkness and yelled, "Call out."

A faint sound came from deep inside the hole. Frankie yelled again and waited. Again, she heard a faint sound.

"There's someone in there," Frankie said.

"Are you sure it isn't an echo?" Jim asked.

"Is anyone there?" Frankie called again.

A faint sound could be heard from inside. Frankie started into the hole, Jim not far behind. Mia and Patrick followed, careful not to back-light the pair in front of them. Baker, Erik, and the other agents stayed behind in case of an ambush.

The darkness enveloped them and only the faint light from the flash-lights guided their way. Periodically Frankie or Jim would call out and, with each step they took, the faint sound became louder. Frankie let the light from her flashlight paint the walls. What appeared to be streaks of blood highlighted their path.

The further beneath the earth they traveled, the narrower the path. The air vents normally present in a mine had long been covered by dirt. Frankie knew at that moment the people Hudson brought here were not intended to be there long. He did not bring them there to keep. He brought them there to die.

When the path looked almost too narrow to pass, Patrick and Jim stood guard while Mia and Frankie advanced. The darkness enveloped them and just as they thought they would have to back out, Mia's light shone on the tear-stained face of a young girl, her knees pulled up under her chin.

Frankie knelt down, brushed the hair out of the child's face and said, "It's going to be okay. You're safe now." She helped the girl stand and began to move backwards. "What's your name, sweety."

"Sasha."

ONE HUNDRED ELEVEN

FRANKIE FELT tears well in her own eyes at the sight of the battered and bruised child. Mia led the way with Sasha directly behind her and Frankie in step behind them. Seeing Mia, Jim and Patrick started moving in the direction of the entrance to the old mine.

Just outside the opening, Jim and Patrick stepped to the left and Mia moved to the right. The moment Mia stepped aside, the frail girl cried out and ran to Patrick, her body wracked in sobs.

"You… came… for… me," she cried.

Patrick wrapped the child in his arms, kissed her head, and with tears streaming down his face he said, "I will always… always…"

Once the sobs subsided, Patrick guided Sasha towards the SWAT medic who did a cursory exam and suggested she go to the hospital for a more thorough examination. Patrick agreed, preparing to climb in the backseat with the child, lest she disappear again.

"Patrick, can we ask her a few questions before you leave?" Frankie asked.

He resisted the urge to say no and instead stepped aside and said, "Sure."

"Sasha, are there any other girls here?"

Sasha shook her head.

"Were there other girls here?"

Sasha nodded her head and then said, "Warren brought me, Celia, Lisa, and Jennifer here when it was still daylight. I think it was around lunchtime. We were all really scared when he locked us inside. But he told us this guy, Roger I think, was going to come get us and take us to another house."

Frankie waited to see if Sasha would say anything more. When she didn't, she asked, "How did you end up staying behind?"

Sasha didn't immediately answer. She looked at Patrick, then out the window. A few moments passed and she said, "I didn't want to go to another house. Warren and Hank used to take us out to *houses*...and it was *always* bad. But the worst house belonged to a guy who said his name was Roger. He was old, smelled weird, and had a temper. I was afraid it was the same guy, so when I heard the door rattle, I told the girls I wasn't going, and I climbed into the hole. They promised not to say anything.

"When I heard his voice, I knew it was the same guy, and I went further into the hole. He had some other guy with him. They grabbed hold of the three girls and led them out. I don't think they knew they were supposed to pick up four because they left and locked me inside. I climbed out of the hole, thinking maybe I could get out the door, but I couldn't push it open. When I heard the door jiggling, I ran and hid in the hole again. I was afraid they were coming back." Sasha began to cry softly. "Do you think the other girls are okay?"

Frankie touched Sasha's hand and said, "I hope so. Do you remember anything about Roger's house? Or how to get there?"

Sasha shook her head. "He always made me put on a blindfold when he took me to a house. I'm sorry."

"It's okay, sweety. You're doing really good," Patrick said.

"There was one thing..." Sasha's voice trailed off.

"Tell me about the one thing," Frankie said.

"There was a radio at his house," looking at Patrick she said, "Like the one you have in your work car."

"You mean like a police radio?" Patrick asked.

"Yes."

"WE KNOW he has at least three young girls on his property. He's a former sheriff, so there's no question he has guns. His son is an active sheriff's deputy, so we can't use locals to assist. In fact, stay off the radios. We can't be sure how many frequencies they may have access to," Jim said.

Everyone except Patrick was gathered inside the squad room at Police Headquarters. A small team was still at Master Key, processing what was left of the scene. They had secured a federal warrant and were planning to execute just after sunrise the following morning. The raid on Cantor's farm would be a joint response, so the SWAT team for the FBI and one of the Tactical Response Teams for KCPD gathered in the squad room for the briefing.

A dry erase board was littered with a diagram of the property, known bottlenecks for entry, and known risk points, though the property also had a lot of unknowns. Thirty minutes into the briefing Erik, who up to this point had been silent, asked if he could offer a possible solution.

"Sure," Jim said.

Erik, who stood a head above everyone in the room, did not need to move for others to see or hear him. "I have a drone I've been playing around with out on my father-in-law's farm. We used it recently to find a lost calf. What if we use one here? Depending on vegetation, it might give us a bird's eye view of at least some of the unknowns."

Chatter could be heard among the crowd. Frankie looked to Mia, who smiled with pride and mouthed, "That's my husband." Frankie grinned back. It was a great idea, and the recommendation was unanimously accepted.

"I don't suppose you have it with you," Baker said.

Erik laughed sheepishly, "Well, even though I can't use it for work, it does just happen to be in the trunk of my car."

Erik's team erupted in laughter.

Jim pulled up a satellite map of the area and located an abandoned school parking lot that was off the normal traffic path to and from the Cantor farm. They would meet there. Erik and one of his team would get as close as they could without being seen, then report back to the school.

"Be there by 5:30AM. We want to execute just after sunrise," Jim directed.

It was late as the team dispersed, plans in place to rally at 4:30 to ride east to the target. Frankie sat at her desk, exhaling the insanity of the day. She wanted, no needed, to go home but she couldn't shake the feeling she was missing something important.

Mia and Erik walked to the door together. Mia spoke softly to Erik, then returned to the room and sat in the chair at her desk in front of Frankie's. Baker and Jim pulled chairs up to the desk as well.

"What's wrong, Frankie?" Baker asked. "I know that look."

"I can't put my finger on it, Sarge, but I feel like I need to talk to Hudson before we go to Cantor's."

"Are you sure it isn't about Danielle or…"

Frankie began shaking her head before Baker could finish. "It's more than that. Sasha said Warren told them Roger was coming to get them, but why from the old mine? Why not where he had been keeping them? Was there something… or someone… there that he didn't want Roger to know about? We know they weren't going to be kept in Master Key long term. It seemed more like a tomb. We're missing something, and I think he has the answers we need."

Mia looked at Frankie and said, "Do you feel up to talking to him tonight?"

Frankie knew Mia would understand and said, "I was hoping you'd say that."

"I can't let you two have all the fun," Jim said. "I'll stay behind and watch on the monitor."

"I'm not going anywhere either," Baker said. To lighten the mood, he said, "You know you two are the cause of the perpetual bags under my eyes."

Frankie and Mia chuckled.

"Let's do this," Frankie said.

ONE HUNDRED THIRTEEN

"YOU MAY NOT REMEMBER ME, Mr. Hudson, but my name is…"

"Of course, I remember you. I've not lost my mind just yet. You're Frank Moretti's daughter. The one with a boy's name."

"That's right. Frankie Moretti."

"How is your old man? I don't think I've seen him since he moved off the homestead."

Frankie detested the phrase "old man" but simply smiled and said, "Dad's doing good."

"It seems like that kid brother of yours is taking good care of the place from what I can see."

"Mmhmm, he is."

"He had a little boy with him the other day. Whose kid is that?"

"I'm not sure who he had with him. Maybe a friend's kid," Frankie said, hoping her face didn't reveal the surprise that Hudson had seen Tyler with Jake. Had he been watching *them*?

Frankie was tired and had zero interest in making small talk with Warren Hudson, but she played along for a few more minutes to give him the illusion he was in control. After all the pleasantries had been exchanged and small talk had dwindled, Frankie and Mia began asking Hudson about the girls they had recovered. He didn't try to lie, in fact almost appeared resolute that he'd been caught.

"This is bigger than you know, girls," Hudson said in a manner that could only be heard as condescending. "You may have bit off a little more than you can chew."

"Tell us more about that," Frankie said.

"Have you ever heard of Miguel Gomez?"

Jim perked up as he watched on the monitor. Gomez was known to him. He was one of the targets they had been listening to on their wiretap, but he had never mentioned his name to Frankie.

Stone-faced, Frankie said, "Tell us about Miguel."

Hudson folded his hands on the table in front of him, leaned forward, and explained, "Miguel found out about my and Hank's little operation and made us an offer we couldn't refuse. You see, we could either sell him the girls or wind-up dead. Needless to say, Hank and I aren't quite ready to meet our maker, so we began collecting girls. We'd use them in our little business until Miguel needed some fresh faces. We'd take him the ones we didn't want or couldn't use for some reason or another. Miguel would pay a modest fee, and we'd move on."

They had been talking for a couple of hours before they brought up Sasha. At the sound of her name, Hudson's face began to pale. It was with Sasha that Hudson tried to lie. He stumbled over his words and said he never had a girl named Sasha.

Frankie pulled a photograph out of her folder and laid it in front of Hudson. "Try again, Warren. Tell us about Sasha... and the three other girls you left at Master Key."

Reluctantly Warren said, "I didn't really trust Miguel, so we'd move the girls just before a big sale in case he tried to follow us. I have a few places in the county I can use, and we always have to keep a few girls for our own business."

Hudson picked up the photograph and a hint of a smile lifted the corner of his lip. He laid it back on the desk and began to laugh, surprising Frankie and Mia. Hudson leaned back in the chair he was sitting and continued to laugh heartily.

"What's so funny, Warren?" Frankie asked.

"I can't believe that idiot left one behind." Pointing at the photograph of Sasha, he said, "She always was the sly one, though. A little too smart for her own good. I should have gotten rid of her a long time ago, but she was such a good…"

Frankie interrupted him and asked, "What do you mean gotten rid of her?"

A sinister look filled Hudson's face as he leaned forward and said, "Maybe you should look inside the barrels."

FRANKIE FOUGHT every urge in her body to leave the room and call the agents at the scene but didn't give into what she knew Hudson wanted. Instead, she leaned back in her own chair and asked, "What makes you think we haven't already looked? Did you really think you'd get away with it? That *you* were smarter than *me*?"

Hudson couldn't be sure but thought Frankie was bluffing. He sat in silence, a sardonic smile on his face.

Frankie didn't move as she mentally calculated the number of barrels she had seen by the entrance of Master Key Mine. She asked Mia, "What was the last count Detective Boden? Ten? Eleven?"

Mia didn't miss a beat, "At least ten, but they're still working the scene so they may have unearthed more. We found some areas of interest inside the mine too."

"That's right. At least a couple different DNA profiles. Although they were just getting started so…"

"It could be a lot more by morning," Mia finished.

Frankie began to close her notebook and gather her things to leave the room. With her pen and notebook in hand she said, "Mia, let's take a break while we wait on the Crime Scene Tech to get here. I'm sure Mr. Hudson would like some water. And maybe a snack?"

The mirth was leaving Hudson's face, but he tried to conceal his concern. Instead, he said, "Yeah. Yeah, water would be great."

Frankie nodded and followed Mia from the room, locking the door to the room Hudson sat in.

"Thanks for playing along, Mia," Frankie said. "Do you think he fell for it?"

"It was a damn good bluff," Mia said. To Baker she asked, "Where's Jim? I thought he was watching on the monitor."

"He went…"

"Sorry guys," Jim walked in from the conference room adjacent to the squad room. "I was just on with the Agent down at Master Key. They hadn't touched the barrels yet. I waited on the phone while they checked one."

"Let me guess…" Frankie started.

Jim paused before saying, "I can't say for certain, but floating inside the one they opened were what appeared to be fragments of human bones."

Frankie stared at the man on the camera, wondering to herself how a man she had known her entire life could be such a monster. He hadn't been warm or affectionate towards Julia, or even particularly kind to her, but she would not have pegged him for a man who trafficked young girls or committed serial murder. Yet, the evidence supported the man who appeared outwardly calm was actually the epitome of evil.

Frankie shook her head and stood to go back into the room with Hudson, but Mia stopped her.

"I need to ask him about Danielle. You can't be in there for that."

Frankie didn't resist. She knew Mia was right and nodded as Jim followed Mia into the interview room. Frankie sat quietly as Mia and Jim questioned the man who tried to kidnap her daughter.

ONE HUNDRED FIFTEEN

JIM INTRODUCED himself and began talking to Hudson about his online presence and the methods he used to lure girls away from their homes. Jim fed Hudson's ego, giving him space to brag about his abilities to convince these naïve girls he was a teenage boy. He seemed to forget Mia was in the room as he reminisced about the naked photos he had collected of hundreds, if not thousands, of young girls. When Jim had what he needed, he deferred to Mia, who led the questioning about the attempted abduction of Danielle. Although he minimized it, Hudson didn't lie. He said he had been chatting with Danielle and although Hank told him to stop, he liked her and was planning to keep her for himself.

Frankie felt every muscle in her body tighten and started to stand up but felt Baker's hand press gently on her shoulder. Without saying a word, she knew he was telling her to stay there. Any movement on her part could jeopardize the case and this single gesture was all the reminder Frankie needed.

Mia took a break after she got as much information as Hudson would give about the attempted abduction. They were all tired and functioning on adrenaline and caffeine, both of which were beginning to fail. Exhaustion was also catching up to Hudson, and Frankie knew this would be a good time to get the final details they would need to rescue the remaining girls.

When Frankie walked in the room, Hudson surprised her by asking, "Why haven't you asked me about Julia and Faith?"

Frankie intended to ask him about her friend and her friend's mother but was not willing to let Hudson dictate how or when he got to talk about it. Instead, she said, "I'd rather hear about your connection to Roger Cantor."

Hudson's shoulders sagged as he detailed the business partnership that had started over 30 years prior, when Roger Cantor was working as a deputy and had put a bid in for county Sheriff. Cantor and Hudson had grown up together but had never been more than passing acquaintances until they were both adults.

"It was summer almost 30 years ago now, I guess," Hudson said. "I was coming back from Springfield and had a couple new…friends with me. It was after midnight and just outside of town I saw police lights behind me. Cantor was working the nightshift and said he pulled me over because I was speeding. I really don't think I was speeding, but that's what he said when he came up to my car. These new… friends… were not exactly happy, so Cantor started asking me a bunch of questions. He called over another buddy of his, Joe something or other, but he didn't stay around long."

Frankie knew who Joe was. He was a good cop who did a lateral transfer to Kansas City. He was an instructor at the Academy and confided to her he had left the sheriff's office because of corruption.

"Anyway, I pulled Roger aside and made him a deal he couldn't refuse. You see, I knew good ole' Deputy Cantor had an affinity for teenage girls. I'd had to talk some sense into him when he pulled over my oldest daughter and made a move on her. Well, it just so happened my new friends were just his type. So, he let us go. He showed up to my house the next day while Faith was at work and the girls were at school, and we struck up a deal. I'd give him access to the girls, and he'd keep my secret."

"Where'd you keep the girls from Springfield?"

"I moved them around a bit, but the first few nights I kept them at the Pederson house." Hudson looked at Frankie, watching her face fill with recognition. "No, the fire wasn't a lightning strike like Frank thought. You kids were too curious for your own good, so the house had to be destroyed."

"Over the years, Roger and I procured new talent and got rid of girls that no longer served us. Eventually, it became quite a profitable business. You wouldn't believe the number of men in the county who would pay for girls. And pay extra the more… youthful their appearance."

Frankie fought the bile rising in her throat and asked, "How did Hank and Greg get involved?"

Hudson laughed as he said, "Hank was a chip off the old block. Always in trouble and looking for a fight. He interrupted a, uhm *business encounter* between his old man and a sweet young thing. We decided it was safer to bring him in and use him as muscle. In retrospect, it might not have been the best decision, but I digress."

"What about Greg?"

Hudson picked at the imaginary pills on his shirt, then put his elbows on the table, folded his hands, and rested his chin on his knuckles. "That's simple, we needed someone to keep us informed of anyone snooping around. The county does not pay its deputies nearly enough, and Greg has a growing family. He didn't know the extent of our venture, but he was paid well to inform us if anyone started asking around."

"How many girls are at Cantor's farm now?"

Hudson sighed then said, "Young lady, I'm an old man and am quite tired of talking about my business. Unless you care to talk about something else, I think I'd like you to return me to my cell."

Jim stood to leave but Frankie asked, "Tell me what happened to Julia and Faith."

CHAPTER
ONE HUNDRED SIXTEEN

Twenty-eight years earlier

JULIA CURSED herself for not telling anyone where she was going, but she was running out of time. Her mother told her they were leaving the next morning, and she had to see for herself what, or who, was in the old Master Key Mine. She grabbed her father's keys out of his jacket and carefully opened the back door. She could hear her parents arguing and hoped they didn't hear the door squeak as she closed it behind her.

The mine wasn't far, but she didn't dare start up the car, lest it draw the attention of her father. Frankie's dad allowed Julia and her sister to keep their four-wheelers at the barn clubhouse, so she snuck up the hill and wheeled it out into the dark night. Julia had never been more grateful for a full moon than on that night as it lit her way up Moonglow Road and away from her house.

Moonlight faded the closer she got to the old mine shaft opening. Julia brought a flashlight, but the beams only cast a few feet of light in front of her, making the approach slow. At the mine entrance Julia fumbled with the lock, which eventually fell open and dropped to the black dirt. The light cast shadows into the dark hole, adding to the fear building in her chest. The only sound was that of her heart and it was deafening.

"Hello, is anyone down there?" Julia said, her voice only slightly above a normal speaking level, nonetheless causing an echo. Increasing her volume she yelled, "Hello, is anyone down there?"

"Who's there?" a female responded.

"Hello?" Julia said. "It's okay, I'm here to help you."

Two young girls, tear stains carving the black soot that covered their faces, slowly approached Julia out of the darkness of the mine shaft.

"We thought... we were... going... to..." the words caught in the throat of one of the girls. Eventually she choked out, "Die."

"Hurry!" Julia said abruptly. "I have to get you out of here."

"Who are you?" the second girl asked.

"My name's Julia. I'll help you get out, but we have to hurry," urgency filled Julia's voice.

Lights flooded the dirt road behind them, the headlights of Hudson's truck visible before the man himself.

"Go," yelled Julia. "Take the four-wheeler or run. Just go!" The two girls hesitated, unsure if they should do as they were being told or take their chances with whoever was in the truck. With more urgency, Julia shouted, "Run!"

The truck approached the turnoff and was barreling in their direction. The two girls ran into the field, and never looked back. Julia jumped on the four-wheeler and tried to outrun her father.

Julie made it back to the barn minutes before her father. She stowed the ATV, then went inside the place she and Frankie had spent hours as children. Instinctively knowing this was her last chance, she scratched a message for her friend onto the chalkboard.

I was there and I saw what you did. I saw it with my own two eyes. You can wipe off that grin, I know where you've been. It's all been a pack of lies.

Julia saw the lights of the truck, dropped the chalk, and crouched down under the window and waited.

"What in the Sam-hell do you think you're doing here, little girl," Hudson asked his daughter.

"Saving two girls from a monster," Julia replied. The words had barely left her lips when she felt her father's hand hit her face. The sound of bone breaking pierced the silent night.

"Give me my damn keys and get in the truck. You're going to pay for this," Hudson growled. "You just cost me a lot of money."

Julia held her face and her ground, "No."

Hudson grabbed Julia by the hair and began to drag her out of the barn and towards the truck. Julia continued to resist, flailing her arms and digging her heels into the earth, but Hudson was too strong. At the truck, he threw Julia's body into the side panel and slammed her head into the steel fender.

"Get. In. The. Truck."

Julia continued to battle her father and shouted, "No," spitting blood at his face.

Hudson hit Julia again, this time rendering her unconscious. He threw her into the passenger side of the truck and drove her back to the house where she had lived since birth. Julia would never regain consciousness. When he got to his house, Hudson carried Julia inside and laid her next to the lifeless body of her mother. He took the knife he had used to kill Faith and stabbed Julia in the chest and abdomen, finishing with a slice across her throat so deep he could see her spine. When he was done, he stood back, admired his handiwork, and plotted how he would dispose of their bodies.

Just before daybreak, Hudson loaded both women into the bed of his truck and covered their bodies with a tarp. He returned to the Master Key Mine and carried each one into the bowels of the mine where their bodies would eventually decay and return to the earth.

Present day

"You never said what happened with Faith," Frankie said. "Why did you kill her?"

"We were having one of our typical arguments. I thought I heard the door but before I could do anything, Faith said she had had enough, and told me she and Julia were leaving the next day. Then she told me she knew about my enterprise and called me a 'sick bastard.' She asked if I'd touched my *daughters* and that pushed me over the edge. I mean, what kind of sick man would touch their own child? I hit her a few times and after she was unconscious, I grabbed a knife and finished her off."

Hudson paused then said, "I think you have all you need, and I'm done talking. Take me upstairs."

Mia and Baker sat transfixed as they watched the scene playing out on the screen in front of them. After Hudson finished telling his story, Jim stood up and took him back to the jail leaving Frankie sitting in the interview room in silence.

CHAPTER
ONE HUNDRED SEVENTEEN

THE PLAN WAS to serve the warrant on Roger Cantor's farm the following morning, without Frankie and Mia, but temperatures had dropped, and due to fog, they would have to fly the drone low and were worried it would be seen. They decided it would be more tactically sound to wait a few hours, so Frankie and Mia went home to get a few hours of sleep. Mid-morning, they loaded up in Jim's SUV and drove east, headed for Frankie's hometown.

Frankie sat in the backseat with Mia and gazed upon the hills and farmland of her youth as they approached the town where she had gone to high school, as had her father before her. She sat quietly as they passed the gas station outside of town where her dad worked when she was an infant, and the house across the highway where her parents had lived. She let her mind wander as they passed landmarks that colored her childhood, the good and bad. When they approached town, she began to focus on the reason they were there, fighting to turn off the loop of memories playing in her mind.

Jim drove halfway around the town square then turned north towards the school near Cantor's farm. The town square was not as busy as she recalled it being when she was a child. There were plenty of open parking places, and only a few people littered the sidewalk that skirted the businesses surrounding the courthouse. As they passed the sign marking the city line, Frankie began to feel more uneasy.

"We're probably ten minutes from the school," Frankie said.

"We know Cantor has guns, and the girls should be in one of the buildings on the property," said Jim.

"From what I remember, the Cantors raised cattle and pigs. They also had land they farmed. Corn and soybeans, I think. According to the satellite photos, the building closest to the house is the one they used for the pigs. There is a barn behind the house too, but it was old 30 years ago."

"Any old cellars or abandoned mines on the property?" Mia asked.

"His house is over 100 years old, so there is likely an old cellar or storm shelter between the house and the barn. Unless he filled it in," said Frankie.

"Do you know if he has any experience with explosives?" Baker asked.

"Not that I know of, Sarge," Frankie said. "Hudson talked about setting fires or causing cave-ins, not blowing things up. But…"

"But what, Frankie?" Mia asked.

"Cantor has access to agricultural fertilizer and diesel fuel for the farm."

The team was quiet, absorbing the information Frankie had just shared. There was no way of being certain Cantor had not created an explosive device. And if he did, it could level the entire place with the click of a button.

"Do you think he might be leading us into a trap?"

Baker did not answer Frankie's question, but instead asked Jim, "What about Miguel? Does he have a history with explosives?"

"No. He prefers to carve people into pieces," Jim said.

"Then let's prepare for anything," Baker said.

ONE HUNDRED EIGHTEEN

THE TEAM ASSEMBLED at the abandoned elementary school set back from the road a few miles from their target. Erik had flown the drone and taken aerial shots of the entire farm. The downloaded photographs were displayed on the laptop, which everyone surrounded, waiting for direction.

"Based on the aerial shots this is our safest approach," Erik said, pointing to the road depicted in the photograph, "We'll be coming in from the north. There is a row of trees that lines the road to the house which should give us a slight tactical advantage. There are two exterior doors on opposing sides of the house. The team will make entry from the front while two of you cover the back.

"There are two outbuildings on the south side of the house about 100 yards from the back door. There appear to be two entries for each of these buildings, but there could be another one on the side as well. I've already called LeGrande, and his team will post up out there. They should be here in 20 and will enter from this access road and come up from the south side. We don't know what, or who, is inside and don't want anyone getting ambushed."

"We believe there are trafficking victims somewhere on the property. We don't know how many or how long they've been there, and part of the crew trafficking them is law enforcement. The victims may think you are there as an extension of their captors and may not be friendly. We need them safe, then separated," Frankie said. She took a deep breath and added, "No radios or cellphones after we leave here. We know he has weapons, but he also has the components to build a bomb. If he does, keying the radio or activating a cell could cause an explosion. Stay alert to anything that seems out of the ordinary, and back out if you have to. We all go home tonight."

Once the additional teams arrived and were briefed for safety, they began the caravan to the house. Silently, Frankie and Mia prayed for protection. Protection for their blue family and protection for those they were going to rescue. When they turned into the driveway, they looked at one another and said, "Let's do this."

The two-story, white farmhouse sat at least a half mile off the blacktop road. The structure needed a fresh coat of paint but looked well-maintained for its age. A covered porch adorned the front, but a lack of vegetation and open railings kept the space open. The lawn was neatly manicured, and the flowerbeds appeared cared for. Frankie shook her head at the contrast between the outward appearance and the reality of why they were there.

The caravan parked in what the untrained eye would view as a haphazard manner, angled to give cover as they made their approach. Each officer knew their role and position and began the execution flawlessly. Erik's team went in formation to the front entrance, while Frankie, Mia, Baker, and Jim ran to the back. The extra team was at the outbuildings at the same time entry was made on the main house.

Frankie heard the flashbang followed by yelling after the front door was breached. Adrenaline was coursing through her veins as she scanned the area for potential threats, returning her gaze to the door. She listened to the team giving commands on the interior of the farmhouse and could hear yelling behind her, when she saw movement out of the corner of her eye. She said Mia's name and nodded to her left, then moved in that same direction. She made it less than 20 feet when she felt the ground tremble and heard the explosion.

Frankie woke up to a cacophony of noise. The formerly blue sky was hazy with smoke, and for a moment she wondered where she was and what had happened. When the realization hit, she clamored to get off the ground and surveyed the perpetual war zone surrounding her.

The air was acrid, and although the house was standing, pieces of glass, siding and wood littered the manicured lawn. One of the outbuildings was rubble, but the other stood with broken windows and holes in the walls. In the direction Frankie had been walking was the site of the explosion. She couldn't be sure, but Frankie believed it was likely the old storm cellar.

To herself, Frankie wondered, *"Where is everyone?"* Aloud she shouted, "Mia? Sarge? Jim!"

Frankie continued to scan the area, looking for her friends. Her blue family. Just as panic began to set in, she started to see movement. She tried to run but struggled with her footing and stumbled. She could see Mia. She was okay.

"Frankie, are you okay? We thought…" Mia said.

Before Frankie could respond, she saw Jim come around the corner of the house and run towards her. Without any regard to those around them, he embraced her, saying repeatedly, "I thought you were gone."

CHAPTER
ONE HUNDRED NINETEEN

BAKER DEMANDED everyone get examined by paramedics at the scene. The blast had shaken everyone, but fortunately no law enforcement was seriously injured. Or worse. Medics wanted Frankie and another officer to go to the hospital for a more thorough exam, but both refused. They had started this, and Frankie had every intention of seeing it through.

"How many were inside the house?" Frankie asked.

"Cantor and one girl," Erik said. "It looks like he was recently filming in one of the rooms, but no one else is in the house."

"Did the girl say anything when you found her?" Frankie asked.

"Two words," Jim said. "Thank you."

Frankie gave a slight nod.

"What about the outbuildings?" Mia asked.

"The standing building didn't have anyone inside. We started looking through the rubble, but..." Erik started.

"Don't say it. We have to find the other girls," Frankie said. Not wanting to say it out loud, she softly asked, "What about the storm cellar?"

"We are waiting on the bomb squad to get out here and make sure it's safe to start digging. We can't be sure he didn't have a secondary device," Baker said.

"Sarge…"

"Frankie, stand down," Baker said firmly.

"I'm going to go talk to the girl that was in the house."

"I'm coming with," Mia said.

Frankie and Mia walked to the ambulance where the young girl sat waiting. They asked the paramedics if they could speak with the girl alone and climbed inside.

"Do you mind if we sit?" Mia asked. "It's been a bit of a rough day."

The young girl nodded.

"What's your name?"

"Celia."

"We want to get your whole story, but before we do, we need to know. Are there any other girls here besides you?"

Celia nodded her head.

"How many?"

"Two, I think."

"Where are they being held?" Frankie asked.

Celia coughed and then said, "They kept us in a room in an old horse barn, but…"

Frankie felt a moment of relief. That was the building that was still standing, but LeGrande had said no one was inside. It wasn't like his team to miss something.

Celia coughed again. Before Frankie could ask her where in the horse barn, Celia said, "He said he was going to move them again."

A wave of panic filled the air.

Mia said, "They looked in the horse barn but didn't find anything."

Celia said, "The door looks like a wall. It would be easy to miss."

"How can we find the entrance?" Mia asked.

"There's a saddle hanging in the middle of the wall."

"Thank you, Celia." Mia said.

ONE HUNDRED TWENTY

FRANKIE AND MIA stepped out of the ambulance and started running towards the barn. Erik, Jim, and Baker shouted, but the women didn't stop. The barn doors were open and once inside, they slowed to a walk. The entrance was lined with empty stalls, sans the last vestiges of hay and glass from the windows that shattered in the explosion. By the time they reached the center of the pole barn Erik, Jim, Baker, LeGrande and his team were inside.

"What the hell is going on detectives?" Baker demanded.

"Celia said there are two girls in here in a hidden room." LeGrande looked at his team with question. Before he could say anything, Frankie said, "She said the door looked like a wall."

"Here," shouted Mia, pointing at a wall about 50 feet from where they stood.

Just as Celia said, there was a saddle hanging center on the wall with nothing around it. Mia and Frankie walked to the wall, looking for a seam or anything that would indicate how to open the space. In concert with one another, they pushed, then pulled, testing each board, but it wouldn't move.

"Is there another wall with a saddle?" Baker asked.

"Let's spread out, men," LeGrande said to his team. "Check every wall. The blast may have blown it loose."

"I know this is it," Mia said. "I can feel it."

Frankie took her flashlight and began painting the wall with angled light, trying to find something that would help identify how to open it. After her second pass with the light she said, "I can't believe I didn't think of this before," and lifted the leather saddle off the door and handed it to Jim. As he took hold of it, the opening in the wall became apparent.

Frankie motioned for everyone to remain back besides Mia. The women slowly entered the small dark space. Huddled in the corner was a young girl with a look of terror on her tear-stained face, holding the lifeless body of her friend.

"Get me a medic!" shouted Frankie as she approached the girls, assuring her she was there to help. "Let me check your friend. I need to see if she…"

"Something hit her during the explosion," the girl cried. "Please help her. She's…"

Frankie checked, and found, a pulse. She leaned in and heard faint breath sounds coming from the child's mouth. She laid her on the floor, scanned the room and said, "Hand me that blanket."

Mia asked, "What's your name, sweety?"

"L…l… Lisa."

"What's your friend's name?"

"She's my… she's my… sister. Jennifer."

Frankie and Mia exchanged a look.

"Lisa, my partner and I are going to get you and Jennifer out of here, okay?" Mia said.

Lisa nodded and watched the paramedics tend to her sister. When Jennifer was loaded onto the gurney, Frankie and Mia helped Lisa walk out of the barn, and out of the nightmare in which she had been living.

CHAPTER
ONE HUNDRED TWENTY-ONE

BAKER INSISTED Frankie and Mia get checked out at the hospital before going home. Both insisted they were fine, but he left no room for argument. When they had been cleared, Frankie and Mia went to the office to notify the families of the missing girls and set up times to get full interviews after they were released from the hospital. They both knew their work was far from complete, with multiple interviews and reports to write, but they could rest easy in the belief all the girls had been rescued. Or at least they hoped they were.

When they had done what was needed, Baker sent both women home to sleep, directing them not to return until after the weekend, giving them three full days off. Frankie turned her cellphone off and spent the entire weekend with Danielle and Tyler. She knew they would be serving a warrant on the Hudson property, but she stayed away from the farm so she would not be tempted to help. The time off proved to be exactly what she needed, and by Sunday morning she felt rested enough to go for a long run. Danielle agreed to watch Tyler, so Frankie laced up her sneakers, grabbed her iPod, and headed to the running path by the river.

With the sounds of Daughtry blasting in her ears, Frankie ran along the murky river and breathed in the air that no one would describe as clean. She pushed her body, forcing the images of the girls who had run away or been cast aside from her mind. Nikki, lying in the rubble. Enya and Kaiti covered in blood. Wendi, unconscious on the ambulance floor. Sasha covered in soot. Celia coughing from the acrid smoke. Lisa holding her sister Jennifer, terror etched in her face. She was haunted by the images of her childhood friend being beaten and stabbed after rescuing two girls whose identities she would never know. Her sweet friend who was left to rot in the mine next to her mother who was one day too late getting them to safety. Their bones being all that remained.

She ran to escape the images of smoke and fire and the sound of gunshots. Frankie pushed down the image of Brad lying in the casket. She ran to escape the heartache left by his passing. Frankie continued to run, tears stinging her eyes at the flash of Jim lying in the woods and the fear she had lost him too. She let go of the fear that had embraced her when she saw the messages her daughter had exchanged with the devil himself and the terror of knowing he had tried to capture her. With each step, the horror of the past few days dimmed. Her heart was pounding in her chest and her muscles were on fire, but she could finally feel the anger relinquish to grief before finally leaving her body.

Frankie stopped at a bench near where she had parked the Jeep. She grabbed the bottle of water she had left under the bench and drank half before taking a breath. Frankie lowered the bottle when she caught someone approaching out of the corner of her eye. The question in her eyes turned to a smile and nod.

"How'd you know I would be here?"

"I took a chance when you didn't answer my text," Jim said. Then, with a shy look admitted, "And I called your house and Danielle told me where you were."

Frankie chuckled and leaned her head against his shoulder. "I'm glad you're here."

Jim nodded and said, "You know I'll always be here for you."

Not lifting her head, Frankie asked, "How'd the warrants go?"

Jim slowly detailed the days Frankie had missed. They recovered several hard drives from Roger Cantor's farm, which they accurately predicted contained child pornography. They did a secondary search of the property surrounding Cantor's farm and rescued six more teenagers; four girls and two boys. All runaways or castaways like the others.

When the bomb squad checked the cellar, they looked over the house and barns. The house looked like it had been rigged to blow, but the bomb builder had fled before it could be detonated.

The warrant on Hudson's farm was a different story. No more girls were located, at least none that were still living. They were still excavating the cellar where Nikki had been found, and they had found another in the woods near where Jim had been shot. The bodies of at least two girls were found, but they couldn't say for sure how long they had been there.

"Frankie, they dug out Master Key too," Jim started.

Frankie sat up and looked at him expectantly.

"They found bones. More than just two body's worth." Jim pulled out his phone, showed Frankie a photo and asked, "Do you recognize this?"

The picture was a chain containing a tiny heart locket with the smallest chip of a diamond. Tears filled Frankie's eyes. She touched the photo on the phone and said, "That was Julia's. Craig gave that to her for her birthday about a month before she died. I don't think she ever took it off."

Jim put the phone in his pocket and the two stared out to the river, both lost in thought.

"I'm starving," Frankie announced. "I think today calls for waffles and peanut butter with the kids. Want to join us?"

"Waffles and peanut butter? Are you kidding me," Jim asked. "Can I just have waffles?"

Frankie started walking towards her Jeep and said, "No, if you are going to be part of this family you have to try it. The peanut butter melts into the pockets of the waffles, and you pour a little warm corn syrup over them..."

Jim put his arm around Frankie, laughed and said, "Maybe I'll just try a bite of yours."

Frankie chuckled, and when they got to the parking lot, she started to say something and realized she didn't have the words so instead she pulled Jim into a hug. When she finally released her hold, she squeezed his arm, smiled, and said, "Thank you."

"For what?"

"For… everything."

Jim nodded slightly.

Frankie climbed into her Jeep and said, "I'll see you back at the house."

CHAPTER
CHAPTER
ONE HUNDRED TWENTY-TWO

FRANKIE ENJOYED BRUNCH WITH JIM, Sophie, and the kids, but behind the laughter that filled her kitchen she felt a twinge of sadness. She had known her friend was dead, but seeing the locket confirmed it, and she knew what she had to do. She pulled Sophie aside and asked if she could stay with the kids for an hour while she ran to HQ.

Outside the house, Jim asked, "You want me to go with you?"

"No, it's okay. I think this is something I need to do alone."

"Okay, I'll be here if you need to talk after," Jim said. He started to leave, then stopped and turned. Placing his hand on Frankie's shoulder he said, "Your friend and her mom can finally rest in peace because of you, Frankie."

Frankie felt her heart in her throat and said, "And because of you."

Inside the jail, she asked the detention officers to bring Warren Hudson to the counter. Hank Cantor had been taken to the Federal holding facility where he was booked and kept in solitary, but Warren was still in their jail. She smiled wanly at the officers who greeted her as they booked in their prisoners, a sudden wave of sadness overwhelming her.

"I told you I was done talking to you," Hudson said.

"That's okay Warren, I don't plan to ask you any questions. I just wanted to give you some information."

"What could you possibly want to tell me?" Hudson asked with a smirk.

Frankie got closer to Hudson and held up photograph of the gold locket for him to see. The color drained from his face.

"We found them. Or at least what was left of them. Julia and Faith will finally get justice after what you did to them."

Frankie waited.

"And we found the seven girls and two boys on Cantor's farm. You all thought you were smart, rigging the cellar and house to explode, but we still found them and none of us died." She started to walk away, then turned back towards Hudson, "Oh, and they also executed a search warrant on *your* farm. I'm sure you know what interesting things were found there. You better get used to orange jumpsuits, *Mr. Hudson*, because that's what you will wear until the day you stop breathing."

Frankie didn't wait for Hudson to respond, but instead asked the detention officers to open the jail door. Stepping onto the elevator, she looked over and saw as they walked Hudson back to the holding cell, his head hung low. Frankie closed her eyes and saw Julia running through the creek towards the barn chasing fireflies. Her laughter filled the night air and in Frankie's mind, Julia would be forever sixteen on Moonglow Road.

A preview of book 5 in the City of Fountains Series
Winds of Change

Chapter One

DUSK HAD FALLEN on the City of Fountains. Streetlights were illuminating one by one and little by little the businesses began to close on the busy avenue and the foot traffic changed from shoppers to those trying to sell drugs, sex, or both.

Inez adjusted her shorts and grabbed the flannel shirt she had hung on the doorknob of the vacant house she had slept in the night before. The air was still pretty warm, but she knew the temperatures would drop the later it got. Inez checked the waist band of her pants for the switchblade she kept, just in case a john tried to hurt her. She had never had to use it, but she knew plenty of girls who had died, or been permanently disfigured because they had nothing to defend themselves with, and she wasn't taking any chances.

Inez began walking, checking the cars as they drove by, waving if the driver made eye contact. She didn't wake up in time to get to the soup kitchen, so she was hungry. She needed to make a date so she could get something to eat, but traffic was still pretty slow.

Inez decided to change her routine a little and started heading south down Prospect. She stopped near the chicken place and when no one was looking, she took a box out of the trash and scooped out the potatoes and little bits of meat still left on the bone. It wasn't much, but it would get her by until she could make some money. When she finished, she wiped her hands on the sides of her shorts and continued to walk south. She walked past a few houses and longingly looked in windows where families were sitting down to watch television or maybe have a real meal. She had that once, and she missed it so much her heart ached.

"Wishin' and wantin' ain't gonna bring 'em back. Get your head on straight Inez," she said aloud and continued to walk.

As Inez approached the Green Duck, she noticed a sedan slow down and take note of her. She smiled and waved as the man driving smiled and nodded but didn't stop. Inez shrugged and when she got to the club, she loitered outside, hoping she could get some business on the way in or out. She knew better than to put all her hope in one place and continued to watch cars as they drove by, smiling when she saw the same sedan slow down as it approached, parking just north of the parking lot.

Inez walked to the driver's side of the car and said, "Hey, baby. Looking for a date?"

"Maybe," the man answered. His eyes bore into hers. "What will it take?"

Inez surveyed the situation quickly calculating what she should charge. The car was clean and so was the man. He was well-dressed, clean-shaven and spoke softly. He seemed safe and like he could pay well.

"Depends on what you're looking for," was her coy response.

"Straight sex and maybe some head."

Direct. Inez liked that. She quickly said, "$50."

The man laughed, his baritone sound filling the air, "Honey that's a bit steep, don't you think?"

"I'm worth it," Inez said, starting to walk away.

"Hey," the man hollered after her. "All I have is $40."

Inez stopped but didn't immediately turn around. She took a breath, exhaled, turned and walked towards the passenger side of the car. Once inside she asked, "What's your name?"

"You can call me Allen."

ACKNOWLEDGMENTS

All the *City of Fountains* novels have been special to me, but this one has taken me farther and deeper than I planned. The idea for *Moonglow Road* was born over weeks of stories over tenderloins and the first words were written shortly after in the home that holds so many of my favorite childhood moments. This book took a long time to complete but my hope is you will feel it was worth the wait.

To the family and friends who have been such an unrelenting source of support as I've followed my passion in writing – you know who you are – thank you for checking on my progress, prodding me to continue writing, giving me storyline ideas, listening intently while I shared plot twists and character arcs, and mostly believing in me and these books even when others looked at me like I was following a childish dream. Thank you for not giving up on me and for not letting me give up on myself.

It can take a village to make a story authentic. To my sweet friend "T," you may see a bit of yourself in this book. Thank you for your advice and feedback on the scenes involving the tactical response team. Your insight makes the story more authentic and richer, and your friendship will forever warm my heart. To Dave and Roger, you have both been there from the beginning of my writing journey encouraging and cheering me on. Thank you both for always being there and for previewing *Moonglow Road* and providing so much valuable advice and feedback.

To my friend and editor Kimberly Hanson. This novel is the polished piece it is because of you. Thank you for all the time, work, and energy you put into the feedback and edits. I look forward to more collaboration and weekend writing retreats!

To my cover artist, Jaycee, at Sweet N' Spicy Designs. You continue to amaze me with your talent. You took photos I captured and created a cover that was beyond what I ever could have imagined. You have brought Moonglow Road to life.

And finally, an enormous thank you to my readers. Without you there would be no reason to continue telling Frankie's story. Thank you for supporting this journey…there are still more to come.

For more information on how to respond to victims of sexual assault please visit www.startbybelieving.org. Your response may make the difference in someone's path towards healing.

ABOUT THE AUTHOR

CJ Johnson was born and raised in the mid-west and spent over ten years working for a major metropolitan police department with the last six spent as a detective in the Sex Crimes Section of the Special Victims Unit. Passionate about her work, she fought hard for justice for every victim – especially those others often overlooked.

In 2012, she left the high-stress, fast paced career of law enforcement investigations to spend more time with her family. As a nationally recognized subject matter expert on sexual assault investigations, she focused on developing and executing training curriculum focusing on sex crime investigations to law enforcement agencies and their officers for the state of North Carolina.

She continues to play an active role in her mission to end interpersonal violence through training, volunteerism, and leading a team of investigators for an organization with an aligned mission while working on the *City of Fountains* series.

BOOKS BY C.J. JOHNSON

FEATURING FRANKIE THOMAS

Thorns of Deceit

No Stone Unturned

Across State Lines

Moonglow Road

Visit:

https://www.cjjohnsonbooks.com